DRAGON OF SEAS

CENTURY
QUARTET
BOOK IV

DRAGON OF SEAS

CENTURY
QUARTET
BOOK IV

Pierdomenico Baccalario
Translated by Leah D. Janeczko

Random House 🏠 New York

Translation copyright © 2012 by Leah D. Janeczko
Jacket art copyright © 2012 by Jeff Nentrup

All rights reserved. Published in the United States by Random House
Children's Books, a division of Random House, Inc., New York.
Originally published as *La prima sorgente* by Edizioni Piemme S.p.A.,
Casale Monferrato, Italy, in 2008. Copyright © 2008 by Edizioni Piemme S.p.A.
All other international rights © Atlantyca S.p.A., foreignrights@atlantyca.it.

Random House and the colophon are registered trademarks of Random House, Inc.

Visit us on the Web! randomhouse.com/kids

Educators and librarians, for a variety of teaching tools, visit us at
randomhouse.com/teachers

CenturyQuartet.com

Library of Congress Cataloging-in-Publication Data
Baccalario, Pierdomenico.
[Prima sorgente. English.]
Dragon of seas / by Pierdomenico Baccalario ; translated by Leah D. Janeczko.
—1st American ed.
p. cm. — (Century quartet; bk. 4)
Summary: Sheng, Elettra, Harvey, and Mistral meet in Shanghai to find the Pearl of
the Sea Dragon and complete the pact before Heremit Devil can stop them.
ISBN 978-0-375-85898-7 (trade) — ISBN 978-0-375-95898-4 (lib. bdg.) —
ISBN 978-0-375-89229-5 (ebook)
[1. Good and evil—Fiction. 2. Adventure and adventurers—Fiction. 3. Shanghai
(China)—Fiction. 4. China—Fiction. 5. Mystery and detective stories.] I. Janeczko,
Leah. II. Title.
PZ7.B131358Dr 2012 [Fic]—dc23 2011031018

Printed in the United States of America
10 9 8 7 6 5 4 3 2 1

First American Edition

This book is for my grandmother,
who sees the stars from very close up.

CONTENTS

And a dark sun, in space, will swallow up the sun, the moon, and all the planets that revolve around the sun. Remember that when the end is near, man will journey through the cosmos and from the cosmos will learn of the day of the end.
—Giordano Bruno, On the Infinite Universe and Worlds, De l'infinito universo e mondi, 1584

Thou did as one who walks in the night bearing a lamp, and by doing so benefits not himself but illuminates others, when thou said: "A new age dawns, justice returns, and the primeval time of man, and a new progeny descends from heaven."
—Dante Alighieri, The Divine Comedy: Purgatory, canto XXII, lines 64–72

DRAGON OF SEAS

CENTURY
QUARTET
BOOK IV

THE FOUNDATION

○

INSIDE THE ELEVATOR ON THAT AFTERNOON FIVE YEARS AGO, ZOE sees only her reflection. Everything is so confused that she's not even sure what time it is. The instant she walked into that man's office on the second-to-top floor of his skyscraper, she lost all track of time. It's as if the world dissolved and was replaced by a parallel world of shiny, polished surfaces. Of metal and glass.

How long did their meeting last? Minutes? Hours? She doesn't know. The only clue is the scorching sensation in the back of her throat, a reminder that she spoke for too long. Or that she answered too many burning questions.

The truth is she said too much. And that's that.

I made a mistake, she thinks, staring at her reflection in the elevator's icy surface. *But I had to talk to him. It was like a snake biting its own tail.*

Yes, a snake biting its own tail.

Zoe doesn't know it yet, but a snake is going to kill her five years from now. It's going to happen in Paris. Her city.

It's a coincidence, if anyone still believes there's any such thing as a coincidence.

I

The elevator descends, as do Zoe and the silent man beside her. Zoe shudders. It's like sinking down into ice.

"It's cold," she says when she feels her breath condensing.

The silent man raises an eyebrow. His name is Mahler, Jacob Mahler. He's an accomplished violinist and a ruthless killer. The two things don't clash as one might expect. "You should be used to it," he says.

The man is alluding to Zoe's recent scientific expedition along the Siberian coast. Or to the place they first met: an Icelandic thermal spa surrounded by snow. Whatever the case, Zoe shrugs and wraps her arms around herself like a little girl.

She looks up. The lights on the elevator panel have stopped blinking on and off. For a handful of seconds they stay on, indicating the ground floor, but the elevator continues to descend.

"Where are we going?" Zoe asks, suspicious.

"Below," Jacob Mahler replies.

Before she can ask anything else, the elevator comes to a halt with a whoosh, its shiny aluminum doors open and Mahler leads her down a narrow corridor. "This way," he says.

Zoe follows him, still hugging herself.

"Where is he?"

"He's coming down."

"Couldn't he have come down with us?"

"Too dangerous."

"What do you mean, dangerous?"

Jacob Mahler slows his pace, brushes against her shoulder and stops. "I mean there would've been too many chances . . . of contact."

Zoe shakes her head. "I see."

2

"No, I don't think you could."

A shaft of light slices through the darkness of the corridor ahead of them. It widens to reveal a second elevator car, out of which comes a tall, smartly dressed man with glossy, perfectly combed black hair, eyebrows that look like they're painted on and black Bakelite glasses that frame his ice-cold eyes. He calls himself Heremit Devil. The hermit devil.

"Pardon me for making you wait," he says.

He gestures at the corridor in front of them. All three of them walk down it. They reach a railing. He switches on the lights and shows her the open space and the ruins they've just finished unearthing as they were redoing the foundation of his skyscraper.

Zoe clutches the railing. She grips it tight. It's cold. Very cold.

Redoing the skyscraper's foundation, of course, Zoe thinks. *And he discovered it.* Coincidence. Pure coincidence, if there's any such thing as a coincidence.

"So now . . . what . . . are you going to do?" Zoe asks as her archeologist heart begins to race.

Heremit Devil stares at her, imperturbable. "You tell me."

1
THE BOY

THE CLOUDS CAST A GRAY VEIL OVER THE SKIES OF SHANGHAI, BUT they're so fragile it seems the least trace of wind could drive them away at any moment.

Sheng runs at breakneck speed to Renmin Park without looking back. It's a frantic, frightened race as he leaves behind the large, round Shanghai Art Museum and looks for a place to hide among the age-old trees in the park. He reaches the white trunk of a plane tree and darts behind it, panting. Then he peers out at the other trees, the path lined with benches, the museum, the square where people are practicing tai chi and wushu.

The boy's gone. Disappeared.

Vanished among the city's twenty million inhabitants.

Good, Sheng thinks, trying to calm down.

The boy is haunting him. Sheng's been seeing him for days now, always just yards away. Inside a shop. Across the street. At the second-story window of a building. He's a young boy with a pale, sickly complexion and he wears a basketball jersey with the number 89 on it. His black eyes have deep bags under them, and his teeth are spaced far apart.

But today, while Sheng was on the museum steps, thumbing through a comic book, the boy walked up to him. "Sheng, is that you?" he said, his voice so low it was blood-chilling.

All it took was one look at him and Sheng was gripped by uncontrollable fear, the mind-numbing kind.

Whoever it was, he's gone now, Sheng tells himself, a little reassured. His eyes are burning, so he covers them with his hand.

Who is he? he wonders again. *And how does he know me?*

Maybe he's a classmate. Someone Sheng has completely forgotten about. One of those students whose names you can't remember. Or who change schools after a few months.

Could be.

It's just that the boy couldn't be one of his classmates. He's at least five or six years younger than Sheng.

A cousin? The son of one of his parents' friends?

Could be, he thinks again, leaning back against the plane tree. Maybe it's someone who stopped by his dad's agency to sign up for a study abroad program.

That's normal enough. Sheng must have forgotten about him, that's all. But then why did he feel the sudden fear? Even more importantly, why does he still feel it? He cradles his head in his hands. It's throbbing. He hasn't been getting much sleep lately. Because of the dreams. Bad dreams, recurring dreams that leave him exhausted in the morning, as if he never even went to bed.

"My eyes ache," he moans aloud.

"You can see me, can't you?" someone nearby whispers.

Sheng springs to his feet.

The boy in the number 89 jersey followed him. He's right there, ten paces away, staring at him.

6

I'm dreaming, Sheng thinks. *I'm dreaming.*

But he isn't. This really is Renmin Park. It's mid-September. In a few days he'll be meeting up with the others. And over the last two months no one's been following him.

"What do you want?" he asks the boy, his back pressed up against the tree trunk. "My name's not Sheng!"

The boy stares at him with his long, dark eyes. "You aren't Sheng?"

"No," he snaps. "Besides, I gotta go."

Without giving the boy a chance to add anything else, Sheng runs off, heading out of the park. His backpack thumps against his shoulder blades.

Trees, benches, people practicing martial arts. Cement buildings. Airplanes disappearing into the clouds. Multitudes of TV antennas. Neon signs. Cars and loud city noises. The sirens from the barges sailing up the Huangpu River.

Without looking back, Sheng keeps running until he reaches the Renmin Square metro stop.

He takes the steps two at a time, slides his magnetic pass through the steel turnstile and pushes on the metal bar before the green arrow even appears. Only then does he turn around, afraid he'll see the boy behind him. But he's not there. He's gone.

He reaches the platform and waits, in a daze. He feels like a fish in a sea of people and finds the loud chatter in the station unbearable. He waits with his eyes closed until he hears the train emerging from the tunnel. At the sound of the doors, he opens his eyes, steps on board and looks for a secluded place to sit, even though he's only a few stops away from home.

"I'm losing my mind . . . ," he murmurs, worried.

His eyes have turned completely yellow.

Mistral shuts the door behind her, takes a few steps down the hall of the Paris conservatory of music and dance and leans against the wall, sighing. Her legs are wobbly and her head is heavy. A thousand thoughts are buzzing around in her mind like crazed bees. She adjusts the boiled wool flower on her dress and tries to think straight.

On the door she just came out of is a brass nameplate: PROFESSOR FRANÇOIS GANGLOF. One of the conservatory's most renowned and most feared faculty members.

In front of her, the sound of a newspaper being lowered. Heels clicking across the floor in small steps. And finally, Madame Cocot, her music tutor, appears.

"Well? How did it go?" Madame Cocot's eyes are bright. She was the one who convinced Mistral to have the audition at the conservatory. That was before Mistral, Elettra, Sheng and Harvey hid out at Madame Cocot's music school to escape Cybel's men. When Sheng fell from the top-floor terrace. And Mistral saved him by summoning the bees to break his fall. Memories so close they seem unreal, almost as if her Parisian summer was just a bad dream.

"It went well," she says, smiling.

The teacher rubs her hands together, making her rings sparkle. "Meaning what, Mademoiselle Blanchard? Would you care to be more specific? Did they accept you?"

"Well . . ." Mistral searches the pockets of her gray dress. "I guess they did."

She hands Madame Cocot a sheet of the conservatory's letterhead, on which Professor François Ganglof has written in elegant handwriting:

Training in music, piano, Italian lyric diction, vocal ensembles type "A," vocal ensembles type "B," stage technique, bodywork for singers. Level two.

"Level two?" Madame Cocot gasps. "Meaning you'll skip the first year of courses? Why, that's wonderful! Come here and tell me everything. What did he have you do?"

Mistral lets the woman usher her into a small waiting room and sits down on a modern, quite uncomfortable chair. "He just asked me what I wanted to sing," she says. "He was sitting at the piano. And I told him I wanted to sing . . . Barbra Streisand."

"Oh, no! I don't believe it!" Madame Cocot laughs. "You had Ganglof play a Barbra Streisand piece?"

" 'Woman in Love,' of course. He played it and . . . and I sang. That's it."

The music teacher scrunches the sheet of letterhead in her hand. "You mean he didn't ask you any questions, like how long you've been singing, who—who brought you here or—or what you'd like to do?"

Mistral shakes her head. "No. It seemed like . . . I don't know . . . like he already knew."

"And he didn't make one of his snide remarks, about your dress or your hair, for example, or about your specifically requesting that he give you the audition?"

"No. He made me sing and then he wrote his evaluation. Then he told me to show up for lessons next Monday."

9

Madame Cocot sinks back into the uncomfortable chair, satisfied, as if it was a cushy mattress. "Incredible. Truly incredible."

"Is something the matter, Madame Cocot? Aren't you pleased?"

Her teacher looks her up and down. "What on earth do you mean? I'm *very* pleased. I've always told you you're my best pupil. But you must understand: Ganglof is a legend in our field. I mean, he—he's never accepted one of my girls just like that before. That's why I was always under the impression he had something against me. But maybe I was wrong."

Suddenly, Madame Cocot claps her hands. "You need to tell your mother! She'll be thrilled."

Mistral isn't so sure of that: she doesn't want such a big change herself, and she doesn't think her mother wants it, either. Not now, at least.

"What is it, Mademoiselle Blanchard? Go on, call her!"

There's a trace of uneasiness in Madame Cocot. A lavish display of happiness that seems to be hiding something else. The glimmer of a teardrop?

"I'm sorry, though," Mistral says, getting up to leave.

"Sorry? But why?"

Passing by Ganglof's door, they hear piano notes and a female voice trying to follow them.

They reach the stairs.

"I'll still come visit you. After all, it's thanks to you that the conservatory accepted me."

"Nonsense, Mademoiselle Blanchard. Don't say such a thing. You're talented, simply too talented to spend any more of your Thursdays—"

"Wednesdays."

"Your Wednesdays, right, with an old piano teacher like me, a teacher who never managed to get into the Conservatoire de Paris." With this, she cocks her head and casts Mistral an amused glance. "In any case, the world is full of pupils who surpass their teachers, don't you think? And now . . . go prepare yourself. Lessons at the conservatory are far more difficult than mine. I wish you the best of luck, Mademoiselle Blanchard!"

Squeezing Mistral's hands, the teacher gives her a little pouch. "I hope you like it. It isn't new, naturally, but . . ."

Inside the pouch is a small silver MP3 player.

"They told me it can hold all the songs you like. The last owner's music must still be on it, but I couldn't find a way to delete it."

"But . . . why? You shouldn't have!"

"At least now it has an owner who'll know how to use it," Madame Cocot insists.

Without waiting for a reply or a goodbye, the music teacher whirls around and walks off between the boxwoods.

Mistral is dazed, to say the least. She switches on her cell phone, but before she can even dial a number, it starts ringing. It's her mother.

"Mistral, there you are, at last! Come home right away, please."

"What's going on?"

"We might have discovered something." Cecile Blanchard ends the conversation without asking her daughter a single question.

As Mistral imagined, the audition at the conservatory is the last thing on her mind, too.

2
THE TRAVELER

"The ancient map of the Chaldeans doesn't work anymore."

This is all Elettra manages to think as she sits on the floor between the two bunk beds in her room. The bathroom light is on and the door ajar. Through the window comes the constant hum of traffic on the boulevard along the Tiber River: horns, scooters.

Elettra sighs.

She grabs the heart top for the umpteenth time, rests it on the center of the map of Italy and tries to concentrate. She knows the tops never answer specific questions: they indicate places and provide clues. But she also knows she has no choice.

"Where is my aunt?" she asks under her breath.

She flicks the top between her fingers and casts it. It starts to spin, its pointy tip following the grooves in the wooden map of the Chaldeans. It whirls silently from one city to the next, from one village to the next, to give its answer. Its revelation.

Where is Linda Melodia, who's been missing since the beginning of summer?

Still resting on the bedroom table are copies of the flyer Elettra posted in half the city. Her aunt's photo, their home number and the words: HAVE YOU SEEN THIS WOMAN?

Many people claim they have. There have been lots of phone calls. And just as many prank calls. The woman's sister, Irene, seems calm, but only one thing is certain: Aunt Linda disappeared without leaving a trace. And given her particular inclination for cleanliness, it's absolutely impossible to find her. Above all, to find out why she left without saying a word or giving an explanation.

"You know she's always been impulsive," Aunt Irene said, as if it was the most normal thing in the world. "She wanted some time alone."

In Elettra's room, the heart top spins, slows down and finally stops. On the city of Verona, in the Veneto region. The umpteenth different answer . . .

Elettra stands up, furious.

Once again, an answer that doesn't make sense. But why? She's getting to the point of thinking that the oracle doesn't work anymore, that its fall onto the sidewalk of Avenue de l'Opéra, which split one corner of the map, irreparably damaged it.

Elettra's tension has risen day by day as the date they plan to meet up in Shanghai draws closer. She's been wearing the same sweatpants and baggy old T-shirts for days now, and she hasn't combed her hair for a week, focusing on the sole objective of hearing news about Aunt Linda before leaving for China.

She holds the top up to the light and peers at it: the faint engraving of the heart that looks like it's pierced by a thorn has led her and her friends to believe it represents life. A life that goes on despite the pain.

13

"Maybe I just can't use it alone," Elettra murmurs.

Maybe. Maybe. Maybe.

The big mirror in the bathroom reflects the image of a girl who's changed. Her black hair has grown since the drastic haircut she gave herself in Paris, but it's still short and accentuates her long neck. Her eyes, which are usually intense, have dark shadows.

Elettra rests her palm against the mirror and savors its cold, reflective surface. When she pulls her hand away, her fingerprints remain on the glass. The secret labyrinth that each of us carries with us.

"What should I do?" the girl wonders with a shiver. "And who am I?"

When she closes her eyes, the only answer she can come up with is a whirl of images: the mixed-up New Year's reservations, the snowstorm, the blackout, their run down Ponte Quattro Capi, Professor Van Der Berger, the briefcase, the map of the Chaldeans, the first four tops. . . .

Elettra is one of the four kids born on February twenty-ninth.

"Why?" she wonders again, well aware that she has no answer.

Angry, she leaves the bathroom and then the bedroom. She walks down the hallway to the dining room, climbs the stairs, passes by her aunt Irene's bedroom door and those of the guest rooms and reaches her aunt Linda's room on the top floor.

She doesn't turn on the light. By now she knows the room by heart. She and her father have gone through it with a fine-tooth comb, drawer by drawer, dress by dress, without finding any clue, any lead, any explanation for Aunt Linda's leaving.

Missing are eight blouses, four heavy sweaters, five pairs of woolen slacks, a few pairs of socks, two pairs of shoes and a week's change of underclothes.

Elettra stares at the bed, the wardrobe, the mirrored dressing table, the Venetian glass collection on the shelf. This is the hundredth time she's been up here.

And it's the hundredth time she thinks something doesn't add up. Something she's not being told. Something she needs to find out.

She quietly steps over to the window, from which she can see the Santa Cecilia bell tower and the four statues that peer down into the inside courtyard of the Domus Quintilia Hotel. They're black shadows in the night. Stone guardians, silent and still, which the first rains of September have begun to cover with damp streaks.

Four statues, she thinks. Then she shakes her head.

She realizes she's obsessed with that number.

September, she thinks again.

In a few days she has to leave for Shanghai. And she's going, no matter what. Aunt Linda or no Aunt Linda. Because she's convinced everything is going to end in that city.

"Did you let them know at the gym?" Mrs. Miller asks her son, walking out the front door with him. "It seems silly to pay if you aren't going."

"I won't be gone for a whole month. I'll be back soon, don't worry," Harvey replies. He kisses her on the forehead and walks toward the taxi.

His mother smiles. "I could call them for you."

"If you feel like it. The number's up in my room, on the bed. Ask for Olympia."

Harvey opens the taxi door and tosses his backpack onto the backseat. "I'm off. The plane won't wait."

"Tell your father I said hello."

"You bet. Oh . . . darn it." Harvey hesitates, looking up at the roof of their house.

"What's wrong?"

The boy motions to the taxi driver to wait a moment and goes back into the garden. "There's something else you should know. I didn't tell you everything, Mom."

"Something else I should know, aside from all this nonsense about boxing?"

Harvey makes a strange smile. He thinks, *Yeah, there's something else, Mom. In Rome I survived an apartment building collapsing; here in New York a Native American mailman danced with his brothers in Inwood Hill Park to protect my life; in Paris I was kidnapped by a crazy woman who had an aquarium full of carnivorous fish beneath the floor in her office and I escaped aboard a hot-air balloon that crashed into Notre Dame Cathedral. And then I lost everything I had with me before I could even figure out what it was.*

"Something else you should know, Mom?" he says with his strange smile. "Just one thing: I'm raising a carrier pigeon up in the attic. Would you feed him while I'm gone?"

"A pigeon? A carrier pigeon?"

"Thanks!" Harvey says, without waiting to hear her protests. He plants another kiss on her forehead and hurries back to the taxi.

Then, when the car joins the traffic, he checks to make sure he has everything he needs for the flight. Ticket for Shanghai, passport, entrance visa for China. Once he's there, at China's biggest port, he's meeting up with his father on New York University's oceanographic ship, on which he has been staying for a couple of months now. It's been his second home ever since he read the latest findings and grew obsessed with the idea that something anomalous is going on with the sea.

In his mind, Harvey runs down the list of everything his father asked him to bring: warm clothes, papers and charts from his study, packages addressed to Mr. Miller both from the university and from people Harvey doesn't know.

"Don't open anything and don't mail me anything," his father said, concerning the last items. "Bring it all with you." On the phone, he almost sounded scared.

3

THE IMPRESSION

"Sheng!" his mother calls out the moment he walks through their home's arched gate. "Where have you been? Sheng!" She rushes toward him, the back of her right hand pressed against her forehead in a pose worthy of a movie starlet. "Sheng! That contraption started up again!"

The boy rests his ever-present backpack on the ground.

"What contraption?" he asks.

It could be anything from the fax to the computer to the DVD player to the stereo, or any device that blinks and ticks.

"I don't know! It lit up and started making terrible noises!" Sheng's mother exclaims.

The boy follows her inside. His house is in the heart of the Old City, Shanghai's original settlement, which has been torn down and rebuilt many times but still has traditional Chinese *shikumen* architecture: two-story houses that are arranged along alleys and have characteristic stone gates and walled-in front yards used for hanging laundry, reading and relaxing. The last two being practically impossible for Sheng to do there, at least since he got back from Rome. That's why he goes to read in the park: at home, he would need to build another wall around himself, one that protects him from the intrusiveness of his father, who's more and more of a full-fledged tourism entrepreneur, and from the anxiousness of his mother, who's more and more "I-don't-know-what-you-two-are-doing-but-I-suspect-you're-going-to-leave-me-all-alone-at-home." Not to mention that Sheng already has good reason to be worried.

"Just look at this mess!" his mother groans in the darkness of the house, which she insists on keeping unlit, convinced that electrical energy is a capitalist demon. She stops a few yards away from a gray plastic device spewing out pages and pages of printouts with Chinese characters.

"It's just the fax, Mom," Sheng says, walking past her.

"It's a fax of what?"

The boy checks the printouts: it's a reservation for a study abroad program his father's cultural exchange agency has arranged.

As he's gathering the pages, Sheng explains to his mother that someone from the agency must have accidentally given out their home number instead of the office number.

She doesn't seem so convinced. "But why did it start up all on its own?"

"Because that's how it needs to work, Mom," Sheng says. "When someone sends us a fax, we receive it."

"You mean other people decide when this contraption starts up?"

"In a way, yeah."

"And we can't prevent it?"

"Well, no . . . not if we keep it on."

19

"It's terrible. Typically Western. It means there's no respect for our privacy."

"Mom, it's a fax machine!"

"Do you think it's normal for someone to barge into our house without permission? I just don't understand you and your father. You call this progress? It's an invasion!"

Sheng sighs. There's no point arguing with someone so stuck in the past. He picks up the sheets addressed to his father and glances over them: the writer is requesting a cultural exchange in Paris so he can learn French.

Still holding the pages, Sheng drops his arms to his sides, as if the flood of memories from his recent, turbulent summer in Paris is dragging him down. The stifling heat, the halls of the Louvre, the race through the city guided by Napoleon's clock, the rickety old motor scooter he and Elettra rode to Mistral's place . . .

He runs his finger under his collar and discovers he's sweating.

The fax spits out the last page.

Sheng notices the date printed at the top of it. September 18.

"Oh, no!" he exclaims.

It's already September 18.

And he forgot he's supposed to meet someone.

"Mom!" he calls to her, breathless. "I gotta go!"

"But you just got home."

"A friend of mine is arriving at the station today!"

"What friend? Tell me it isn't one of those—"

"Mom, please! But yeah, he is. He's one of those Coca-Cola, jeans, comic books and computer friends!"

His mom is so horrified, she looks ready to faint. "You aren't bringing him back here to sleep, are you?"

"No, he's staying at a hotel."

"Of course, and I bet he's staying at one of those hotels for big-spending billionaires."

"Mom, there are more big-spending billionaires in China than where they live!"

His mother stares at him, a suspicious look in her eye. "I don't know you anymore, son. I don't know you anymore."

Sheng goes back to the gate, slings his backpack over his shoulder and gets ready to leave a second time. But before he opens the door, he peers out at the alley. It's a couple of meters wide, gray and crowded with people.

"At least take these," his mom says, handing him a little bag full of rice balls. "That way you'll have something to eat."

Sheng smiles at the kind gesture. "Thanks, Mom."

They're probably awful, like most of his mother's cooking, but it's the thought that counts.

"You wouldn't happen to be in love, would you?" his mother asks, ruffling his jet-black hair.

Sheng turns away, his face flushing. *Is it so easy to see?* he thinks, running outside to go to the central station.

"Is that you, Mistral?" Cecile Blanchard asks when the girl walks into the apartment. She's in the dining room, leaning over the table, which they've turned into the base of operations for their investigation. "I was looking all over for—" She stops, puzzled by her daughter's elegant dress. A second later, she slaps her forehead with the palm of her hand. "Your exam!"

"Audition."

Cecile rushes over to hug her. "How could I forget! Well, how did it go?"

Mistral smiles. "They accepted me."

"Why, that's wonderful! Then we need to . . . celebrate!"

"Mm-hmm." Mistral nods, putting down her purse made of aluminum pull tabs from Coke cans.

Her description of the audition is calm. She doesn't show any enthusiasm or particular emotion. Or criticism for her mother's forgetfulness, for that matter. As she talks, she goes over to the dining room table.

"You told me there was news," Mistral says, once she's finished. "Have they found Elettra's aunt?"

"No news on that front," her mother replies. "I heard from Fernando a little while ago."

"Then what is it?"

Cecile points at some photographs spread out on the table like petals on a big daisy. "Do you remember Sophie?"

"Not exactly," Mistral says.

"That colleague of mine . . . tall, blond, thin, always dressed in black . . . In any case, she works with fabrics. She travels the world looking for the best wools, the finest cottons and so on. She's studied the compositions of different synthetic fabrics for so long now that she's practically a chemistry expert. She uses lab equipment you couldn't begin to imagine."

Cecile picks up some photos and sits down beside her daughter. "So I gave her you-know-what to analyze."

Mistral pictures what her mother is alluding to: the Veil of Isis. The mysterious cloth they found folded up in a niche at

22

Saint-Germain-des-Prés, along with the black statue of a woman whose face was worn with time.

"Sophie ran some in-depth analyses." Cecile smiles.

"And . . . ?"

First picture.

"She says the cloth is old, but not that old. A blend of cotton and silk from at least seven or eight centuries ago. Let's say . . . from the early twelve hundreds. Marco Polo."

"Okay," Mistral replies, catching her breath. "Keep going."

Second picture.

"She says that for cloth it's extremely well preserved. The lines here and here coincide with the folds, and judging from how worn they are, the cloth was probably folded up like that for a long time. There are openings in two places on this side, near the edge, as if buttons or cords were slipped through them to keep it suspended . . . or tied to something."

"Like a sail?"

"It could be, but sails normally have a whole row of openings for the lines, above and below, so they can unfurl. This seems more like a flag than anything else. A really big flag, but still a flag."

Cecile hands Mistral a colored chart.

"Sophie detected high amounts of sodium carbonate in the fabric. Salt, basically."

"Like it was exposed to seawater for a long time."

"Exactly."

Mistral and her mother stare at each other.

Then Cecile goes on. "In any case, that isn't the most interesting thing Sophie discovered. The most interesting thing, which we overlooked, is that just above the openings there's an almost-invisible gold pattern in the fabric."

"A gold pattern?"

Third picture.

"Look here and here. And then here. On this side of the fabric are small golden fibers interwoven with the cotton and silk. In a long line from top to bottom on this end. Grouped together on the opposite end. They form circles, some whole, others broken."

Mistral sees them clearly in the enlarged photographs. The tiny thread patterns form some sort of outline on the veil's lower-left-hand side and, on the other side, a series of tiny designs, or . . .

"Are they letters?" she asks, running her fingertip over the pictures.

Cecile nods. "I think so. But they're incomprehensible."

She picks up a large illustrated book, thumbs through it and sets it down in front of Mistral. It's opened to illustrations of Chinese characters. "They don't look like these. . . ." Then she flips back to the cuneiform writing of the Assyrians. "Or like these. They look like . . . something in between."

"We definitely have to tell the others," Mistral murmurs.

"Wait, that's not all," Cecile says, closing the book. "Sophie ran one last test, even though it was pretty risky. Fortunately, no one noticed. She subjected the veil to reflectance spectroscopy and X-rays, plus a brief thermography. They're tests normally done to determine how breathable new fabrics are. They detect traces of perspiration, water, bloodstains, pigments and things like that. Well, Sophie certainly wasn't expecting the results she got."

"What did they say?"

Last picture, complete with explanatory sticky notes: in the center of the cloth is an impression probably left by the dehydrating oxidation of the cellulose in the cloth's surface cotton fibers. Mistral gasps with shock. In the center of the veil is the shape of something that looks like a giant serpent with a square head and four legs. It's at least three yards long.

"What do you think?"

"How did it end up . . . impressed on the cloth?" Mistral says.

"That's what Sophie's wondering, too. It can't be a statue, because statues don't perspire. But if it isn't a statue . . ."

It's a dragon, Mistral thinks.

But she's too afraid to say it out loud.

4

THE ELEVATOR

○

ELETTRA WAKES UP IN THE MIDDLE OF THE NIGHT, HER HEART pounding.

Her bedroom is dark and silent.

She rolls over between the sheets, buries her face in the pillow. What was she dreaming about? She doesn't remember. Something confused. Mistral was there. So was Harvey. They were being forced to sit in the backseat of a car with tinted windows. Moving past them was a city that seemed to be made only of lights. An incomprehensible city whose buildings and skyscrapers looked liquid. Like they were made of water.

Elettra stretches in her bed, feeling a dull ache in her lower back. Tension. She keeps accumulating tension that she can't find a way to release.

She rolls over a second time and then a third, her eyes wide open.

She tries to think of something comforting. Harvey's face, for example. But no matter how hard she concentrates, she can't picture his features clearly in her mind.

Elevator, she thinks, perking up her ears. *Who's using the elevator at this time of night?*

Elettra rubs her eyes, trying to remember: she went up to her aunt's room, then she went straight to bed, without watching TV or opening the book she was supposed to read for school over summer vacation. She looks for the alarm clock.

Three in the morning. Impossible. No one could be awake at this hour. In fact, everything is quiet. She must've been dreaming.

But instead, she hears it again: a distant hum, the counterweight activating as the elevator car begins to descend. Elettra listens carefully. Whoever's using the elevator at three in the morning, they're going down to the dining room. A guest who got in late? Her father going for a midnight snack? Or Aunt Irene who's not feeling well?

Elettra slips out of bed, looks for the pair of purple-and-lilac-striped socks she wears instead of slippers, slowly opens the bedroom door and, when she sees a dim light moving by at the end of the hall, runs to the other end of it in the blink of an eye. Her nightgown flows like a shadow past the grated windows that overlook the courtyard.

Whirrr . . .

Whirrr . . .

The hotel is full of creaks and the noises old houses make. Woodworms in the furniture that escaped Aunt Linda's savage disinfestations, wooden beams shifting, floorboards groaning for no apparent reason. Old things love to let it be known that they're still alive.

When she reaches the dining room, Elettra hides behind the

big credenza that her aunt Linda would cover with white doilies and pile high with cakes and pastries for breakfast but is now just a dark, ominous-looking piece of furniture. She's just in time to glimpse a shaft of white light that's crept into the room through the elevator's wrought iron door before the little elevator car disappears. And since the dining room is on the ground floor, the only possible direction it could've gone is up. Toward the bedrooms.

And so, Elettra crosses the dining room, reaches the stairs and peers up. Beside her are the reception desk and the basement door, which is hidden behind some neglected-looking houseplants. She doesn't hear footsteps in the hallways, so Elettra climbs a few steps to take a better look. But no matter how high up she goes and how carefully she listens, she doesn't hear the customary creak of the wrought iron door opening and closing or the sound of keys unlocking the door to a room.

In fact, she discovers that the elevator didn't stop on the second floor. Or even the third.

Impossible, Elettra thinks. *It can't have disappeared.*

And yet, total darkness reigns in the third-floor hallway, where she can hear their German guest snoring steadily.

Elettra hurries back down to the dining room. But there's no trace of the elevator here, either.

And the Domus Quintilia doesn't have any other floors, above or below.

It's dark, I'm stressed and my mind is just playing a nasty trick on me, Elettra tells herself. *It's here somewhere. I just can't see it.*

And yet . . .

She's tempted to make another round of the hotel's floors but holds back. Instead, she walks past the breakfast credenza with the intention of going back to her room and trying to fall asleep. But halfway down the hallway, she stops.

Bewildered.

She stares straight ahead at her bedroom door, which is still ajar, but out of the corner of her eye she's noticed something unusual outside the window. Something *very* unusual.

In the old well in the center of the courtyard, a light has gone on.

The minute Harvey walks into the intercontinental terminal of the airport in New York, he looks for his check-in desk. Number fourteen. He waits in line, has his ID checked and his wheeled suitcase sent directly to Shanghai. His only carry-on luggage is his backpack, which contains a book and the sealed documents his father asked him to hand-deliver to him. His backpack is passed through an X-ray machine before the boarding gates, while he, in jeans, double T-shirt, wool sweater, is frisked. He also needs to take off his shoes and have them pass through an X-ray machine before he can go any farther.

He sighs and makes sure his toothbrush is still in his shaving kit.

So far, so good, he thinks, stopping to tie his shoelaces.

While he's waiting for his flight to start boarding, he stands at the windows and stares at the landing strips that welcome planes from all over the world. He tries to guess which one is his and looks around for a couple of comfortable chairs, texts Sheng to let him know he'll be landing at the Shanghai airport in eight hours, sends a second text to Elettra and, after a moment's hesitation, writes to Mistral, too.

He doesn't tell his friends what his real plans are. He just lets them know that once he gets to Shanghai, he'll go see his father first and then meet up with them to . . . try to do something.

Harvey isn't sure he's made the best choice, but he's happy he made up his mind. It was a tough, hard decision, but he's learned to live with the responsibility of having to do tough, hard things. He's learned to accept his own unusual characteristics, which set him apart from other kids his age. No other boy can hear the Earth talking to him. Or hold a dead plant in his hand and see it spring back to life and grow before his very eyes.

An announcement over the PA and the formation of a long line of people show that they're starting to board. Harvey gets in line, hands over his ticket and passport, follows the flight attendant's directions, picks up a copy of the *New York Times* from the mountain of free newspapers, finds seat 14E and sits down. He tucks his backpack under his seat so his book will be easy to reach during the flight, switches off his cell phone after checking if any of his friends have replied, fastens his seat belt and opens the newspaper, skipping all the articles about politics. He scans down the pages with the same lack of enthusiasm as someone thumbing through a comic book they've already read or a women's magazine in a men's barbershop.

"Excuse me . . ."

Harvey lowers his paper. A woman who looks like she could fit the role of a cantankerous teacher in a cartoon is asking if she can get through. Harvey unbuckles his seat belt, gets up, smiles as he lets her take her seat and opens the paper again. The woman starts to grapple with her seat belt.

"Dammit," Harvey says, making her turn to look at him.

The article is brief, just a few lines long. THE BRONX. FIRE IN GYM.

Harvey reads it all in a flash.

"Dammit!" he bursts out again when he learns that the gym in question is Olympia's. His gym.

The woman in the next seat glares at him, but Harvey doesn't have time for formalities. He takes his cell phone out of his pocket and turns it on. He looks through his contacts for Olympia's number and calls her.

"You can't keep your cell phone on during takeoff," the woman in 14F points out.

Harvey turns the other way. "Pick up," he says as he listens to the slow succession of rings. "Come on, Olympia, pick up."

When his boxing trainer answers on the fifth ring, he can finally breathe again.

"It's Harvey. I read the news in the paper. What happened?"

"Harvey! I tried calling you at home! Where are you?"

"On a plane for Shanghai. I just boarded and . . . darn it, can't you sit still one minute?" he snaps at the woman next to him, who's trying to get up.

Meanwhile, Olympia says over the phone, "You've got to be careful! It was those damn women."

"What women?" Harvey asks. Then he shouts, "The ones from Lucifer? Nose's women?"

The woman next to him waves her arm to catch the flight attendant's attention.

31

"Exactly. They dumped gasoline all over the gym and set fire to it. When no one was there training, luckily," Olympia says.

"How can you be so sure it was them?"

"They called me at home to let me know."

Harvey's head is spinning: the women working for Egon Nose, the man who was sent in to track them down in New York. The lord of nightclubs.

"Nose got out of prison, Harvey," Olympia goes on. "Three days ago. And he didn't waste any time. This was only a warning. For us . . . and for you. Is there anyone at your place?"

"Just . . . my mom," Harvey whispers.

"Warn her. Warn her right away! It could be dangerous!"

Harvey ends the call, dazed. He calls his home number.

"Excuse me, sir," says a kind voice above him. "You need to turn off your phone."

Harvey looks up at the flight attendant, but he's so lost in thought that he doesn't even see her.

The line is free. One ring. Two rings. Three rings.

"Sir," the flight attendant says again, "I need to ask you to hang up."

Harvey raises his palm defensively and holds up his finger, motioning for her to wait a second, it's important.

Four rings. Five rings.

On the sixth, the answering machine picks up. "This is the Miller residence. We're not at home right now. Leave a message after—"

Harvey almost loses his grip on the phone. From her seat, the woman in 14F reaches over and snatches it out of his hand. "That's enough, young man!"

"Gimme my phone back, now! It's important!" Harvey protests.

But the cantankerous woman snaps it shut and hands it to the flight attendant. "Here, you keep it. And don't worry, miss. I'm a math teacher. I know how to handle troublemakers like him."

Harvey is dumbstruck. He'd love to tell her off and take back his phone, but he doesn't have the strength to do anything: he sits there, perfectly still, as if paralyzed, staring at the wings of the plane as they begin to shudder over the runway.

Egon Nose got out of prison.

And he's really angry.

5

THE DOUBT

An intercontinental phone call pierces the Earth's atmosphere to be picked up and relayed by a private satellite in orbit over the skies of China.

"Heremit," a voice replies.

"Heh, heh, heh, old boy!" Dr. Nose exclaims. "It's a voice from the grave!"

"Egon."

"Always in an excellent mood, aren't you?" says the old owner of Lucifer. His voice brims with tension. "Want me to tell you how I've been over the last few months?"

"No."

"Aren't you happy to hear from an old friend?"

"Not exactly."

"Heh, heh, heh! Heremit! You surprise me. You think I called just to say hello? That wouldn't be my style, don't you think? My style is elegant. Sober. High-class. Oh, I'm sorry you can't see me on your monitors . . . but as you know, things have changed and I haven't had the chance to equip my new office with all those electronic contraptions you like so much. So you'll have to make do with hearing my voice."

"What do you want?"

"I have good news for you. Heh, heh, heh!"

Silence.

"First: I had Olympia's gym burnt down. But I don't think you're interested in that. Let's just say I did it mostly to . . . re-establish my priorities. Second: I'm about to do the same thing to your boy's house."

"Stop."

"Stop?" Egon Nose protests, his big nose trembling. "I can't stop! Not after what they did to me. Besides, you certainly can't stop me."

"I'm the one who had you released, Egon."

"Heh, heh, heh! Of course, Heremit. You got me out of prison and I'm grateful to you. But may I remind you that you also got me in there, thanks to your orders: get my hands on a top and follow a boy from Grove Court . . . who, coincidentally, just left town."

"When?"

"Half an hour ago."

Silence.

"You still there, Heremit?"

"Do what you want, Nose. New York is no longer my concern."

With this, the conversation ends. Heremit Devil has other things on his mind. Things that are unfolding. And things that don't add up.

Harvey left town. To meet with the others in Shanghai, no

35

doubt. But where? There's only one thing Heremit hasn't yet learned: the Chinese boy's identity.

The man paces his office on the second-to-top floor of his tall building and stares at the city spread out on the other side of the picture windows, trying to decide what to do. Then he picks up the phone again.

"Mademoiselle Cybel," he says in a low voice, hanging up a second later.

Various objects are lined up on his desk.

"The Ring of Fire," he says, going down the list as he strokes the object also called Prometheus's Mirror. It's a fragment of an ancient mirror set in a frame that can't be more than a hundred years old. *Possible*, Heremit thinks. Its original frame might have broken. And the more recent one must have been designed to fit into the statue of Prometheus at New York's Rockefeller Center.

"The Star of Stone," Heremit continues. An ancient, primordial rock. A rock that's hollow, like a vase.

"And then Paris . . . ," Heremit murmurs. The object from Paris is an old wooden ship.

Why a wooden ship? he's been wondering for weeks now. *And how are these three objects connected?*

Next to the ship are six ancient wooden tops. Heremit runs his fingertip along their delicate engravings: dog, tower, whirlpool, eye . . . those are the ones that were in Professor Van Der Berger's possession; rainbow, which was in the antiques dealer Vladimir Askenazy's possession; skull, which has been in Heremit's family's possession.

"A hundred years," Heremit Devil says aloud. "These objects

36

are useful only once every hundred years. The mirror, the stone, the ship and, finally . . ."

The underground level of his skyscraper.

Zoe told Heremit that last time, in the early 1900s, the objects weren't found. Therefore, game over. The universe turned, the stars moved. And they had to wait another hundred years.

"But today," Heremit Devil murmurs, "the objects should all be here."

The elevator opens with a whoosh.

"Is something the matter, my dear? Is something the matter?" the mammoth Mademoiselle Cybel asks, gliding across the room in her flashy white-and-blue-flowered dress and butterfly-shaped glasses. Without waiting for a reply, she goes over to one of the two chairs in Heremit's office and sits down on it with unexpected grace. "You asked for me?"

The man doesn't turn around to look at her. He concentrates, as much as possible, on the objects on his desk. Finally, he breaks the silence. "I don't understand."

"What don't you understand, Heremit, dear? What?"

The man sits down in his chair. "I need the kids."

"Ah," Mademoiselle Cybel remarks, straightening her glasses. Then something crosses her mind and she takes them off, pulls a little mirrored compact out of her purse and checks her makeup. "You said that—"

"I know what I said."

Cybel snaps the compact shut, satisfied. No lipstick smudges on her cheeks. "As you like, dear, as you like. Let's go get them, then. Do you still have someone in New York?"

"Miller is already on his way to Shanghai."

"Then we can get Mistral Blanchard." The woman chuckles. "From what I know, she's probably at home. Or taking those singing lessons of hers. I'll send someone at once, if you like."

Heremit Devil doesn't respond.

"I think we'll need someone in Rome, too, for our Little Miss Electrical Current."

Heremit Devil has perfectly combed hair. Black Bakelite glasses that frame his eyes. He wears a dark Korean jacket buttoned all the way up.

"Yes," he says.

But something off-key lurks in that single syllable.

6

THE VOICE

"Not bad, Mademoiselle Blanchard, not bad at all! You're my finest student!" Mistral says, laughing, as she lies on her bed in her room.

She's changed clothes and now wears a sweat suit with tiny light blue flowers. She's opened a notebook, the kind she uses to write down everything that happens to her, and is sketching Professor François Ganglof's face. If she closes her eyes and thinks back to the audition, she can still feel her legs trembling. She was certain she got a number of notes wrong. And that her voice was too sharp, shrill, almost unpleasant. She was nervous, of course, but the professor told her, "Emotions are vital, Mademoiselle Blanchard. That is what one must convey when singing. The world is full of fine singers. Excellent singers. Powerful voices with perfect intonation. But not voices full of emotion."

Mistral flips through her notebook, going back in time. Then she stretches and steps over to the window. Above it, just beneath the gutter outside, the beehive is closed now, sealed up with wax. Indifferent to the changing of the seasons, the bees have already decreed the end of summer.

"Darn you," the girl grumbles, thinking of everything she detests about autumn and winter. She walks to the living room.

Her mother is out doing a little shopping. The purse made of soda can tabs is there, where Mistral left it. The Veil of Isis is draped over the backs of two chairs like an old blanket hung out to air. Sophie's photographs are scattered over the table, next to the books on calligraphy and alphabets and the one on the language of animals that Agatha, Professor Van Der Berger's friend, sent to her from New York. Mistral opens her purse to look for the MP3 player Madame Cocot gave her.

She turns it on, plugs in her earphones and goes back to her room, whistling. She scrolls down the list of songs saved on it: titles and artists she's never heard of. Classical music, it seems. She sets it on shuffle mode and tumbles into bed.

Murmurs, applause, and then a piano strikes the first notes of a nocturne by Chopin. Mistral listens to it, enchanted. A loud symphony follows, and she skips over it. Again, a piano. Sweet and extremely slow.

In the background, a few coughs from the audience. Fourth piece: powerful and romantic. Mistral looks at the display and reads the artist's name. PRELUDE AND FUGUE BY SHOSTAKOVICH, PERFORMED BY VLADIMIR ASHKENAZY.

Mistral reads it a second time. She knows that name, but . . .

The pianist plays, then coughs, the audience bursts into applause. The MP3 player moves on to the next track.

"Hello, Mistral," a voice suddenly says. "If you're listening to this, it means I had to leave."

Mistral barely manages to hold back a shriek. She bolts upright in bed and rests her feet on the floor.

"I just pray you're still in Paris," the voice continues. "Listen carefully: you need to do something important. There's a small square on Boulevard de Magenta. It's called Jacques Bonsergent. Go there as soon as possible. But be careful . . . because *they're* probably already following you."

Mistral is on her feet now, standing stock-still in front of her mirror. Her eyes are open wide with fright.

"In the square you'll find a newsstand," the voice from the MP3 player continues. VLADIMIR ASHKENAZY, the display reads. PIANIST.

But what Mistral hears is a voice she knows all too well.

It's the voice of the antiques dealer from New York. Vladimir Askenazy.

7
THE WELL

THE WELL IN THE DOMUS QUINTILIA'S COURTYARD IS ANCIENT.
A stone cylinder a meter and a half tall that rests on two steps and
is topped with three intertwined wrought-iron bars with a pulley
attached to them.

Elettra stares at the light coming from the well. But only for a
few seconds, because then the light disappears and everything—
the well, the courtyard, the wooden terrace, the vines, the four
statues that guard the Domus Quintilia—goes dark again.

Elettra steps outside, barefoot. She walks over the old, smooth
paving stones, then over the gravel, where weeds stick up imper-
tinently around her father's rickety old minibus. In the air, the
distant sounds of horns honking, people laughing.

Elettra climbs up the two steps on her tiptoes. She rests her
hand on the stone rim and peers down into the well. The opening
is covered by a black grate. And below the grate, only darkness.
No light, not even a distant one.

"Can you hear me?" a voice says just then from inside the well,
almost making her lose her balance.

Elettra looks around. She counts the windows with their closed shutters. She counts the floors of the Domus Quintilia. She counts the doors, the arcades. The statues.

Her jaw drops. Who said that?

She leans even farther down over the well and rests her hands on the grate. She listens.

The voice echoes out again. "Linda, can you hear me?"

Elettra claps her hand over her mouth. She can't believe what she just heard.

"Linda, answer me, please," the voice in the well whispers.

Then it falls silent. Everything falls silent. And the distant sounds from the boulevard along the Tiber River return to the courtyard. For the second time, a faint light comes up from the well. A creak, like one from wheels. The sound of the elevator doors.

Elettra looks through the windows into the dining room. She sees light from the elevator rise up from belowground and stop on the second floor. Its little doors open and close. Aunt Irene's wheelchair glides across the floor. Her bedroom door opens and closes.

Elettra sits down on the steps of the well, trying to decide what to do. How do you make the elevator go down another floor? And what's down there?

She goes back inside the hotel and steps behind the reception desk. She picks up the green lighter next to her aunt Linda's pack of cigarettes, the flashlight, opens the basement door and shines the light on the steep stairs that lead down into the maze of dusty rooms.

43

Elettra flicks the light around on the sheet-covered furniture. She remembers Aunt Linda calling to her while she was down there last year. Elettra was hunting a mouse.

"You sure are stupid," she tells herself, wondering where the underground room might be. "You never noticed a thing, did you?"

She starts walking down the stairs.

"I just want my cell phone back," Harvey hisses on the intercontinental flight once they've taken off and the seat belt sign has been turned off.

The Air China flight attendant is opening and closing aluminum drawers full of soft drinks. She's very cute, petite and smiling.

"Of course, sir," she replies, "but I need to inform you that making phone calls is not allowed for the duration of the flight."

"That's eight hours!" Harvey exclaims. "And for me, eight hours might be too long."

"I don't make the rules. During the flight, you can use a computer on condition that it isn't connected to a printer, listen to music from a portable media player or watch one of the movies we're showing. We have all the latest releases and—"

"Don't you understand what I'm telling you?" Harvey snaps. "I need to call home and I need to do it now. My mom might be in danger!"

He shows the flight attendant the article in the *New York Times*. "You know why somebody set fire to this place? Because of me."

"I don't know what to tell you, sir."

"Stop calling me sir!" Harvey says, almost shouting. "I'm just a kid who needs to call home. Is that so hard to understand?"

"Try not to raise your voice. . . ."

The flight attendant takes the intercom out of its cradle and says something in Chinese. Then she walks over to two stewards, whispers to them and points at Harvey, who's standing at the back of the plane, next to the bathroom door, which is ajar.

"Okay," he says, sensing what's going on. "She's calling for backup."

Passing by outside the windows are blankets of white clouds as far as the eye can see.

Harvey waits for the two men to walk up to him and ask, again, what he needs.

"I just . . . need . . . to make . . . a phone call," he says.

"On this flight—" the burlier of the two men begins.

"I know! But this is an emergency. AN EMERGENCY. I wouldn't dream of bothering you over nothing."

"We suggest you go back to your seat," the burly man says.

"We can bring you some water, if you like," the thin one says.

"They're showing *Harry Potter*."

"You should like that."

Harvey shakes his head. "You aren't listening to me, are you?"

A moment of turbulence makes them all lose their balance. The burly man elbows Harvey, and it's far from accidental.

"Forgive me," he says, but there's a hint of warning in his eyes. So the going's getting tough.

"Can I at least have my phone back?" Harvey asks.

"We suggest that you—"

Harvey raises his hands. "Okay, okay, I get it."

The burly man smiles.

Harvey analyzes the situation. Closed drawers, drinks cart, burly steward, thin steward, bathroom. He looks at the lock on the bathroom door, estimates the distance between the thin man and the door.

Then he decides. He steps closer to the thin man and points at his pants pocket. "Why do I have to keep mine switched off when yours is still on? Look! It's blinking."

The man thrusts his hand into his pocket, pulls out his phone and checks it. "What are you talking about, kid?"

Harvey moves like lightning: he shoves the drinks cart toward the thin steward and snatches the cell phone out of his hand. Then he dives into the bathroom and instantly locks the door.

The bathroom is tiny, but it offers everything he needs. A minute of peace.

"Sir!"

"Come out, sir!"

The stewards shout and pound on the door.

"Just a minute!" Harvey replies.

He switches on the phone.

Dials his home number.

"Sir! Don't force us to knock the door down!"

"Sir! My phone!"

Harvey waits for the line to start ringing.

"C'mon, Mom. . . ."

"Open up at once!"

"Oh, man!" Harvey grumbles seconds later. He stands up and

looks at himself in the mirror. He flicks open the lock and is almost knocked down by the burly steward, who grabs him by the sleeve of his sweater.

"Okay! Okay! I'm coming out!" Harvey says, holding the cell phone well in sight. "Here you go." He smiles wryly. "No reception."

8

THE PASSENGER

◯

After changing from Line 4 to Line 1, Sheng reaches the South Railway Station a few minutes after two o'clock. He walks away from the waiting areas on the basement level and ends up below the giant dome in glass, aluminum and polycarbonate structures. It's one of the world's largest waiting rooms, 270 meters in diameter and almost 50 meters high, supported by a web of columns and tie rods that look like they're floating. Bright and clean, it's a massive hall capable of holding over ten thousand people, with direct access to the thirteen incoming train platforms. On the opposite side is the VIP lounge and, on the upper floor, the departure platforms. It's impossible to run into anyone by chance here.

Sheng calmly walks through the murmuring river of people and reaches track 13. The screen above it indicates that the train from Beijing will arrive in just under a quarter of an hour, right on time.

He looks around, tense. A man with a mustache gestures strangely to him. He's sitting at a sushi stand by the picture windows of the Soft Seat waiting area. Sheng doesn't recognize him at first glance and is about to walk past him when the man with the mustache clears his throat loudly. He wears a big gray-on-gray tartan hat, a shot silk shirt, a dark overcoat and a pair of pointy black shoes that look like they've come straight out of an early-century gangster's wardrobe. When Sheng smiles at him sheepishly, the man holds up his chopsticks and spreads them open in a V-for-victory sign. Then he puts them down, winks at him and gestures at the wheeled wicker stool beside his own. When Sheng goes to check the arrivals board one last time, the mustachioed man leaves the stand and walks up to him, annoyed.

"Would you grace me with your presence at the stand, most honorable Mr. Sheng?" he asks point-blank.

"*Hao!* Ermete!"

"Sorry, but who were you expecting?" says the engineer from Rome, in his latest disguise. "Brad Pitt?"

Ermete walks him over to the stools, chuckling. Then he shows him a train ticket. "Did you know you can only wait in the Soft Seat hall if you have a 'Soft Class' train ticket? They wouldn't let me in, so I stopped off at Mr. Sushi's." The Roman engineer turns to the man behind the counter, points at a couple of fish dumplings and asks Sheng if he wants anything.

"No thanks."

"Rice noodles," Ermete De Panfilis says, ordering for him.

"But I said no!"

"No eats, no seats. So how's it going, old pal?"

"Not bad, you?"

"Ready to get back to it?"

"I dunno. What about you? Aren't you tired of changing from one disguise to another?"

"What are you talking about? This is nothing for a role-playing gamer like me. Still, I've had some serious problems. . . ."

"Your broken leg?"

Ermete waves it off with his hand. "Are you kidding? I mean my mother. She didn't want to let me leave the country. But then I managed to convince her by saying I was coming here to find a millionaire girlfriend." Ermete automatically pulls his cell phone out of his pocket, checks it and puts it back. "And here I am, just as planned."

"Have you seen the city yet?"

"I know all about it. Shanghai is sinking by a centimeter every year, it has a population of twenty million, you all go out to eat on Friday nights and you don't have street names."

He shows Sheng a printout with a picture of his hotel on it. "I booked a room on this street, which is simultaneously called Huaihai Middle Road, Central Huaihai Road, Huaihai Zhonglu and Huai Hai Zhong Lu."

Sheng laughs. "You could've stayed at the Grand Hyatt, like the others."

"At those rates?" exclaims the engineer/radio ham/archeologist/comics reader/gaming master Ermete De Panfilis. "I'm paying out of my own pocket for this trip to save the world . . . or whatever it is we're supposed to be doing. Besides, the Grand Hyatt is on the wrong side of town, near where Mr. Congeniality lives. A place it's best to steer clear of . . ." Ermete points to track 13 and adds, "For a little while longer."

In the silence that follows he gobbles down a few portions of raw fish. Then, noticing that Sheng is looking around nervously, he asks, "Hey, everything okay?"

"I can't sleep," Sheng admits. "Too stressed."

The engineer slaps him on the back. "You'll get over it. The others will be here tomorrow."

"Harvey texted me. He should be getting in tonight. But first he's going to see his dad, who's still at the port, on the oceanographic ship. There seem to be some anomalies."

"What's Harvey got to do with that?"

Sheng shrugs. "He's taking some documents to his dad, who doesn't trust anybody."

"Hmm . . . interesting," Ermete says under his breath, digging into Sheng's rice noodles. "You weren't going to eat these anyway, right?"

"No."

The engineer starts to slip the first noodles into his mouth, which makes it hard for him to speak. "It'll all . . . go great . . . you'll see."

Sheng shakes his head. "I don't think so. We don't have a chance, this time. . . ."

"You're forgetting the ace up our sleeve."

At the end of track 13, a white train enters the station.

"Right on time."

Ermete tosses a handful of yuan onto the counter and gets up from the stool.

"Are we sure we know what we're doing?" Sheng asks, following him.

"You tell me," Ermete replies.

The train stops, its brakes squealing, and the doors open, letting the first passengers out. Standing out against the gray sky, they're like dark shadows of different heights. They whoosh past

Ermete and Sheng and let themselves be swallowed up by the city.

"My father always used to say," the Roman engineer says softly as he braces himself against the oncoming flow of commuters, "that there are only two kinds of people who keep their cool when their house collapses."

Sheng looks up at his friend. "Being . . . ?"

"Stupid people and people who know why the house is collapsing."

"And which one do you think we are?"

"The second, I hope," Ermete admits.

A shadow that's come out of the train stops right in front of them. He shouldn't be there. He shouldn't even exist. He has very short gray hair beneath his baseball cap, a dark, murky green-gray raincoat and black leather boots whose heels make no noise. Tucked under the shadow's arm is a case containing a violin that was custom-made by a luthier in Cremona. Its strings and bow are razor-sharp. He breathes in the air, satisfied, and says, "Home at last."

He wears leather gloves. He doesn't hold out his hand.

"Is it just us?" Jacob Mahler finally asks, seeing that neither Sheng nor Ermete is brave enough to speak.

Cecile and Mistral Blanchard come out of the Line 5 metro stop in Place Jacques Bonsergent. There really is a newsstand: it's just to the left of the exit, with an ad for *Le Monde* above it.

After Mistral told Cecile what she found stored on her MP3 player, the mother and daughter split up the earphones. They left their apartment without even changing clothes: Mistral in the flowered sweat suit, her mother in cargo pants and a long-sleeved sweatshirt. They brought along an oversized shoulder bag with the Veil of Isis and Mistral's notebooks in it.

"Hit play," Cecile tells her daughter. "Let's hear what he says next."

Mistral presses the center button on the MP3 player and listens to the New York antiques dealer's recorded voice.

"The woman at the newsstand is called Jenne. Go up to her and tell her you're Professor Van Der Berger's niece. Ask her for his spare house keys. Don't worry, it's nothing unusual. Alfred had the habit of trusting newsagents. If she asks about him, say he's fine but out of town. Don't mention New York. Rome, if you like . . ."

Mistral looks at the newsstand and sees that no women are working there. There's a young man with a beard.

"Give it a try," her mother says.

Mistral asks anyway and, just like what happened in Piazza Argentina in Rome, a moment later she's holding a copy of the professor's keys. And a mountain of newspapers he ordered.

Play.

"Go straight down Boulevard de Magenta, toward Place de la République. Stop at number eighty-nine. To get inside, you need to type seven-one-four-five into the entry phone."

Pause.

The time to reach the address, find the entry phone, punch in the access code and step into the courtyard.

Play.

"Go to the door all the way at the back. Use the small key to unlock it. Then go upstairs. The big key opens the door on the top floor. No, I'm sorry . . . there's no elevator."

Pause.

Mistral and her mom walk across the courtyard, find the door already open and start climbing the narrow spiral staircase. The handrail and steps are worn from use.

Play.

"You must be wondering why I left you this message. That's a good question. Don't expect just as good an answer, though. All I can tell you is that I probably should've been there, in Paris, but the situation got out of our control. I had to go elsewhere. Not trusting the mail system, I entrusted an old friend of ours."

Mistral climbs up past the second and third floors.

"The truth is, it's very difficult to help you kids without telling you anything. They instructed us that we can only leave you clues and hope you follow them . . . and get further than we did."

Mistral climbs up past the fourth and fifth floors.

"Just like you, there were four of us. Who are we? That's easy: we're the ones who faced the Pact before you did, in 1907. Yes, you heard me right: 1907."

Mistral climbs up past the sixth floor and reaches the seventh floor.

There's a closed door.

"Today, the Pact is called Century. That isn't its real name. It's the name we gave it . . . when the problems began."

Mistral pulls the keys out of her pocket.

"The four of us knew nothing about the existence of the Pact when we started out. But, like Alfred always used to say, anything can be learned."

Mistral slides the big key into the lock.

"Be careful around your house, Mistral. Don't trust anyone."

The girl turns the key. One, two, three times.

"And don't stop singing, ever."

She opens the door a crack and sees a small apartment with parquet floors. Inside, the air is stale. The windows are barred.

"Keep going, Mistral," Vladimir's voice continues. "Because in 1907, we didn't."

9
THE SHADOW

New York.

Mrs. Miller isn't used to the house being so empty. With her husband out of town, Harvey out of town, too, and Dwaine gone for years now, she feels like the last person on Earth. It's nighttime now, the night Harvey left, and the restaurants in the Village in New York have switched on their first lights. She's going to eat in. She would be embarrassed to eat at a restaurant all alone. Besides, it would make her even sadder.

There are two messages on the answering machine. The first is just a strange noise. The second is from Harvey's boxing trainer.

"Ma'am, this is Olympia MacMahon. I'm sorry I'm calling at this hour, but I thought I should warn you about a possible danger. Watch out for an old guy named Egon Nose. I repeat: Egon Nose. He might do something nasty to your place. If you use a security service, call them. Or check into a hotel for a while. Believe me, this isn't a joke. If you want to talk to me, my number is 212-234 . . ."

Strange message, Mrs. Miller thinks. *Disturbing, to say the least.* She tries the number Olympia left, but it's busy, so she goes upstairs to her son's bedroom to look for the gym's number. When she's in Harvey's room, she hears a strange noise coming from the attic but thinks nothing of it.

The number isn't on his bed.

Mrs. Miller opens his desk drawers. She's surprised to notice the corner of a passport sticking out of a padded envelope addressed to Harvey. She opens it.

"Heavens!" she exclaims.

It's a photocopy of a fake passport with Harvey's face and the name James Watson. Mrs. Miller scans down the other information, alarmed.

Then she empties out the drawer and the ones below it.

What is Harvey doing with a fake passport? And what's the meaning behind the young woman's warning about that man called Nose? What kind of people is her son mixed up with?

There's another suspicious package: a private investigator's kit. Micro-flashlights concealed in the most unimaginable objects. An all-purpose micro-screwdriver . . .

The phone rings, making her shriek.

"Hello?"

They hang up.

Mrs. Miller's heart beats faster.

The first thing that comes to her mind is to call her husband. The second . . . is that someone's on the roof.

Gun, Harvey's mother thinks instantly. But she knows perfectly well there's no gun in the house.

Again, noises on the roof.

Wait, Mrs. Miller tells herself, trying to muster up her courage. She looks at the pull-down ladder that leads up to the attic door.

Maybe the noise is just Harvey's carrier pigeon. Maybe it's hungry. It's getting restless in its cage and I thought it was footsteps on the roof.

She climbs up the ladder and opens the door. Everything is dark, with the exception of a shaft of light coming in through the skylight. The woman gropes around for the light switch.

Her hand gets caught in something.

She screams.

She flicks on the light.

They're just strings. Strings everywhere, with photographs of Elettra hanging from them.

Mrs. Miller lays a hand on her chest. How foolish of her to be so frightened. They're just pictures. And the girl is so pretty. Harvey is clearly very fond of her.

The attic ceiling is so low that she's forced to walk hunched over. Where on earth is the pigeon's cage?

Another noise, this time louder, from on top of the roof.

She stares at the skylight, terrified. She moves toward it, trying to figure out where the noise—and she screams.

There's a man outside the dormer.

An enormous man.

Who kicks open the window.

Letting a crow with a cloudy eye fly into the attic.

Paris.

A small group of people is staked out on Rue de l'Abreuvoir in Montmartre, the artists' quarter. They're sitting at a corner café called La Maison Rose and keeping tabs on the building across the street, which is covered with creeping ivy tinged a fiery autumn red. They've been sitting on the green plastic chairs for hours. And now their boss is asking for an update.

"No one's here," one of them says over the phone. "No Mistral Blanchard."

He pulls the receiver away from his ear as a deafening shower of protests comes from the other end of the line.

"Very well, Mademoiselle Cybel, I understand: she'll turn up. All right," he concludes. "We'll wait for her."

Rome.

The shadow of a long-haired woman sneaks along the southern boulevard by the Tiber before turning down the lane to Piazza in Piscinula. She's careful not to be noticed and keeps close to the walls.

It doesn't take her long to spot the Domus Quintilia sign. Or to check whether the front door is locked.

10

THE ROOM

I<small>T'S COLD DOWN THERE</small>.

The basement is a maze of rooms, each one damper and more deserted than the last. Dark niches, flaking walls, furniture with open, empty drawers. Black-and-white photographs and old documents that the mice have begun to gnaw on.

Elettra looks for a passageway leading to the spot below the well. To her surprise, it doesn't take long to find it. It's behind a massive wardrobe positioned at an awkward angle by the wall. There's a gap between the wall and the heavy wood, and she needs to squeeze through it, ignoring the spiderwebs and the dust.

The passageway leads into another room, its floor covered with rugs.

The air isn't as musty here. On one end, the metal doors to the elevator. On the other end, a little wooden door that leads who knows where. A lightbulb hangs from the wall.

She's below the courtyard of the Domus Quintilia.

Elettra shivers. She shines her flashlight on the ground and goes over to the wooden door. Before trying to open it, she listens.

Not a sound. Not even someone's breathing as they sleep. She pushes on the door gently, opens it a crack, slips her flashlight inside.

Another room.

To the right of the door, the light switch. Elettra shines her flashlight all around.

In the center of the room is a big, wooden desk. On it, an open address book, a portable satellite telephone and an old black Bakelite phone whose cord trails off into the darkness.

On the back wall is a world map with all the cities crossed out in black ink. On the continents are dark lines, dotted lines, arrows, incomprehensible annotations. Four yellow pieces of paper are attached with just as many pushpins to Rome, New York, Paris and Shanghai.

Then, a blackboard, on which Aunt Irene has written and circled in chalk: SEE TO IT THAT SHENG GROWS UP.

On the last wall are dozens of photos of children, their faces crossed out with a red marker. A sign above the pictures reads LIST OF THOSE BORN ON FEBRUARY 29.

Beside it, a filing cabinet. One of its drawers is open a crack. Elettra steps into the room and walks over to the cabinet. She opens the drawer, shines her flashlight into it and takes a peek. It contains dozens of pink file folders labeled ELETTRA.

Inside the folders are photos, notes, episodes from her life, all organized year by year. A picture of her mom. Her parents at their wedding. The first mirror she burned out. There's even a photograph of Zoe with three red circles drawn around her.

Her aunt Irene has written meticulous notes on all the material.

> Powers of fire: strong magnetic fields.
> Watch out for her outbursts of anger. She
> tends to lose control (December 28 and 29,
> March 20, June 19).
> Close friendship with Harvey, or stronger
> feelings?

Elettra is horrified. *They know me. They've been watching me and studying me since I was born. But why, Aunt Irene?*

She yanks open the other drawers: Harvey's life, Mistral's, Sheng's.

> Harvey Miller. Powers of earth. Suspected bouts
> of depression (December 4, April 9). Introverted.
> Inclination to act alone.

> Mistral Blanchard. Powers of air. Possible
> psychological consequences from kidnapping in
> Rome (December 30). Indispensible that she do
> well on her exams at the Paris Conservatory.

> Sheng Young Wan. Powers of water. As yet
> unmanifested. Only known episodes: anomalous
> coloration of his pupils. Replaces Hi-Nau, the
> chosen one.

"Hi-Nau?" Elettra asks aloud.

Flipping through the folder, she finds the picture of a young boy with Asian features, black hair and deep-set eyes.

Elettra hears the wheelchair creak behind her. She doesn't even try to put everything back in its place. There's no time.

She stands there, stock-still, until the wheelchair reaches the doorway.

"It wasn't supposed to be Sheng," Aunt Irene says softly, behind her. "That boy, Hi-Nau, was tremendously powerful. More powerful than the rest of you."

Elettra turns around slowly, very slowly. Her aunt—or the woman who claims to be her aunt—is staring at her. Her face is aglow from a candle on the arm of her wheelchair.

"Us *who,* Aunt Irene?"

"The four of you. The four disciples."

"What does that mean?"

"It means you are the four children of Ursa Major . . . and the others are hunters trying to track you down."

"Auntie, what does all this mean?"

"Quite simply, that we're all stars."

"Please don't talk in riddles."

"It's the only way I'm allowed to talk to you."

"Why? Who are you, really?"

"I'm one of the four who came before you," the old woman says, wheeling herself into the room with both hands.

"The four what, Auntie?"

"The four disciples," Irene answers with a weary smile.

Then she raises her hand in a strange gesture, the candle goes out and Elettra instantly slides to the ground, fast asleep.

"We suggest you take a nap now," the two Air China stewards threaten. After his prank with the bathroom, they searched

63

Harvey's things and insisted he move to the back row of the plane so the service staff can keep a constant eye on him.

"Thanks for understanding, guys," he says.

"We'll have some fun when we get to Shanghai, wait and see," the burly steward adds.

"I'm already laughing."

"I've never liked smart-aleck kids."

"Well, I've always had a weakness for mountains of muscles."

The steward glares at him and walks off. Harvey puts his father's books and journals into his backpack, along with his notes and opened letters. There are all kinds of things: studies on global air pollution, catastrophic graphs, charts on the present status of the greenhouse effect, a book documenting temperature changes and tides, an astronomical abstract, a list of solar eclipse dates between 1950 and 2050, and a long newspaper article about intelligent rocks, on which his father has underlined several passages and written his name followed by a question mark.

Harvey glances over it. The author claims that many ancient myths about gods born from stone might have a deeper meaning; that is, that men were actually born from stones that fell from space. Stars of stone that contained microorganisms complete with DNA, waiting to crack open and return to life as soon as they came into contact with water.

"Whoa," Harvey murmurs. He flips through the rest of the material, growing more nervous with every page.

11

THE CAFÉ

Jacob Mahler hands the taxi driver a slip of paper and says, "We feel like having a decent coffee."

Then, in silence, he waits for the car to make its way from Shanghai's south side to the French Concession. Passing by outside the window are congested streets, skyscrapers in iridescent colors, the characteristic bridge spanning the river with spiral ramps, anonymous cement buildings with all kinds of shops and, finally, the French residential quarter with its old colonial dwellings.

The taxi pulls up in front of the Bonomi Café, located in a villa from the early 1900s, with large, elegant rooms and little tables on the lawn. Immersed in the colossal city, it looks like the classic fairy home in the middle of the woods with a pointed red roof and sponge-cake doors.

Mahler gets out of the car without even looking around and walks up the path leading inside as if it was his own home.

"Hey!" grumbles Ermete, the last one left in the taxi. The engineer pulls out a wad of banknotes and tries to find out from the taxi driver how much they owe him. Then he runs inside the café. Mahler and Sheng have chosen a secluded room with elegant wooden furniture. Their table offers a view of the garden and is surrounded by low stools in red leather.

The three order two coffees and an ice-cold soda.

"What do you want to know first?"

"Why does he live on the second-to-top floor of his building?" Ermete asks.

Jacob Mahler raises an eyebrow.

"I mean, if the building's all his, why doesn't he live on the top floor?" the engineer insists.

"Another question?"

Sheng leans forward nervously and asks, "What kind of business is he in?"

"Triads and *banghui*," is Mahler's succinct reply.

Ermete shoots him a puzzled glance.

"Chinese mafia," Sheng explains.

"Not exactly," Mahler says. "The *banghui* were secret business societies. Illegal business, naturally. Their names speak for themselves: the Daggers, the Opium Dragons. . . . They were all that remained of the ancient societies who did business with the English, or the French, back when they still traded here. They came about when the East India Company was shut down. The first wars broke out to gain control of the Indian opium that the English brought to the port in their battleships and sold at the mouths of the river. Bloody wars in which many of the *banghui* were wiped out. But not all of them. Not the Devils, as they called themselves so that the Westerners would be sure to remember them. The Devils. Half English, half Chinese: a mixed family, and one of the city's most ferocious ones.

66

The years passed, but they stayed standing. Even when the Green Gang arrived."

Jacob Mahler takes a long pause, stirring sugar into his coffee. "It was 1888. The Shanghai boatmen's guild, the most feared of all the local mafias—they were the ones who started the Opium Wars so they could take over the whole city. But they didn't manage to, not completely. When the Second Opium War broke out, the Devils kept a low profile. They left the opium business to others and started to build houses that they'd sell later on. To both sides. The century passes by, the First World War, the Second. Instead of houses, skyscrapers. The real estate business does better than the drug trade, and while the secret societies dealing in opium are being crushed one by one, the Devils keep on building. Up until today, when the dynasty is cut short. And comes to an end. With our man."

Mahler finishes half his coffee with one swig.

"He calls himself Heremit. Nobody knows his real name. He's the one who sent me out to track you down."

"How old is he?"

"Fifty?" Jacob Mahler replies. "I'm not sure. There aren't any birth certificates or residency records. There aren't any documents at all. The building he lives in doesn't even show up on Shanghai's city maps. And if you look for him by satellite, well . . ." He chuckles. "The satellite's his."

Sheng gulps.

Ermete, on the other hand, starts fiddling with his spoon. "I've always wanted my own satellite. To see things before anyone else does, you know? Do you think it's true they can actually take pictures of the license plates on your—"

"Why does he call himself Heremit?" Sheng asks.

"You know what a hermit is?"

"No."

"In Europe, a hermit is someone who shuns the world, who lives secluded from everyone and everything. Heremit Devil created his skyscraper. That's his world. He's never left it."

"What do you mean?"

"I mean that as long as I've known him, at least, he's always lived in it. I think he was born in it. He studied with private tutors. He's fluent in eight languages. He was in the building when he planned its interior. The private elevator. The top two floors. He personally designed every room, every hallway, every air-conditioning system. Every level. Every security procedure. He's got everything he needs in there: eight different restaurants. All kinds of exercise equipment . . . not that he works out. He has a movie theater. A massive library. A museum with works of art from all over the world. A giant swimming pool. You name it, and he's had it installed inside that building."

"But how can he run his . . . business if he always stays indoors?"

"His business runs itself." The killer smiles, as if surprised by how foolish the question is. "If he needs to get in touch with someone, he knows how to do it. He has a satellite at his disposal. He has computers that you and I won't be using for another ten years or so. And when he needs something done in the outside world . . . he calls in people like me."

Sheng tries to catch Ermete's eye. "But this time his plans fell through," he says.

"I don't know what plans he made. Maybe he thought sending in one of Egon Nose's women would be enough to get rid of me."

Jacob has already given them a recap of how he managed to escape the American gangster's female killers. How he hid in the woods, waiting, and how he decided to go out and track them down, ultimately meeting up with them in Paris.

"I worked for him for years," Jacob Mahler continues, "without ever asking questions. Never. Not even when he sent me to Rome with instructions that verged on the insane. Kill an old professor. Get a briefcase. Make sure the briefcase contains four wooden tops and an old map covered with engravings."

Pause. A long pause.

"I never really understood what that briefcase meant to him," the man continues, "except that he needed it to get something even bigger. At first, I thought it was some kind of treasure, but I was wrong. Someone like Heremit Devil would never lift a finger just for money. He already has more than he could manage to spend in his whole life."

"Lucky him," Ermete says. "I could ask him for a hand paying rent for my shop."

"In any case," Mahler concludes, "now he's got the tops."

"We've got to get them back," Sheng whispers.

Jacob shakes his head. "Impossible. Surveillance cameras are everywhere. The elevator that goes up to the top two floors only opens with a registered, authorized digital fingerprint. And only Heremit can grant the authorization."

"Stairs?"

"One service stairway, sealed off by sixty-four doors with coded locks. A different code for each floor. Not to mention his ferocious security team. And Nik Knife. 'Four Fingers.' The knife thrower."

"Why 'Four Fingers'?"

"Because he misaimed once. And to punish the hand that got it wrong, he cut off a finger."

In Paris, on the seventh floor of 89 Boulevard de Magenta, Vladimir Askenazy's voice falls silent. Mistral and her mother look at each other, hesitant.

The apartment seems completely empty. It has two bedrooms and a small bathroom. The front door opens onto a living room with an open kitchen, a wall table, a floor lamp and an empty white bookcase. In the middle of the living room are a couch covered with a sheet and a coffee table with a television and an old VCR on it.

Mistral slowly closes the door behind her. The floorboards creak beneath her feet. Mother and daughter cross the living room to peek into the second room. It's a bedroom that has two beds with a nightstand between them. On the walls, a poster for a Georges Méliès film: *L'éclipse du soleil en pleine lune.*

On the bed they find a map of Shanghai and two red passports that have their faces but different names.

"Mom!" Mistral cries. "Look!"

"Fake passports . . . one for me and one for you," Cecile Blanchard says, flipping through the pages. "Complete with an entry visa for China. Well, they've certainly done a good job."

"What do you mean, Mom?"

"They're telling us it's dangerous to travel using our real names. And maybe even to go back home, at this point . . ."

There's little else in the apartment.

"What I don't understand," Cecile says in a low voice, "is why all the spy games. If they wanted to give us fake passports, they could've sent them to us at home."

"Maybe they were afraid someone else might get hold of them. . . ."

"So it was safer to send you a message recorded on an MP3 player, a message you might have deleted? Or never have listened to? We were leaving for Shanghai tomorrow anyway. And we've already bought our tickets."

Mistral shakes her head. "I don't know, Mom. Really, I don't know."

"Well, I don't think it's a good idea to travel using fake documents. It's dangerous."

"More dangerous than traveling under our real names?"

"Whatever the case, it's illegal. And we aren't going to do anything illegal, Mistral."

Cecile is opening all the kitchen cabinets. Plates, glasses, silverware. A package of Italian pasta. Oil, salt, pepper. A can of tomatoes that hasn't expired yet. Pots in different sizes. Everything needed to cook for a short period of time.

"This apartment hasn't been used for at least a year," the woman remarks.

Mistral checks the VCR to see if there's a tape in it. She hits the play button.

"There's something in here . . . ," she says as the television turns on.

A quivering line appears on the screen, followed by a man sitting on a couch holding some sheets of paper. Mistral and Cecile

71

recognize the room. The man is quite old, with a sparse beard and a checked jacket. He clears his throat and looks at the papers in his hands. Next to him on the couch is a series of photographs.

"Pull in closer," he says to the person working the camera.

Zoom in on his face.

"It's Professor Van Der Berger!" Mistral exclaims, recognizing him.

In the video, the professor asks the cameraman to leave. There are footsteps, and the apartment door opens and closes.

Finally, the professor begins to talk.

"My name is Alfred Van Der Berger," he says a bit wearily, "and I was born on February twenty-ninth, 1896. My family fled Holland and moved to New York in 1905 . . . and it was in New York, two years later, that I learned of the Pact. It happened in a movie theater. I went there to see a short film entitled *L'éclipse du soleil en pleine lune,* which at that time and to my child's eyes was an amazing sight to behold. The film was set in a school for astronomers. A great professor strides in, his robe covered with symbols of the zodiac and constellations, and then everyone goes up to the roof with long binoculars to observe the sun and moon as they join together in the sky. After that, you see the stars drifting down to earth with people riding them."

Professor Van Der Berger coughs.

"When the movie was over, there was a woman in the theater whom I'd get to know better many years later," he continues. "A young woman with a lazy eye. She was Siberian, from a little village named Tunguska, and she'd traveled from Russia to New York for the sole purpose of meeting me. That day, she left me two wooden tops and a name, the name of a shop owned by Russian carpenters who'd recently moved into town. Working there was a boy named Vladimir. He was my age, born on February twenty-ninth, like me. He'd received a top, too, and an old wooden map covered with inscriptions."

"Goodness . . . ," Mistral murmurs. Her mother leans over and puts her arm around her.

"Who gave it to him? The same young woman who gave those things to me in the darkness of the movie theater?" the professor asks in the video. "Thanks to one of Vladimir's cousins, who worked on Ellis Island, where all the American immigration permits were issued, we discovered that the woman had arrived from Italy on a ship that had set sail from a place called Messina. After writing letters and making our first intercontinental phone call, we determined that the woman had met a Sicilian girl named Irene in Messina. She gave her two tops and a name. Mine. Only one person was missing: the fourth one. Zoe called Irene at the end of the year. She said she found her name beside two old wooden tops she discovered in her toy box."

The professor lapses into silence as he shuffles through the pictures beside him.

"Do you want me to pause it?" Mistral's mother asks.

"No," the girl says. "Let's keep going."

"What we didn't realize back then is that we were part of a master plan. An ancient plan, as we would realize much later. A plan that had begun many centuries earlier, in the time of the ancient Chaldeans, who lived three thousand years before Christ. A plan that first came about in the Orient and whose name was connected to the name of a god: Mithra. Which means 'pact.' 'Alliance.' Today we call it Century, after the name of the place

73

where the Pact was broken. Like all respectable alliances, this one had its rules: every hundred years, four Sages had the task of finding their four successors and giving them four tests. The masters were sworn to silence. They could only guide their disciples and observe their behavior. If the children passed the tests, they would discover the masters' ultimate secret. If they didn't pass the tests, the masters would explain to the disciples only what they, themselves, had managed to discover, and not the entire plan behind the Pact . . . and little by little, this would decrease the chances of figuring everything out."

Again, Van Der Berger takes a long pause.

"The woman who was my master—and Irene's, Vladimir's and Zoe's—knew only a small part of the ancient Pact: the part that her master had passed down to her in the early eighteen hundreds, when he gave her the map and the tops. She wasn't aware of there being any other master alive. She set out to find us after the big solar eclipse of January fourteenth, 1907 . . . when, she said, she dreamed about us."

The professor turns toward the door to make sure no one has come in.

"Naturally, it took us a long time to believe her story, especially the fact that the young woman could be over a hundred years old. Her reply to that was very simple: when you become a master of the Pact, even to the smallest degree, you age more slowly than other people. That's the gift Nature gives us for undertaking the task."

The professor looks around nervously and goes on. "As I was saying, in 1907, we had only one master and only the tops as clues. And we did nothing, or practically nothing. We failed the

Pact, just as our master's companions had done, and their masters before them. But then we realized that the Pact was more than a simple secret agreement among men. We discovered that Nature had some kind of . . . punishment in store for us."

Alfred Van Der Berger holds up a photo of an ice-covered valley.

"June thirtieth, 1908, in the Siberian town where our master lived, there was an enormous explosion that flattened two thousand square kilometers of forestland. Even now, no one can explain what happened that day."

Another photo: buildings and cities in ruins.

"The same year, on December twenty-eighth at five twenty-one in the morning, Messina, Irene's city, was struck by one of the most devastating earthquakes in its history. The resulting tsunami submerged the coast for miles. At least seventy thousand people died. During the earthquake, Irene's back was injured, as were her legs. She could still walk, but only thanks to her incredible willpower and the force of Nature that flowed through her veins. The more she aged, the more painful and difficult it became for her to move."

Alfred Van Der Berger puts down the photographs and stares straight into the camera. "The four of us could only think one thing: that it was our fault. That we didn't do what we were supposed to do. We had special powers, but we didn't put them to good use. Walking down the streets ravaged by the earthquake, I could hear the Earth weep. At that point, we started searching, even though the time wasn't ripe anymore. We learned to use the tops, and with their guidance we found the Ring of Fire in Rome and the Star of Stone in New York. We spent a long time searching Paris and just as long searching Shanghai, which in those years was war torn. But that's as far as we got. And so, we put everything back in its place and created a series of clues to do what we were instructed to do: choose four successors and give them the clues without saying anything else. But things unexpectedly came to a head. That's why I'm making this tape. The last time we saw each other, we were in Iceland. It was an important moment; we could feel it in our bones. The century was coming to an end and the chosen ones had to be selected from among the ones on the list we brought with us. Zoe was the last to arrive, and when she did, she told us the Pact would begin in Rome."

Professor Van Der Berger's face moves offscreen for a moment. He's picked up an inflatable globe from the floor.

"The four cities aren't simply four cities. They're symbols of the four elements: Fire, Earth, Air and Water. They're all north of the equator, below the polestar and the constellations of Draco and Ursa Major. That's why the chosen ones are also called the Children of the Bear. The constellation contains seven stars, and there are just as many tops. What do the stars have to do with it? It's simple. . . ."

Mistral listens to Professor Van Der Berger's words, unable to breathe.

"I believe that by studying the stars, the Chaldeans discovered man. The same laws apply to men and stars. This is the meaning of the signs of the zodiac. I believe their scholars—the Magi, as we call them—discovered something they kept secret, protected by this succession of masters. A secret, yes. A secret that we gradually forgot, failure by failure. But the failures of those who came before you won't prevent you from discovering it. I'm convinced the students can surpass their teachers."

There's a knock on the door. Frightened, the professor spins around in his seat. Then he looks back into the camera and whispers, "May Nature be with you, children. And may it protect you always!"

Alfred Van Der Berger gets up from the couch and switches off the camera.

Mistral and Cecile stare at the blank screen.

"We've got to show this to the others," Mistral says.

Cecile nods.

"In Shanghai," the girl adds, holding up the passports.

1 2

THE MINIBUS

◯

WHEN ELETTRA OPENS HER EYES, SHE'S SITTING IN THE FRONT SEAT of her father's minibus. Outside the window are the lanes of the Grande Raccordo Anulare, Rome's ring-shaped highway. She blinks, surprised.

"Hi," Fernando Melodia says from behind the wheel.

"What's going on? Where am I?"

"We're going to the airport," her father replies, perfectly calm.

"The airport?"

"You have to leave for Shanghai, don't you remember?"

"But . . ." Elettra looks around, bewildered. "I'm supposed to leave tomorrow."

"It's already tomorrow."

Then, slowly, the girl remembers the elevator, the light in the well, the room in the basement, her aunt Irene showing up.

"I can't believe it, Dad!" she exclaims. "I was at home. And Aunt Irene was there, too. We were—there's a room with a phone, below the well! The elevator goes straight down there!"

"Oh, sure," Fernando says. "We've got a couple Martians up in the attic, too!"

"Dad, I'm not kidding! Aunt Irene is . . . one of them!"

"One of who?"

"She's one of the four . . . Sages . . . the masters . . . the Magi! The ones who got us tied up in all this."

Fernando skillfully passes a Japanese car. "Could be," he admits, returning to his own lane.

Elettra stares at him, stunned. "You know about it, too," she guesses. "You've always known."

"Known what?"

"Stop playing dumb!"

"Oh, great. Your mother always used to tell me that, too."

Elettra crosses her arms, furious. "You guys can't keep treating me like a little girl."

"Well then, try to calm down. Otherwise you'll make the minivan's engine boil over."

"You know about that, too?"

"What? That you let off fire and flames whenever you get mad?"

"That I *really* do it. Literally."

Fernando drums his fingers on the steering wheel. "It's hard not to notice."

"And you've never said anything about it? You can't pretend nothing's happening, Dad. Aunt Irene claims she's over a hundred years old, do you realize?"

"I hope I make it that long."

"That's not the point. The point is that down in that room

79

under the well, there are photos of all of us. Of me, Mistral, Harvey, Sheng . . . and another boy, too. A boy I'd never heard of before, but maybe . . . Of course!" Elettra shouts, pounding her fist on the dashboard.

"Hey, are you trying to set off the air bag?"

"And then I was fast asleep," Elettra remembers, struck by the memory. "Just like that, I was fast asleep."

"Yes, you were fast asleep until a minute ago. And it might've been better if you'd kept on sleeping all the way to the airport."

"Last night, Aunt Irene called you, you went down to get me, you loaded me into the minibus and now you're sending me away to Shanghai so I won't find out anything else about that room. Which I bet you've cleaned out already."

"You're sounding a bit paranoid, Elettra."

"I saw it! There were pictures of me with comments from you guys. You even know I like Harvey."

"That's no big secret, if you ask me."

"And you're wondering if I have stronger feelings for him, like I was a lab rat under observation. I can't stand you! You or Aunt Irene!"

Fernando whips his head around. "Now you're going too far, Elettra."

"Why won't you tell me what you guys did to Aunt Linda, then? What did you tell her? Where did you send her?"

"How should I know? I was in Paris with you!"

"Oh, right, sorry!" Elettra grumbles. "You never know anything. You're always the one who's never told anything. The artist! The man hopelessly wrapped up in his novel, which he'll never finish writing!"

Fernando Melodia stares at the road without replying. Elettra does the same, obstinate and furious.

"You have no idea what it's like to feel this way," she says after a while.

"You need to get something from under your seat," her father says.

The girl leans over, gropes around and pulls out an old cookie tin. "This?"

"Open it."

Inside the tin are dozens of Chinese coins in different sizes.

"Aunt Irene wanted me to give them to you."

Elettra picks up a few of the coins and studies them. They look—and are—very old. They're in different shapes and colors, and some of them have holes in the center.

Beneath the coins is a red-lacquered wooden tile with four black-bladed knives painted on it, along with a folded letter and a passport tucked inside of it.

"What's this for?" she asks.

"The letter should explain everything," Fernando says, still driving.

Dear Elettra,

It's with great regret that I say goodbye to you this way. But the time we've been given has almost run out. I hope you'll find the answers you're looking for. In the box are all the clues from Shanghai in 1907. Use them as you see fit: no one is better than the four of you at interpreting the Pact's clues. None of us got so far. And none of us knows the meaning behind the objects you found, nor the intentions of the man who stole them from you.

Forgive me for keeping you in the dark about everything, but Vladimir and I are convinced that we should follow the rules to the letter: silence and patience.

If there really is a plan with any meaning, this is the only way we'll discover it.

May Nature be with you.

And may it protect you always.

P.S. Your aunt Linda is fine. She just went to meet her real family.

When they land in Shanghai, they make Harvey get off the plane last. The burly steward brusquely escorts him to a back room in the customs area.

"We're going to have some fun, just wait and see," the steward whispers, shoving him inside.

The room is almost completely bare. There's just a small desk with a little man sitting behind it. Behind him, a large portrait of the Chinese president, who's smiling. In front of the desk, a terribly uncomfortable-looking chair.

"Have a seat, Mr. Miller," the little man says in English with a strong state official's accent.

Harvey does as he's told, his teeth clenched. The steward and the man begin to speak to each other in Chinese so he can't understand them. From time to time they point at him. After ten minutes of this, the official takes a large sheet of paper out of his small desk. Then he picks up the phone and dials a number.

"Listen," the boy pipes up, "I need to call my mother. And my father."

The steward cuffs the back of his head. "No cameras in here," he sneers. "We're going to have some fun, wait and see!"

Harvey tries to stand up, but the man plants both hands on his shoulders, pinning him in his seat. Just then, the little official talking on the phone turns pale. He motions for the steward to leave the boy alone.

Harvey stands up, rubbing his neck. "You big ox."

"Don't get smart with me!" the man threatens, pointing his finger at him.

"Quiet!" the little official orders them both. He hangs up the phone and waits.

Another ten minutes later, the door opens. The official snaps to his feet, his face pale.

The newcomer is a lean Chinese man dressed entirely in black. His shaven head reveals a glimpse of a circular bull's-eye tattoo. He has four fingers on his left hand and wears strange cork rings on the others.

Ignoring both Harvey and the steward, the man with the bull's-eye tattoo points at the man behind the desk and utters a few incomprehensible words powerful enough to persuade both the little man and the burly steward to leave the room.

Harvey smiles, relieved.

"Do you feel better, Mr. Miller?" the Chinese man asks.

"Yeah, actually. Would you let me make a phone call?"

"Please."

Harvey dials his home number. He's surprised to hear a man answer.

"Heh, heh, heh! Young Mr. Miller!" Egon Nose exclaims from the phone in New York. "What a pleasant surprise! You have a nice home, I must say! What a shame there's nobody here. Nobody at all! Care to tell me where you've all gone?"

"Nose!" Harvey shouts. "What are you doing in my house? Get out, now! I'm calling the police!"

"Oh, really? You want to call the police? In Shanghai?"

The Chinese man puts his finger down on the telephone's cradle, ending the conversation.

"I think that is enough," he says, his voice monotone. "We are going."

"Going where?" Harvey says, waving his arms and trying to make another call. "You don't understand! There's a man in my house!"

The Chinese man whips out a sharp knife and presses it against the young American's rib cage. "I think you are the one who does not understand, Mr. Miller."

84

Harvey is left breathless.

The pressure from the knife eases.

"Let's go," the man hisses, pushing him toward the door.

"Where to?"

"Home."

FIRST STASIMON

"Irene? Hello, Irene? Can you hear me?"

"Vladimir? Is that you?"

"Yes, it's me. I have great news: our master is still alive! She's here in Siberia. She's very old and very frail . . . but she's alive. She even sent a man to Paris."

"Now I see who did it."

"Who did what?"

"The kids met him. He had the heart top with him."

"Your top?"

"Yes, my top."

"Is it the connection, Irene . . . or are you crying?"

"Yes, Vladimir, I'm crying. Elettra discovered the room. I had to . . . make her fall asleep. And have Fernando take her away."

"What did she see?"

"The photographs. And my notes."

"She would've found out sooner or later. Better this way than hearing about it from Mistral."

"I know, but looking in her eyes and seeing that she didn't trust me anymore . . . that she was afraid of me . . . it was terrible. And now that she's gone, I feel so alone. And so full of doubt."

"We're all alone and full of doubt, Irene."

"Take care of yourself, Vladimir. And take care of my sister."

"Your sister?"

"She's on her way there."

13

THE TRAIN

"OH, NO, PLEASE DON'T BOTHER," LINDA MELODIA SAYS IN ITAL-
ian, smiling. She's in the third-class car of the train from Moscow that's going—or should be going—to Omsk, not far from the
Kazakhstani border. "There's no need for you to get up."

Naturally, the woman beside her doesn't understand and simply smiles, slipping off her skirt to put on a pair of light blue flan-
nel pajama pants. Linda tries to avoid looking at her, but deep
down she's shocked by how casually the woman is changing her
clothes in front of everyone. She doesn't say a word, partly because she wouldn't know what language to say it in. The woman's
husband, who is already in pajamas and has a mustache that looks
like a pair of sabers, has tried to speak to Linda in Italian, but as
it turns out, all he knows are the names of a few soccer players,
which he's repeated to her at least twenty times. The two are
in the seats beside Linda's, and in front of them is a wool-lined
cradle with a baby girl sleeping inside it.

Now the woman is working on her pajama top and Linda has
to dodge her elbow. Still, it's a quick process and in under a minute the woman has taken off her good dress and put on her train

clothes. She folds the dress and shoves it, crumpled, into the luggage rack over their heads.

Linda is horrified. "You can't leave it like that," she murmurs, biting her lip. "You'll ruin the crease!"

But the woman beside her couldn't care less about the crease. She tosses everything overhead, including her shoes, and ends up barefoot, as are her husband and many of the other passengers in the train car. Rows of shoes hang by their laces, jackets and shirts are draped over seats, swaying with the train's every lurch. The air is filled with the hum from the heater and has a mix of smells that are anything but pleasant: sweat, cheap soap, gasoline, salted fish, smoked mutton and other odors better left unidentified. The train car doesn't have compartments—just rows of high-backed wooden seats divided by a central aisle and small folding tables. In Linda's row, across the aisle, four men have been playing chess for hours. That is, two are playing and the other two are watching. And although there's probably a No Smoking sign somewhere, the players appear to have no intention of obeying it.

Linda sits in her little corner, trying not to touch, look at or breathe in anything. Her large suitcase has been stowed in the train car behind theirs and her small traveling bag is on her lap, sealed tight. She's so tense that she's on the edge of her seat, ready to spring to her feet at the slightest contact.

On the other hand, the woman next to her seems more relaxed now that she's in her pajamas. She even offers Linda a cup of coffee as thick as motor oil.

"Oh, no, thank you!" Linda exclaims, horrified but polite.

She stares at the cup as it's passed halfway around the train car and back again to be refilled. When the woman's husband holds the cup out to the baby in the cradle, Linda can't stand it any longer. "No! You can't give coffee to a baby!"

The man with the mustache stares at her, not understanding, so Linda takes the cup away from the little girl and sits down again.

"Ah, *da!*" The mustachioed man smiles, thinking Linda wants to finish the coffee herself. Holding back a shudder, she raises the cup to her lips and pretends to take a sip.

"*Daaa!*" the mustachioed man cheers as his wife offers her some more.

Linda politely declines and tries to concentrate on the monotonous landscape passing by outside the window. It's the endless expanse of the taiga: green fields, shrubs and countless rivers dotted here and there with tiny villages of little wooden houses or huge cement buildings devoid of beauty, the work of some overzealous local party administrator.

Once the thermos has been put away, Linda studies the train car again. The chess players smoke like chimneys as they calculate their next moves. A thick cloud of smoke hangs in the air over their wooden seats. A few of the travelers noisily flip through newspapers as big as bedsheets.

Linda imperceptibly unzips her bag. She takes out a slip of paper folded in eight, on which she's written down her departure and arrival times. But once the train set off, she realized that for some strange reason both schedules are in Moscow time, which means two time zones ago, so the times on the clocks at the various stations don't coincide.

Sighing, Linda tries to sort it out in her mind: ten more hours on the train, she thinks. Or eight. Or twelve.

She huffs, completely downcast.

Then she reflects. She's surrounded by strangers who don't speak her language. But maybe she could try to make herself useful.

She unzips her bag a bit wider and pulls out her little Italian-Russian phrase book.

"Hmm . . . so . . . ," she begins, staring straight at the woman in blue pajamas. "So, par . . . don . . . me."

She nods and repeats, with greater emphasis, "Pardon me!"

Then, with an inquiring tone, "Pardon me?"

Finally, she closes the phrase book. The woman smiles. Her husband smiles.

The chess players smile.

Did they understand? Linda Melodia wonders. She gets up, grabs the woman's clothes, pulls them down and folds them properly.

14
THE ARRIVAL

Sheng is dreaming.

And it's the same dream as always.

He's in the jungle with the other kids, a jungle that's silent, noiseless. A jungle they cross through almost running, as if being chased. Beyond the tropical vegetation is the sea. Sheng and the others dive in, swim over to a tiny island covered with seaweed. They see a woman waiting for them on the beach. Her face is covered by a cloak, a veil hiding her features. And she wears a close-fitting gown with all the animals of the world printed on it. This time, the woman's hands are empty and she raises them to bless Sheng's friends, who slowly pass before her: first Harvey, then Elettra, then Mistral. Sheng tries to get out of the water, but he can't: it's like he's being crushed, trapped by the weight of the sea. When the others have passed by, the woman turns toward him. And . . . and Sheng wakes up with a start.

He's in his room, in his house, the walls so thin he can hear his father snoring in the next room and his mother bustling around downstairs in the kitchen. If Sheng listens carefully, he can hear her feet shuffling across the floor.

He rolls over in bed, restless. The computer monitor on the table in the corner is a pale rectangle the color of ghosts. Their laundry is hung out to dry on dark clotheslines strung across the courtyard. TV antennas stick up from the rooftops of the old neighborhood's squat houses like a modern, flowerless rose garden.

Sheng buries his head under the pillow. He thinks back on the dream. On what it might mean. Slowly, he starts to sweat.

He gets out of bed, crosses the narrow hallway that leads to the bathroom and goes down to the kitchen, still half-asleep.

"What time is it?"

His mother motions for him to lower his voice: his father is still sleeping.

"Six in the morning."

A layer of dew covers the pavestones in the courtyard. Outside the rectangular windows, the alley is already bustling with people, with bicycles, with strange goods carried on people's shoulders or on old motor scooters.

"Sheng, are you sure you feel all right?" his mother asks, serving him a bowl of dark bancha tea directly from the pot. Then she surprises him by resting a dish with two mooncakes in the center of the table.

She smiles.

"I'm practicing for the Chung-Ch'iu Chieh festival," she whispers.

The Mid-Autumn festival. When fruit and treats are laid out on the home altars for visitors to enjoy.

He picks up one of the cakes between his fingers. It's firm, heavy. Looks good.

"Sugar, sesame seeds, walnuts, lotus seeds, eggs, ham, flower petals, plus . . . my secret ingredient," his mother says, running down the list as if she was reading from a cookbook.

Sheng takes a bite. Not bad. But with his second bite he tastes something strange in the filling, something vaguely pungent.

"Mpff . . . what exactly . . . did you use . . . as your secret ingredient?"

"Oh, who remembers? I improvised a little!"

With the fourth bite, the cake becomes a pasty glob that sticks there on the middle of his tongue. It won't come out and it won't go down. Sheng tries to loosen it with a sip of bancha tea and after a few failed attempts he finally manages to swallow it.

"Well? How is it?" his mother asks, still whispering.

Sheng stares at the other mooncake on the dish, terrified. "Not bad," he lies, stashing the uneaten half of the first one in his pajama pocket.

As he drinks his tea, he mentally goes over the day ahead of him and breaks into a sweat. He hasn't heard from Harvey and he thinks about everything he needs to do: pretend to go to school, meet up with Ermete and again with Mahler. Cross the river, try to figure out a way to get into the skyscraper. Wait for the others to arrive.

But then what?

He quickly finishes his breakfast, goes back up to his room, gets dressed without looking at himself in the mirror, grabs his backpack with his books and stops a moment. But his every thought is interrupted by his father's steady snoring, which echoes through the room. To Sheng, it sounds like he can barely breathe.

And so, he goes downstairs and walks back into the kitchen, ready to leave.

His mother stops him. "Where are you going, Sheng? It's too early for school."

"I can't sleep, Mom. I might as well go out."

"You're just like your father," the woman whispers. "At your age he couldn't sit still one minute."

Sheng pecks her cheek and goes out into the alley. He looks around. Vendors selling eyeglasses, billboards, shops with trousers displayed on aluminum hangers, colorful fabrics, people walking their motor scooters.

And across the street, him. Leaning against some cardboard boxes of fluorescent tube lights. The pale boy in the number 89 jersey.

The boy who's been following him.

On the second-to-top floor of a black skyscraper in the heart of Pudong, the new area of Shanghai, the phone used for confidential calls rings. Heremit Devil closes the little door to the children's bedroom where he normally sleeps, walks down the long hallway covered with childish, scrawled drawings and writings, and reaches his desk.

"Heremit," he hisses into the phone with a trace of breathlessness.

"I have the boy," a man's voice replies.

Nik Knife. Four Fingers. The knife thrower. The head of his security team.

Very good, Heremit thinks. *The first one has arrived.*

"Bring him up."

"Can he keep his own clothes? He traveled by plane."

"Have him decontaminated first."

95

"It will take half an hour."

"I can wait."

Heremit ends the conversation. He leans against the desk and dials another number.

"Cybel?"

"My dear fellow! My dear, dear fellow! To what do I owe the honor? I'm on the twelfth floor of your delightful beauty spa! I didn't know you appreciated such things! I'm having my nails polished with—"

"Any news about the girls?"

"Always in a good mood, aren't you, Heremit? Why don't you come here and enjoy a nice drainage massage? Or a chocolate treatment? Your ladies here tell me it's simply divine."

"Cybel. Any news about the girls?"

Cybel puffs. She cups her hand over her mouth and whispers into the receiver, "I simply didn't want to answer you with them around."

"Do it."

"You trust people too much, Heremit! If you keep this up, sooner or later someone—"

"Cybel. The girls."

"It sounds like you're giving me an ultimatum. Well, then, I'll answer you: no. No news. We haven't managed to get them."

"Why not?"

"Neither one is at home. The French girl and her mother haven't come back. As for the Italian, early this morning she got into her father's minibus . . . but she didn't catch a flight. I repeat: she didn't catch a flight."

"Then why did she go to the airport?"

"To help her father pick up some guests?"

"Why aren't they home yet?"

"Because not everyone is like you, Heremit, dear! People go out, my sweet! They go out! Being out of the house doesn't necessarily mean setting off for Shanghai."

Heremit checks the calendar. September 19. Two days until the year's last equinox.

"They should have left by now."

"But they haven't, my dear, they haven't! How can I get it through to you? I have my men. And neither Elettra Melodia nor Mistral Blanchard is on a plane, a train, a ship or a race car headed for Shanghai."

Heremit hangs up. Only two days left.

And he still has no idea what to do.

"'Claire and Lauren St-Tropez . . . ,'" the immigration officer at the Shanghai airport reads aloud as he checks the two passports. He glances at Mistral and her mother, studying the photographs. He thumbs through the pages with incredible slowness and checks their visa. Finally, he stamps it and quickly signs it.

"Welcome to China." He smiles and hands them their passports.

The two hold back a sigh of relief and hurry off, turning down a corridor with neon lights. Shanghai Pudong International Airport is a triumph of glass and crystal. It has a massive wave-shaped roof that looks like it's resting on thin air and overlooks countless landing strips. It takes the mother and daughter a good ten minutes just to reach the baggage claim area. They still have on the clothes they wore when they visited the apartment on Boulevard

97

de Magenta because they thought it best not to go home. Their only luggage consists of a suitcase they bought at the Galeries Lafayette and filled with new clothes, all paid for in cash so as not to leave a credit card trail.

When they reach the conveyor belts, Mistral and Cecile Blanchard realize they aren't alone.

"Elettra!" the girl shouts, spotting her friend among the people waiting for their luggage.

The two say hello and hug. Despite the trip, Elettra seems to be in good shape: raven-black hair down to her shoulders, a white cotton crew-neck sweater, cream-colored slacks tucked into a pair of tough-looking black ankle boots with lots of laces. Mistral and Elettra spoke just before boarding, agreeing to meet at the airport and go to the hotel together.

The French girl smiles. "Actually, it's Claire, not Mistral," she says, peering around.

Elettra smiles sheepishly. "And I'm Marcella."

They giggle.

"The others?"

"I haven't heard from Harvey since yesterday," Elettra replies. "As for Sheng and Ermete, they should already be at the Grand Hyatt."

"It looks like a wonderful hotel, at the top of a skyscraper."

"What are we waiting for?"

"To figure out which way to go?"

Having claimed their luggage, the three ladies walk into the massive arrivals hall: a long white two-level space with illuminated totems showing commercials on their giant screens.

"We need to follow the signs for the Maglev," Elettra says, trying to orient herself amid the river of people, "which happens to be the world's fastest train."

According to their guidebook, the Maglev travels at 431 kilometers an hour, using the world's first and as of yet only magnetic levitation railway. Seven minutes to travel the thirty kilometers between the airport and the city.

"That way," Mistral says, pointing at a sign.

They wheel their suitcases onto an escalator, walk across the mezzanine and turn down a long corridor, which is strangely deserted. And the few people walking down it are all foreigners.

"The Chinese don't seem to like this train very much," Elettra murmurs, struck by the contrast with the crowded, bustling hall.

They reach the Maglev station, a cascade of red Chinese lanterns overhead. Cecile gets in line to buy their one-way tickets. Next, an escalator leading downstairs and a moving walkway. Finally, they reach an aluminum and glass barrier along with around forty other people. The train is there in moments: a white snake with a tapered nose that silently stops beside the magnetic track.

They get in.

The train car has two different-color seats: yellow and white. The yellow ones are the famous VIP "soft seats." Cecile, Mistral and Elettra sit down on the other ones. Then the world's fastest train sets off.

"I wonder what it's like to travel on magnetic tracks?"

The answer comes soon enough: it's wobbly.

Feeling queasy, Mistral looks at the black and green display that indicates the train's speed. Outside the window, the landscape whizzes by faster and faster. Streets, trees, buildings.

"Two hundred kilometers an hour," Elettra says as the Maglev rocks like a boat.

"Three hundred kilometers an hour," Elettra says again.

In comparison, the cars moving down the highway look perfectly still.

"Four hundred and thirty-one!" Elettra exclaims.

Then the train begins to slow down and, seven minutes after its departure, it stops at the Longyang station. The three grab their luggage and step out of the train.

"What now?" Mistral asks, looking around.

They see two taxi signs, but it isn't clear which way they need to go. The train heads back to the airport, leaving behind a few clusters of people, suitcases in tow, who all appear to be wondering the same thing as Mistral.

"Let's follow them," Elettra suggests, pointing at two travelers who look more confident than the others.

Five minutes later, they wind up in a desolate asphalted parking lot without any signs.

"Over there!" Cecile suddenly shouts, seeing a taxi entering the parking lot.

They rush toward it like desert nomads who've found an oasis.

"To the Grand Hyatt, please!"

The taxi driver smiles and merges into a flood of cars that ends up stuck in a traffic jam after a few hundred yards. Shanghai is ahead of them, but it still looks far, far away.

Mistral, Cecile and Elettra look around glumly.

"What point is there in taking the world's fastest train if you have to add another hour by taxi to get where you're going?" says Elettra.

15

MILLER

IT'S ALL VERY DIFFICULT TO UNDERSTAND, BUT MRS. MILLER IS
trying her best.

She's sitting in a leather armchair in a foul-smelling bar with
the man who came into her house through the skylight, saving
her life in the process.

His name is Quilleran, he has Native American blood in his
veins and he claims to be Harvey's friend. One thing is for sure:
he's their mailman.

"Believe me, ma'am, there was no other way for me to get in,"
the man repeats for the umpteenth time. "Egon Nose was already
at the gate and he would've seen me."

This is the part of his story that Harvey's mother finds incomprehensible. "Would you mind explaining why this—this Egon
Nose would have something against me?"

"Not against you, ma'am. Against your son."

"Is it because of the passports?"

Quilleran shakes his head. "It's a long story. If he hasn't told
you, I can't be the one to explain."

"Then what can you do, apart from making me run away from my own home over the rooftop?"

"I've already apologized."

"And I've already accepted your apology; otherwise I wouldn't be here talking to you."

"You need to stay in a safe place until things have calmed down. And go to the police station right away."

"To tell them what?"

"That someone's threatening you."

"I'm calling my husband," Mrs. Miller says.

Quilleran hands her his cell phone.

Mr. Miller is on the ship's deck together with Paul Magareva from the Polynesian Oceanographic Institute. The two have been talking nonstop for hours. Professor Miller's report is grim.

"'Last year,'" he reads, "'saw a record number of typhoons in the Pacific. Fifteen hurricanes of the highest category in the Atlantic as opposed to an average of ten; a hundred and eighty-two tornados in August, fifty-six more than the record year of 1979, and two hundred thirty-five in September, a hundred and thirty-nine more than in 1967; unprecedented forest fires in Alaska; a devastating earthquake in Iran and the tsunami in the Indian Ocean; extreme droughts in North Africa with swarms of locusts, at an estimated loss of eight point five billion dollars, of which insurance covers only nine hundred and twenty-five million. All together, we're talking a hundred and forty-five billion dollars in damages. Plus, the last ten years have been the hottest ones since 1861.'" George Miller tosses the report on the table. "Is that a big enough catastrophe for you?"

Paul Magareva looks at the Port of Shanghai. "Well? Are you convinced there's a planet on a collision course with us?"

"Honestly, no. But I'm convinced we're on a collision course with ourselves."

"What's happening now has happened before," his Polynesian colleague insists. "It's like when a computer has too many useless programs on it. There's only one thing to do: delete everything. Call it a great flood, call it the extinction of the dinosaurs, but that's the way it is."

"You read too much science fiction, Paul."

"And you don't read enough of it!"

Professor Miller's cell phone rings. "Who could this be?" he wonders, not recognizing the number.

The professor answers. It's his wife. She sounds alarmed. He listens. Nods. "I'll call the embassy right away," he says.

Through the car's dark windows, Harvey sees only shadows. Shadows of massive streets, buildings, grates, construction sites. The outlines of cranes. Rows and rows of trees that suddenly appear and disappear just as suddenly.

There's also a shadow behind the wheel, but Harvey can't see him from his seat beside the Chinese man with the bull's-eye tattooed on the back of his head. So far, the trip from the airport to wherever-it-is has lasted thirty-two minutes. One thousand nine hundred and twenty seconds, which Harvey has counted one by one so he won't lose his concentration. Discipline and self-control. Olympia taught him that.

Obviously, beneath his cool composure, he's angry. Very angry. He didn't expect to have to deal with Egon Nose again.

He wishes he told the others what he planned to do. But he didn't. And now it's definitely too late to warn anyone.

My dad knows, he thinks as the city's shadows slip by outside the tinted windows. *My dad knows something big is going on. He'll know what to do.*

The Chinese man sitting beside him as silent as the grave is clutching Harvey's backpack, which has his father's books in it.

The car slows, turns gently and plunges down. An underground parking lot, Harvey guesses.

From his silent traveling companion's movements, he can tell they've arrived. The car door opens. Harvey is accompanied into an elevator a few steps away. He only has time to take a quick glance around: an asphalt ramp, fifty parking spaces, shiny, black vans.

Daylight. It's already morning.

Then he's swallowed up by the elevator.

16

THE GRAND HYATT

◯

ERMETE AND SHENG ARE SITTING AT A SMALL CRYSTAL TABLE
that looks like it's floating in the middle of the clouds. It's the
spectacular, panoramic lounge in the Grand Hyatt, the world's
tallest hotel.

The moment they see Elettra, Mistral and Madame Blanchard
walk in, they stand up and wave them over. It's a warm, welcom-
ing hello with all their usual wisecracks. Then Cecile goes to the
reception desk to check in under their false names before taking
their suitcases up to the room. Meanwhile, the two girls sit down
at the table so they can decide what to do.

"Harvey?" Elettra asks.

Ermete and Sheng exchange glances. "That's the first mystery.
He should've landed in Shanghai last night, but his cell phone is
off and he hasn't texted us."

"That's not good."

"Especially since we don't have much time to lose."

Sheng rubs his eyes and looks around. Then he holds back a
yawn, making his whole jaw tremble.

"How do you feel?" Mistral asks him.

"Fine," he says, stifling a second yawn. "I'm just a little . . . sleepy."

"You look exhausted."

"Yeah, that's the word for it," he says.

"What about that dream you keep having?" Mistral asks.

Sheng nods. "Still having it."

The girls look at Ermete and then at each other. "Maybe we should figure out why you have it in the first place."

Sheng stares at the tips of his new shoes. Nobody's noticed he isn't wearing horrible sneakers.

"It might have something to do with your eyes," Elettra guesses.

"Hey!" Sheng snaps. "Can we change the subject or do you really need to give me the third degree?"

"It isn't the third degree. It's just that there's no such thing as blue-eyed Chinese people," Elettra continues. "You do realize that, don't you?"

"How would you guys know?" he grumbles. "Actually, there's no such thing as what you call 'Chinese people,' either."

"There aren't?" Ermete asks. "Then who are the Chinese?"

"It just so happens that we 'Chinese' don't have a word for Chinese. We use the word Han, but that just means a certain number of ethnic groups who at some point in history were ruled by the Han dynasty."

"So how do you say someone's Chinese or not Chinese?"

"We don't. What point is there in saying someone's Italian, or French?"

"It's really important to us Europeans."

"To us it isn't. And if you really want to know, we don't even have a word for *China*."

Ermete laughs. "You're kidding, right?"

"Not at all. *China* is a word *you* came up with to talk about the place *we* live. It isn't Chinese. It isn't Wu."

"What's Wu?"

"Shanghai's dialect, which is different from Beijing's dialect. And Hong Kong's, and—"

"Wait, wait . . . ," Mistral cuts him off. "If there isn't a Chinese word to say *China*, then how do you say *China*?"

"It depends on what we mean, exactly. We can use *Zhongguo*, the 'middle country,' and *Zhongguo Ren*, its inhabitants. But it doesn't mean *China*."

"It's like the street names!" Ermete grumbles. "Two hundred ways to say the same thing. Nothing's simple here. It's all mutable, fluid."

"Well, after all, we're in the city of water," Elettra reminds the others. "Which is also the world's biggest river port. In any case"—Elettra peers around—"do you think we should talk here?"

"I doubt they bugged the place just for us," Ermete says.

"Besides, nobody could even know we're here," Sheng says.

Elettra hesitates. "I need to tell you something," she says.

"So do I," Mistral adds.

The two girls give the others a recap of their discoveries. The only thing Elettra leaves out is the other Chinese boy, Hi-Nau. When she's finished, Sheng looks at her and exclaims, "Your aunt is one of the four Sages!"

Ermete is sprawled out in his armchair. "After all the trouble we went through, we could've just asked her!"

"But she wouldn't have told us anything. Not being able to talk to us is a part of the Pact."

"Okay," Sheng says, turning to Mistral, "but Professor Van Der Berger didn't seem to care. He ended up telling us what happened."

"But only because he's dead," the Roman engineer reminds everyone. "I don't know if the Pact still counts after you die."

"In any case," Mistral says, "the Pact was broken. In a place called Century."

"Could it have happened in that apartment in the Century Building in New York?" Ermete murmurs.

"That's not important," Elettra says. "There are two important things right now: Sheng and this box." She puts the cookie tin from her aunt in the middle of the table. "Inside of it are the clues they had back in 1907. But they didn't know what to do with them."

"Like in Paris, with the clock?"

"Exactly," Elettra replies. Clutched between her knees is her backpack with the map of the Chaldeans and the only top they have left, the heart top. "But before we open the box, I think we should talk about Sheng's dream some more."

He grumbles. "Again?"

"I think it's fundamental. In her files, my aunt talked about powers. I have the power of Fire, of energy."

"And you can make lights explode," Mistral whispers, remembering what happened in the library in New York.

"You have the power of Air," Elettra says to Mistral. "And

because of your power, when you sing you can make creatures of the air listen to you."

"Like that Indian guy in New York!" Sheng says. "Quilleran, who could talk to the crows. Was he one of the Sages, too?"

"No," Mistral says, "he said that a friend taught him how to speak to the crows, and I think I know who it was."

"Who?"

"Vladimir."

"The antiques dealer?" Ermete is astonished.

"Yes, him. And do you know why? Because I'm convinced that the four masters who came before us had these powers, too. Take Professor Van Der Berger: he could talk to the Earth. And make plants grow, I think. Just like Harvey."

Ermete holds up both hands. "Hold on, hold on. I'm not following. Harvey has the power of Earth . . . like the professor, right?"

"Exactly," Elettra confirms.

"And you're saying Mistral has the power of Air, like Vladimir, the antiques dealer."

"What about you, then?" Sheng asks Elettra.

"I have the same power Zoe had."

When he hears her name, the engineer thinks back to the day he spent with her in Paris. "Fifty-eight euros' worth of flowers down the drain," he grumbles. Then he turns to Sheng. "So that leaves you with the power of Water . . ."

"Guys, I can't even swim."

Everyone looks at Elettra.

"Like your aunt Irene?"

"Exactly," the girl replies, raising her finger. "Maybe she could explain your recurring dream."

Sheng nods. "Yeah, maybe."

"Partly because I think your power is somehow connected to sleeping, Sheng. My aunt made me fall asleep with a wave of her hand."

"And don't forget your yellow eyes," Mistral breaks in, flipping through one of her notebooks.

Sheng cringes, turning red. "You want me to strip so you can examine me better?"

"We're just trying to help you!"

"In my dream there's always a lot of water," Sheng says, suddenly serious. "We swim over to this island. It's just that . . . well, once we reach it, you guys get out, no problem, but I . . . I don't. I can't. I'm trapped."

"Now you see why it's important for you to talk to my aunt? Even if she answers you with riddles, like all of them have done so far, they might be riddles that are easy to solve."

The four sit in silence, turning things over in their minds.

After a while, Cecile walks over to the table, smiling. "Would you like me to take your suitcases up to the room for you?" she asks.

Elettra stands up. "Please, don't bother, ma'am. We'll take care of it." She winks at Mistral, inviting her to follow her. Then she turns to the other two and adds, "Will you wait for us down here a minute?"

As soon as the elevator door closes, Elettra explains to her friend, "I didn't want Sheng to hear me."

"What is it?"

"In my aunt's secret room, I found out that Sheng is a replacement for another boy, whose name is—or was—Hi-Nau."

"Sheng wasn't supposed to be Sheng?"

"Exactly. Before making me fall sleep, Aunt Irene told me that Hi-Nau's powers were really strong, even stronger than all of ours."

"Then why isn't he here?"

"I don't know."

"You could ask her."

"I'll try, but the thing is . . . this might explain why Sheng is insecure."

"What, you think the rest of us aren't? I haven't used the language of animals for weeks. I get scared even thinking of doing it."

"But you *can* do it! I was scared by my energy, too, but I used it. The same thing goes for Harvey! But Sheng . . . what can he do?"

The elevator door opens, leaving the two friends agape. The hallway looks onto the lobby fifty meters below. It's like being in a theater with a breathtaking view: a spiral of carpeted terraces, gold lamps and sparkling windows. Outside, the sky is growing dark and the city is lighting up. Millions of multicolored neon signs are getting ready for another incredible night.

Elettra and Mistral lean against the railing, captivated.

The elevator Cecile took has yet to arrive.

"So did you see that boy, Hi-Nau?" Mistral asks, staring down at two colorful specks, which are Ermete and Sheng.

"Just a photograph, but I don't think I'd recognize him. What I'm afraid of . . . is that Sheng might get discouraged if he knew he was some sort of fill-in."

Mistral nods. "You're right. . . . Oh, here's my mom."

The elevator lets out a chime and opens.

The two girls turn around.

Cecile Blanchard is pale.

Beside her is a tallish man in a long green-gray raincoat and a baseball cap pulled down over his eyes.

"Happy to see me?" Jacob Mahler asks, stepping out of the elevator.

17

THE DEVIL

A WHITE-TILED PASSAGEWAY DIVIDED BY DARK GLASS PANELS. To the right is a silver conveyor belt. To the left, aluminum shower-heads mounted on the wall. On the floor, a layer of crystal-clear water about ten centimeters deep. It looks like the entrance to a public pool.

A voice from the speaker on the wall tells Harvey to undress, but he thinks they must be kidding, so they have to tell him a second time. Surprised, he slips off his shoes and puts them on the silver conveyor belt.

"And the rest," the voice from the speaker orders.

Nik Knife is a perfectly still mask behind him.

"You're kidding, right?" Harvey Miller asks, laughing nervously.

The Chinese man simply rests the backpack on the belt. "We do not have much time. Mr. Devil is waiting for us."

Harvey nods. Devil's house, devil's rules.

He pulls off his sweater and two T-shirts, ending up bare-chested. He sticks it all on the conveyor belt. Then come his pants.

"Walk through there." The Chinese man points to the middle of the passageway with the pool of disinfectant water.

While Harvey is walking, an X-ray of his skeleton appears on the dark screens that divide the passageway.

The aluminum showerheads spray him with a pungent-smelling jet of steam. A shower of water mixed with some kind of germicide. Then a jet of scented steam and, finally, hot air to dry him off.

Meanwhile, six latex-gloved hands rifle through his clothes, open his backpack, pull everything out and put it back in its place. The soles of his shoes are scanned with a beam of orange light. Pants, shirts, sweater and backpack are sprayed with the same disinfectant steam.

Harvey is given his clothes back at the end of the passageway.

"You can get dressed now," says the Chinese man, who now wears latex gloves on his hands and a mask over his face.

"Really nice of you," Harvey jokes. "Do you all have to do this when you walk into his place?"

"Only the people he wants to see quickly," the Chinese man replies, as stony as a statue. "We are much more careful with the others."

He pulls off his gloves and mask as he waits for Harvey to finish getting dressed.

"My hair's still wet," Harvey complains when he's pushed toward a second elevator with gold doors. "I could catch a cold if I go outside like this."

"We are not going outside," the Chinese man growls.

The elevator doesn't have floor buttons. The door closes and the elevator zooms up automatically.

Twenty-nine seconds. Thirty. Thirty-one, Harvey counts, feeling the pressure on his knees.

Finally, they reach Heremit Devil's office.

"Why, look who's here, look who's here!" Mademoiselle Cybel exclaims the moment Harvey steps out of the elevator. "My favorite American boy!"

He wasn't expecting to see her here. But Nik Knife's grip on his elbow makes him keep moving.

"Mademoiselle Cybel," Harvey snarls, moving toward the chair the large woman is sunk into. "Always a pleasure to see you."

The woman laughs, making her double chin quiver.

"Looks like I'm pretty good at letting myself get kidnapped at airports," Harvey continues, annoyed. "At least I don't see any poisonous spiders this time."

"Look carefully." The woman laughs again. "Look carefully, Miller Junior."

Harvey's eyes dart around the room: a breathtaking view of the city. The river to the west. A large park to the south. Other skyscrapers. The Shanghai television tower. It takes him only a few seconds to figure out the building's location on the map of Shanghai, which he learned by heart.

Heremit's office is a spartan, sterile room. TV screens turned off. Shelves practically empty. Desk polished. Phone. And a series of objects, most of which are familiar to him, lined up on the desk. The Ring of Fire, the Star of Stone, the tops, a wooden ship . . .

Then the man, who's had his back to Harvey the whole time as he contemplates the city lights, turns toward him very slowly.

The hermit devil.

He doesn't speak. He just fixes his gaze on Harvey from behind his thick black Bakelite glasses. His silent stare teems with ice-cold insects that crawl up Harvey's back and sting all his nerves.

"Nothing in particular, sir," Nik Knife says, resting Harvey's backpack on the floor. "Except the printout of a reservation at the Grand Hyatt tonight."

Mademoiselle Cybel whistles. "Why, Miller Junior! Treating yourself well, hmm? Very well, I'd say!"

"And this," the Chinese man concludes.

He's holding the small paper and foil packet that contains the last two of the seeds Harvey found in New York.

Mademoiselle Cybel peeks at them through her gaudy glasses. "They look like little seeds for big weeds. Seeds, weeds," she chirps, as if she's just come up with history's greatest rhyme. "You certainly are a strange boy, Miller Junior."

Heremit Devil slowly steps toward the packet. He does so walking in a perfect circle, with Harvey as its center and the distance between them as the radius.

"What are they?" he asks.

Nik Knife puts the seeds on the desk.

"Seeds for weeds," Harvey says, on the razor's edge.

"Cheeky," Mademoiselle Cybel remarks with a hint of admiration.

Harvey tries to hold Heremit Devil's gaze, but he can't. He's forced to look down at his disinfected gym shoes.

"Destroy them," Heremit Devil orders Nik Knife.

The Chinese man turns to carry out the order and Harvey caves in. "You shouldn't do that," he says.

Heremit Devil circles back to his favorite window, following the same path in reverse. "What are they?" he asks for the second time.

"They're tree seeds."

"Why shouldn't we destroy them?"

"Because they're my good luck charm. I always plant trees when I travel."

"Then you'd better find a new good luck charm, my boy," Mademoiselle Cybel interjects, laughing. "Find a new good luck charm . . . and fast!"

Heremit Devil whips his head around, instantly making her fall silent.

"Tell me about this tree."

"My father says it's a really ancient species. The ginkgo biloba."

"Your father is an esteemed professor," Heremit Devil observes. "And he's very concerned, I imagine. On that ship."

He juts his chin toward the window, at the river below. It looks perfectly still.

"We weren't talking about my father."

"And he's right," Heremit continues, his voice flat and monotone. "We're all very concerned. Strange natural phenomena. Violent tornadoes, the climate inexplicably changing, ice caps melting, sea levels rising, rivers drying up. We have good reason to be concerned."

No one in the office says a single word. Heremit continues his slow monologue. "The air in this city has become unfit to breathe. Seventy-five percent of the inhabitants of Shanghai suffer from chronic insomnia because of the lights from the bars and restaurants. We're all worried. Worried enough not to sleep at night."

Heremit Devil clasps his hands behind his back and cracks his knuckles. "All we need . . . are answers. Simple answers to simple questions: Who are you? Where are you? Where did you come from? Where are you going? Why? That's the fundamental reason we're here: to answer these questions."

As he listens, Harvey lets out a nervous laugh. *This guy's insane*, he thinks.

"Let's not waste any more time, Miller. I know all about the Pact, about the four of you, about the four masters. I know what they did, where they are now, how they chose the four of you. I know practically everything, except the reason why they chose you and the meaning behind this collection of . . . things." He points at the objects lined up on his desk and continues. "I understand the mirror: look at yourself, realize who you are. Discover your true nature. And the stone that fell from the sky: know where you came from, from comets that journey through space, like the scattered seeds of a tree that seek the earth. But then we come to this ship. Knowing where you're going? Across the waves? Down some unknown river shrouded in fog?"

Harvey's never seen the ship before. He imagines it's the fourth object, the one for Water that was hidden in Shanghai. But given how nervous Mademoiselle Cybel is, he senses that something doesn't add up.

"I should have everything," Heremit Devil continues, "but everything is slipping through my fingers. Including time. I've spent five long years making assumptions. And frankly, I've grown tired of it."

Heremit's gaze locks onto Harvey's. It's a long, questioning gaze. A hard, heartless gaze but also—surprisingly—a pained one.

"You're telling me, Heremit my dear, you're telling me!" Mademoiselle Cybel exclaims. It's like crystal shattering. Ice breaking at the wrong moment. "We're all tired. Just think, five years! Five years!"

The woman bolts up from her chair, her giant silk dress rustling. "I'll leave you alone now! I think I'll go try out a new relaxing massage."

To Harvey, Mademoiselle Cybel's agitation is even further proof of his suspicions. "Is that the Ship of Shanghai?" he asks, deciding to go for broke.

"What's that, Miller?"

Heremit Devil's question sounds rhetorical, as if the man already knows everything. In fact, he turns to his Parisian collaborator and orders, "Cybel, wait."

The woman is just a few steps away from the gold elevator. Her face is covered with a layer of uncontrollable perspiration. Nevertheless, she manages to pretend she doesn't understand. "Why would that be the Ship of Shanghai?"

"Because Shanghai is the city of water," Harvey says, "while Paris is the city of wind and—"

"Heremit, dear!" Mademoiselle Cybel says. "Certainly you can't believe the boy! Zoe found this ship right where it was hidden. Right where it was hidden."

"Which would be . . . ?"

"On Île de la Cité!"

Harvey snickers. The only thing on Île de la Cité was the pointy spires of Notre Dame. He can tell that Heremit doesn't believe the woman's story but is letting her leave anyway. "Of course. You may go, Cybel."

"Heremit—"

"You may go."

The woman snaps at Harvey. "Are you calling me a liar, boy? Mademoiselle Cybel, a liar?"

When the silk elephant disappears into the elevator, Heremit asks, "What was in Paris?"

"I can't tell you," Harvey answers.

"Fair enough," he says. "We're enemies. And one should never help one's enemy."

Heremit Devil steps over to his desk. He picks up the wooden ship and hurls it with incredible force against the picture window, shattering it in a thousand pieces.

"Junk!" he screams. "Useless junk! What was she trying to do, trick me?"

No one answers. Pieces of the ship tumble across the floor, some even reaching its farthest corners.

In under ten seconds, Heremit Devil has already calmed down. "Take care of it," he orders Nik Knife, pointing toward the trail of perfume that Mademoiselle Cybel left behind. "And when you're done, go to the Grand Hyatt. Mr. Miller's companions might have arrived already."

Nik Knife slips out of the office as swiftly as a sense of foreboding.

"Leave my friends alone," Harvey growls, trying to sound threatening.

"Friends, Mr. Miller? Are you really convinced there's any such thing as friends? Of course, you're young . . . you have yet to learn what friendship is. It's just a mask concealing envy. It's the glove of the thief who robs you of your life and leaves no trace behind."

18
THE ASCENT

"So what's in this thing, anyway?" Ermete asks, picking up the cookie tin and shaking it. The old Chinese coins inside of it clatter.

"We'd better leave it alone until the girls get back," Sheng suggests.

"Would you at least smile?"

Sheng smiles. *"Hao!"*

"So tell me, is that a Chinese word?"

"Who knows? But you know what? I've been thinking of what our names mean. *Mistral* is the name of a wind. *Elettra*, as in electricity . . ."

"Uh-uh, wrong," Ermete corrects him. "It comes from the Greek word for 'yellow amber.' It means 'radiant.' When amber is rubbed, it has the property of electricity, of attracting light objects."

"You're a walking science book."

"Do you know what my name means? Hermes, messenger of the gods, the god of eloquence. Does *Sheng* mean anything?"

"It's a sort of wooden flute with lots of vertical shafts. Or"—Sheng flashes an all-gums smile—"it can mean victory."

"So you're called Victoria, like a girl?"

"Very funny!" Sheng says, laughing. "More like Victor, as in . . . the winner!"

His cell phone rings.

"Harvey?" Ermete asks.

Sheng shakes his head. It's an unknown number. "Hello?"

It's Jacob Mahler. "There should be a man in the lobby who's dressed in black. Shaved head. See him?"

Sheng mouths the name "Mahler" to Ermete and repeats in a whisper, "Man in black . . . shaved head . . . in the lobby . . ."

They steal a glance around.

"There are lots of people in the lobby."

Not a sound comes from the other end of the cell phone.

"There," Ermete says a moment later, pointing at a massive but not-too-tall Chinese man standing by the elevators.

"I see him. He's here," Sheng says into the phone. "What's going on?"

"They found us," Mahler says. "It's Four Fingers. Is he looking your way?"

"No."

"Then he doesn't know what you look like."

"What do you want me to do?"

"Don't look at him. Grab all your things and get out of the hotel."

"What about the others?"

"I'll take care of that. Be at Rushan Lu, at the corner of Meiyuan Park, in a couple hours."

"Elettra and Mistral—"

"They're here with me," the killer concludes before hanging up.

Many floors above, in the spectacular hallway that leads to their rooms, Mistral feels like she's about to faint.

Jacob Mahler. The man who kidnapped her in Rome. Who threatened to kill her, locked her up in a room in the Coppedè district. The man who was supposed to be dead.

He's there now, just a few steps away from them, standing beside her mother.

"Hello, Mistral." He even has the nerve to speak to her.

Mistral looks the other way. She feels Elettra take her hand.

"Everything's okay," the Italian girl tells her. "He—"

Mistral doesn't want to hear it. She whirls around. She refuses to speak to that man.

She doesn't trust him.

She'll never trust him.

"Get him out of here," she says, standing by their door.

Mahler looks down at the lobby. "In the room, quick," he orders.

They do as he says, but once they're inside, Mistral locks herself in the bathroom. She stares into the mirror over the clear glass sink and turns on the water. Under any other circumstances, she would think the bathroom was stunning. But all she can think of right now is Jacob Mahler, who's right outside the door, talking to Elettra and her mother.

"The second you try to leave, he'll be on your tail," the man is saying.

"How do you know that? We used fake names and passports."

"Harvey, too?"

"What does Harvey have to do with it?"

"Was he supposed to stay at this hotel, too?"

"Yes, why?"

"It's obvious. He isn't positive you're here, but he's assuming you'll come. And he's willing to wait. In fact, he sent in the best man he's got left to look for you."

Mistral's heart races faster and faster. She clearly remembers the moment she woke up in that bedroom in Rome, when Mahler came in to interrogate her.

"Don't trust him, guys . . . ," she murmurs from behind the bathroom door. "You shouldn't trust him."

The noise of the hot water running in the sink drowns out the rest of the conversation. Steam fogs up the mirror and every-thing else.

"Mistral?" Elettra asks a moment later, knocking on the door. "Everything okay?" Then, when there's no reply, she adds, "He's gone."

Mistral opens the door a crack. "We shouldn't trust him."

"He's our only hope."

"That's not true; he's not our only hope. Your aunt gave you the clues from 1907. We have those. And we still have one of the tops."

"Yes, but Jacob . . . he knows the city. And Heremit Devil's men."

"He's one of Heremit Devil's men."

"He used to be."

"Where did he go?"

"He's making plans with your mom."

"What kind of plans? What does he have in mind?"

"He says we can't go down there."

"So . . . ?"

"So . . . we go up."

"Up? We're on the seventieth floor! And once we get there?"

Elettra stares at her without replying.

"Once we get there?" Mistral asks again.

19
THE BAT

"Do you know the way there?" Ermete asks as he darts out of the Jin Mao Tower, where the hotel is.

Ahead of him, Sheng crosses Lujiazui Green Park and heads toward the wide lanes of Jujiazhi Lu.

They've taken Irene's cookie tin and Elettra's backpack with them.

"You think he saw us?"

"No, but if you wait up for me, I might avoid having a heart attack."

Sheng slows his pace a little.

"The address he gave you, is it very far away?" the engineer asks.

The two reach the intersection on the other end of the park. Six lanes of traffic. The first headlights zooming through the fading daylight. Tree branches swaying in the thick, damp, gentle breeze. The smell of rain in the air.

"Everything's far away here."

"I mean, do you want to walk there?"

Sheng scratches his head. "I guess so."

Ermete opens his tourist map of Pudong, which he picked up at the hotel reception desk. "Where is it?"

"This way."

"And where are we now?"

Sheng puffs. "C'mon, you know I'm no expert at reading maps."

"Fine, but where are we?"

"Here, I think."

"What do you mean, you *think*?"

"Um, no. Here. Maybe."

Ermete stomps his foot.

"This is a city of twenty million people," Sheng says in his defense. "Besides, Pudong isn't my neighborhood."

The engineer nervously runs his finger down the street names. "Why do you write them all in Chinese, anyway?" he grumbles. Then he looks up. Standing out against the dark sky, the Grand Hyatt's tall profile looks like a giant precious gem.

"It sure is something . . . ," Ermete murmurs, letting his gaze linger. "These skyscrapers are nothing short of incredible. Now I know why they call it the New York of the East."

"Well, they call it the Paris of the East, too," Sheng adds. "But we should get moving if we want to reach Meiyuan Park in two hours."

He waits for the green light and crosses the street.

Behind him, Ermete yawns. "Did you know that walking makes people sleepy?"

"I wish," Sheng replies, his eyes red from exhaustion.

They walk along, the backpack slung over Ermete's shoulders and the cookie tin tucked under Sheng's arm. Tiny black specks in the jungle of mirrors.

"The last time I checked, I weighed forty-five kilos," Elettra says from the ledge of the eighty-seventh floor of the Jin Mao Tower. The damp wind keeps pushing her hair forward over her eyes. Night descended upon the city like a shroud in under forty minutes. The girl's voice is trembling. Around her, the Pudong skyscrapers are pillars of light. The immense city is spread out before her, immeasurable, infinite. Five paces in front of her is empty space. And on the very edge of that empty space, a shadow is crouched down.

It's Jacob Mahler. He's perfectly still, like a predator. He watches. He waits for the guests on the observation deck above them to leave. Beside him is a large backpack he picked up from his room. And a violin case.

"What about you?" the shadow asks Mistral.

The French girl is as pale as a ghost. Her oval face makes her look like a porcelain statue. Her fine, windswept hair covers her eyes. She keeps her hands pressed against the wall and the bag containing the Veil of Isis slung over her lean shoulder. Ten paces to their left and overhead, the hotel's searchlights look like beams from a spaceship.

"Mistral?" Elettra asks. "How much do you weigh?"

"I don't know," she says. "I've never weighed myself."

Jacob Mahler stands up, balancing on the edge of the tower's eighty-seventh floor as if it was the most natural thing in the world. "You can't weigh more than she does," he says.

It's as if he still remembers Mistral's weight from when he carried her out of the professor's apartment in Rome.

He holds his violin case out to the girl, but she refuses to take it. Jacob doesn't insist. "You hold it," he tells Elettra.

Then he begins to fasten the other backpack onto his shoulders, tightening the belt and straps.

"I need the bow," he orders Elettra.

The girl clicks open the lock on the violin case, raises the lid, then brushes the hair out of her eyes and looks at the wooden instrument that was handmade in a shop in Cremona, S-shaped openings on either side of its unusual metal strings. Beside the violin is a razor-sharp bow.

Elettra hands it to Mahler, who uses it to slice his green-gray raincoat into strips. With astonishing swiftness, he fashions two crude harnesses.

From the street, a distant siren. The skyscrapers' mirrored windows glimmer.

"Put them on," Mahler tells the two girls.

"We can't actually be doing this," Elettra says, shuddering.

"They'll hold."

"What if they don't?"

"Hug your friend," Jacob Mahler orders.

"What?"

"Hug her."

Mistral keeps her eyes shut and shakes her head. Elettra gently wraps her arms around her.

"Tighter," Jacob Mahler says, behind her.

Elettra squeezes Mistral tight. Then, suddenly, she feels weightless. Mistral stifles a scream. A viselike grip has grabbed

129

them by the sides and lifted them up. After a few seconds, Jacob Mahler puts them back down.

He used only one arm. "If they don't hold," he says, nodding at their harnesses, "I'll hold you."

At Rushan Lu, on the corner of Meiyuan Park, is a high-rise from the 1970s. A dozen stories, no taller. Gray and anonymous, apart from a tall radio/TV antenna that looks like a plume swaying on its roof. The main door at the top of the stairs is closed. And there's no intercom.

"What now?" Ermete asks.

"We wait?" Sheng suggests.

The two sit down on the lowest steps, far from the fluorescent lights illuminating the entrance, far from the swarms of tiny insects dancing all around them.

"We could take a look inside the box," Ermete says. "What do you say?" He rests the cookie tin on his lap and opens it: coins in different shapes and sizes, and the red-lacquered tile with four small black stylized knives.

"That's it?"

"I guess so."

They hand the coins to each other, one by one, reading the dates against the light.

"Old," Sheng remarks, "and English."

"What do you think they're for?"

"I have no idea. No idea at all. Besides, today the city's totally different from what it was like in 1907. I don't think very much from back then is still around."

Ermete examines the stylized knives on the red tile.

"We don't like old things," Sheng continues. "When a building needs renovations, we tear it down and build a new one that's identical to the old one."

Ermete nods, putting down the tile. "So to use these clues, the first thing we need to do is get a map of the areas of the city that were around back in 1907 . . . and are still around today."

"Exactly," Sheng agrees. "That won't be so hard. The Huxinting Teahouse, the Yuyuan Garden, the Jade Buddha Temple, a couple old English buildings by the river in the Bund area . . . and a little something among the houses in the French Concession."

"Not such a big area to investigate, then," Ermete murmurs, handing Sheng the red tile.

"Oh!" the boy says, staring at it.

"Does it mean anything to you?"

"Nothing good," Sheng says in a low voice. "Four daggers."

"Meaning?"

"The Daggers is the name of the group of rebels who started up the revolt against the Westerners in the late eighteen hundreds."

"Great."

"And there are four of them." Sheng shakes his head.

"So what?"

"It's a superstition: in Shanghai, the number four brings bad luck because it's pronounced like our word for death."

"Death?"

Sheng nods, a bleak look on his face. "The word also means . . . to lose."

Base jump.

That's what they call leaping from tall buildings with the kind of equipment now strapped to Jacob Mahler's back. To some, it's an extreme sport. To others, the only possibility of getting out of a skyscraper without attracting too much attention.

"Ready?" Jacob Mahler asks from the ledge of the hotel.

"Yes," Elettra answers.

Mistral doesn't say anything. There's no need.

"On three, all you have to do is run forward."

Ahead of them is empty space. The wind. The city. The river. The girls are held in place by the harness made of strips of Jacob Mahler's raincoat and by his arms.

Elettra can't even think.

"One . . ."

Mistral moves her lips slowly. She's singing beneath her breath.

"Two . . ."

Maybe she's summoning the spirits of the air, Elettra thinks. *Shanghai's insects. The seagulls.*

"Three."

Jacob lunges forward. Elettra runs up to the edge of the Grand Hyatt, not even breathing. But by the time she even realizes she's running, she's already out there. In the void.

The wind swirls around her head, her body clasped in the strong arms of Jacob Mahler, the killer with the violin, the man who survived being shot in the gut, the explosion in a building in the Coppedè district. The man everyone believes was killed by Egon Nose's women. The man who, instead, hid in the woods, perfectly still, waiting.

A dead man walking.

And who's trying to fly.

Their forward thrust lasts less than a second. A long, eternal second. Then the fall surprises Elettra like a scream. It's like being dragged down into the dark of night. A blinding whirl of lights springs to her eyes.

It's a matter of another second.

Of two seconds.

Three.

Then Jacob Mahler lets go of the two girls, who plunge down along the vertical walls of the Jin Mao Tower, bound together with strips of green-gray fabric.

Upside down, Elettra sees her reflection in the building's windows. Mistral is still singing.

Four seconds.

And the parachute finally opens.

A big black bat, which glides over the green lawns of Lujiazui Park and slips between the tall buildings like a ghost.

With three pairs of legs dangling in the void.

20
THE CALL

"Did you have Mademoiselle Cybel killed?" Harvey asks.

Several minutes have passed since Nik Knife left the office. And Heremit Devil hasn't said a word. Not one.

They're the only two people in the room.

"Are you going to have me killed, too?"

Heremit Devil slowly looks up at him.

"And then who are you going to have killed?" the boy insists.

"You should know all about death," the man replies. "Shall we talk about Dwaine?"

To Harvey, hearing his late brother's name is like a punch in the stomach. He feels bitter rage boiling up inside of him. But he can't let himself react. Heremit is a cold, heartless, contemptible creature who's just trying to provoke him. Harvey's boxing trainer taught him how to act. Don't listen. Don't react. Keep your head up. Stay light on your feet. Focus. Don't listen. Don't react. But strike blow for blow.

"Sure, why not?"

The hum of TV screens switching on. New York. Rome. Paris. Shanghai. Images of places Harvey recognizes. The remote control zooms in on an image here, an image there. Rockefeller Center. Cybel's restaurant in Paris. Tiberina Island. The images flash by one after the other in a fury of zapping.

"Just one day left until September twenty-first, Miller."

"And two left until the twenty-second."

"Very amusing. But useless."

The remote clatters onto the desk. Heremit Devil's hand sweeps over the tops and grabs the one marked with a skull.

Harvey gives a start. He's never seen that top before.

"When you were a child, Miller, did you already have one of these? One of the tops of the Chaldeans?"

Don't listen. Don't react.

"No, you didn't. You weren't a lucky child. You were just a child born on a very strange day. A day that doesn't exist. A strange child. Very strange. A child who grew up with everyone smiling at you, but they were really thinking, 'He's so strange.' Isn't that right?"

Keep your head up. Stay light on your feet.

"But when it came to your brother, everyone said, 'Oh, he's smart. Very smart. He's going to make us proud. Not like Harvey. Leap year. Bad luck.' Like the tail on a comet. Something that sticks to you forever. You don't think that, but others do."

Strike blow for blow. "You're pathetic," Harvey says.

The man spins the top on the desk. "And you didn't have this. Your masters gave it to you much later. In an old, worn leather briefcase. After a long journey from Paris to Rome. Hoping to get there in time. Four tops. One for each of you. Which one was yours?"

Heremit Devil holds up the other tops one by one. "The

135

soldiers' quarters . . . or tower, as you call it? Here's the million-dollar answer, you ignorant fool: the Chaldeans didn't have towers. Was this one yours?"

"Nobody has their own top. The tops belong to everybody."

"To everybody? Of course! That's what I used to believe. Instead, someone decided they were only yours, that they belonged to Harvey Miller. And Mistral Blanchard. Elettra Melodia and . . . finally . . . the Chinese boy."

When the office is quiet again, Harvey thinks he hears a faint, distant yet persistent call. A voice is calling his name, but with a pained, suffering tone.

"Who's calling me?" he asks Heremit Devil in a hushed voice.

The skull top has come to a halt in the center of the desk.

"What's that?"

"I hear someone calling my name," Harvey says. And as he does, he sees the man's stony mask quiver. He watches the man reach out, his perfectly manicured fingers trembling slightly, press a button on the intercom and bark the order, "Take Mr. Miller to his room."

Keep your head up. Light on your feet. And when the time's right, throw your punch.

"There are things you still haven't figured out, aren't there?" Harvey asks, taking a step toward the man.

Separated from him by the perfectly polished desk, Heremit Devil shows no sign that he even heard him.

"There are things you still haven't figured out, and you don't know what to do," Harvey says again, with greater conviction. "You know about the Pact, the four Sages, us. . . . You had us followed, you stole everything from us, you had our masters and your

136

own rotten thugs killed . . . and after all that, after five years, you still don't know what to do. And you don't know what you did it for. Am I right?"

"Watch what you say, boy."

The elevator door in the office opens silently.

"Who is it that's calling me?" Harvey asks again before two strong hands grab him by the shoulders and drag him out of the room.

To someplace.

In the black skyscraper.

21

THE CODE

It's a night full of life, illuminated with neon streaks in different colors. Shanghai is a tangle of serpents of light. The signs are buzzing masks. Hidden behind the tree-lined boulevards with their five-star hotels, sparkling marble-floored restaurants and perfectly manicured flower beds are smaller, darker streets. The forgotten alleys. Alleys lined with the service exits of bars, kitchen doors. Where tired waiters chat to each other in Wu, English, French, Russian, Italian. While stiletto heels and designer shoes tread the sidewalks along the main roads, the forgotten alleys are silent. Only shadows walk there. Shadows pulling other shadows behind them: billowing fabric, nylon cords. The wing of a parachute, to be quickly folded up and hidden among the plastic skeletons of garbage bins.

Elettra and Mistral stand guard on the forgotten alley where they landed, not even sure what they have to be afraid of. In their minds, they relive second after second of their descent between the skyscrapers.

In the shadows, the human bat finishes tucking away the parachute and motions to the girls to follow him.

138

They walk along in the darkness, hearing muffled music pulsing on the other side of the thin walls. Jacob Mahler reaches a well-lit street. He crosses it and walks past a row of trees. Once again, darkness.

When he reaches a large roundabout, the man seems to reflect on which way to go. Then the trio turns left, crossing over a green area illuminated by bright, flat disks they can walk over. All around them, the treetops look like shrouds. A stairway covered with graffiti. And a long sidewalk that leads back to the street. On the ground level of the block of buildings are restaurants. Mahler walks into the first one, whose flashing sign depicts a blue pig. He sits down on one of the stools facing the sidewalk and orders meat dumplings and tea for all of them. Then he turns to the girls and points at the skyscraper just across the street.

It's a completely black building.

Tall, shiny and black. Heremit Devil's skyscraper.

"That's it," Mahler says.

A middle-aged waiter serves them three glasses filled with a strange, yellowish beverage and a basket of steamed dumplings to be eaten with chopsticks or their hands.

"Now I understand," murmurs Mistral, who refuses to touch the food.

"What?"

"Why it's called Century." She turns to Elettra and points at a sign on the corner, which is written in two languages: Chinese and English.

CENTURY PARK

"The name of the place where the Pact was broken . . . ," Elettra murmurs.

139

"It happened five years ago," Jacob Mahler says in a low voice, "when that woman, the archeologist, responded to an ad in the paper."

"An ad?"

"Heremit ordered work to be done on the building's foundation. In the process, they unearthed an ancient dwelling. He put an ad in the papers to find someone who could explain what he found."

"And Zoe replied to it."

"I went to meet her in Iceland and then she came here."

"And she told him everything."

Jacob's silence is his answer.

Mistral shakes her head and lets out a shrill laugh. "And then," she whispers, "you went to Rome to kill the professor. And to kill us."

"I wasn't ordered to kill you."

Mistral looks at him intently with her big, clear eyes. And her stare summarizes everything she's thinking.

"I was just carrying out orders," Jacob Mahler says.

Another long moment of silence. Elettra and Jacob eat slowly, order more dumplings. Across the street, the skyscraper's shiny black steel seems to swallow up even the reflections of the street-lights.

"Time for us to meet up with the others," Mahler decides when they're done. "Once you're with them, find a place to spend the night."

"What are you going to do?"

"I need to see an old friend of mine"—Jacob checks his watch—"in exactly two hours."

"Who's the old friend?"

Mahler pays in cash. They leave the restaurant, walk down Century Avenue on the opposite side of the street from Heremit Devil's skyscraper and turn down an alley going in the other direction.

"Who's the old friend?" Elettra asks again.

Jacob Mahler doesn't answer.

He isn't used to talking much.

Elettra catches Mistral's eye. The French girl walks along, staring at the toes of her gym shoes. "Don't trust him," she whispers.

Sheng and Ermete are still sitting on the steps.

They've unfolded the tourist map of Shanghai and covered it with circles: one for each building constructed before 1907.

"*Hao!* Finally," Sheng says when he sees Jacob Mahler show up, followed by the two girls. They don't seem to be in a very good mood. And the man with the violin is dressed differently than before. "What happened to your coat?"

Running. Jumping. Plummeting. Gliding. At the very thought of what they went through, Elettra's skin starts to tingle with shivers.

"Are you guys okay?"

Ermete and Sheng show them the work they've done on the map. Meanwhile, Mahler punches a code into the panel by the door. He has everyone follow him up to an apartment on the ninth floor.

It's a big, empty room with wires all over the floor. In the center of it, on a tripod, is a round naval signal lamp that faces the window. A table without chairs. A dozen or so black spray canisters. A row of identical suits still wrapped in cellophane hung on an aluminum rod.

Mahler waits until they're all inside and shuts the door behind them. He doesn't turn on the light.

No lightbulbs to be seen.

"There should be something to drink in the refrigerator. The bathroom's over there."

"Is it without lights, too?" Ermete asks.

He gets no answer.

Jacob Mahler rests the violin case on the table, undresses, removes the cellophane from one of his other suits and puts it on. Then he feeds his old clothes into a paper shredder.

"Where are we?" Elettra asks him.

"My place," the man replies.

"Nice," Sheng says.

"Yeah, real cozy," Elettra points out. "Beautiful wires on the floor . . . no furniture getting in the way, not even a lightbulb . . ."

Sheng rests the cookie tin and Elettra's backpack on the room's only table.

"You can stay here for a couple hours, tops," Jacob Mahler says. "Then you have to go."

He walks over to Elettra, talking to her as if she was the head of the group. "There's a red button by the door. When you leave, push it. Then close the door. And don't open it again, no matter what."

"Or else . . . ?"

"You'll get blown up, too."

Mahler buckles his belt.

Mistral steps over to the signal lamp by the window. In the

distance, among the other buildings, she recognizes the shape of Heremit Devil's black, crystal skyscraper.

"You're going over there, aren't you?" she asks, not expecting an answer.

Mahler slips by her without making a sound. "That's why I came back."

"But yesterday you said it was impossible!" Sheng exclaims.

"And I'll say it again: it's impossible. Unless there's someone inside who can open the door for you."

"Your friend," Elettra says.

Jacob Mahler nods. He checks his watch.

Then he leans over behind the lamp, throws its large switch, and the heating element inside of it starts to heat up, glowing bright red. In half a minute, the lamp is ready and it projects a shaft of white light through the windowpane, straight at Heremit Devil's building. A push-button control is connected to the switch. When it's pressed, the light blinks off and on again. Off and on again.

Off and on again.

Sheng is the first one to figure out what's going on.

"Morse code," he says, his voice low. Then he runs over to the window. "To communicate with someone inside Heremit's building! Brilliant idea!"

Mahler doesn't reply. He continues to switch the signal lamp on and off, focusing on his message.

"What are you transmitting?"

"I'm asking him what his name is."

Five pairs of eyes stare at the black skyscraper between Century Park and Century Avenue. Most of the windows on the lower floors are dark. Only the second-to-top floor is completely lit up.

For a long time, nothing happens.

Then the light in one of the rooms suddenly turns on, turns off, turns on again.

"There he is," Jacob Mahler remarks.

"What's he saying?" Elettra asks, fascinated by the silent messages crossing through the night.

"'H . . . A . . . ,'" Ermete reads. And without even looking at Elettra, he explains, "Morse code is a role-player's bread and butter."

"H, A . . . and then?" Sheng speaks up.

"Harvey," Jacob Mahler says, smiling.

22

THE FRIEND

"Someone's at the door," Irene Melodia says. She turns in her wheelchair, looking for Fernando. "Fernando?"

He glances up from the stacks of papers all around him. "Hmm?"

"Someone's at the door."

"I didn't hear anything." He points at his papers. "I—I was . . ."

The Domus Quintilia is closed and strangely silent. All the guests have checked out, and Fernando and Irene decided not to take in any more, not until things are back to normal, at least. During the wait, Elettra's father is turning his efforts to working on his interminable novel in the only lit room.

Once again, clangs from the iron knocker on the front door fill the courtyard. This time, Fernando hears it, too. He stands up and rubs his eyes. "Who could it be at this hour? And why don't they use the bell?"

"If you like, I'll go down to see," Irene says.

The man stretches and walks out of the room, grumbling. But a moment before shutting the door behind him, Irene calls out, "Don't open it right away. Be careful."

Fernando goes downstairs to the reception area, sees a broom propped up by the door and, thinking the person knocking might be up to no good, grabs it. He weighs it in his hands. Better than nothing.

He crosses the dark courtyard, passing under the yellowing vines, reaches the front door and clicks open its old, heavy lock.

"Sorry, we're clo—" he begins to say the moment the light from the nearby streetlamp creeps into the courtyard.

Outside is a gypsy woman.

"Oh, no . . . look . . . don't even ask," Fernando says, hurrying to close the door.

A gold earring glimmers through the woman's grimy, curly hair. "I am a friend of your daughter," she says.

The man leaves the door open a crack, hesitant.

"Your daughter, Elettra," the gypsy woman adds.

Fernando opens the door a little wider. There's something familiar about her face. He has the impression he's seen her before. Then he remembers: she's the gypsy woman who often begs in Piazza in Piscinula or on the bridge over the Tiber. Now he recognizes her. He also seems to recognize the sweater the woman is wearing. Is it Elettra's? Or Irene's?

"That's my sweater . . . ," he finally mumbles.

The gypsy looks down at her clothes. "It is? Oh, I didn't know. . . . I'm sorry. Elettra gave it to me."

"My daughter—"

"She is in Shanghai, I know." The woman smiles. It's a yellow, ugly smile, but it's unusually friendly. She pulls a black appointment book out from underneath her sweater and hands it to Fernando. "Look at this. I stole it."

The man stiffens.

"Read it! You are in danger!" the gypsy woman insists.

"Listen, if this is some kind of joke . . ." Fernando leans against the doorframe and opens the appointment book. It's full of entries.

WEDNESDAY: E.M. LEAVES AT 8 A.M.,
RETURNS AT 1 P.M.
F.M. STILL AT HOME. WRITING?
THURSDAY: NO MOVEMENT
FRIDAY: F.M., E.M. DEPART AT 5 A.M.
F.M. RETURNS ALONE AT 7:38 A.M.

"What is all this?" Elettra's father asks.

The gypsy woman points to nearby Piazza in Piscinula. "This book belongs to the waiter over at that restaurant, the one who just started working there. I stole it from him not long ago. They are watching you."

"What?" Fernando gasps.

"Look at the last page," the woman insists.

TOMORROW: F.M. AT THE OPEN
MARKET AT 6 A.M.?
GO IN AND GET THE OLD WOMAN.

Fernando Melodia gapes at the page.

"I think you should leave," the gypsy woman says. Then she adds, "At once."

23

OUTSIDE

In Heremit Devil's building, Harvey is in the dark again.

He stares at Shanghai's skyscrapers, the many lights switching on and off.

And he wonders if those windows might be hiding other messages.

Other Morse codes.

When Jacob started to blink his light, Harvey had just walked into the room. He didn't notice it right away, even though he'd gone over the plan for weeks and knew exactly where to look. Jacob explained it to him because he was sure that once Harvey was captured, Heremit would lock him up in that very room. He explained how to attract attention on the plane, how to act toward Heremit and, once he was alone, what direction to look in as he waited for the coded message.

On. Off.

On. On.

Off.

On.

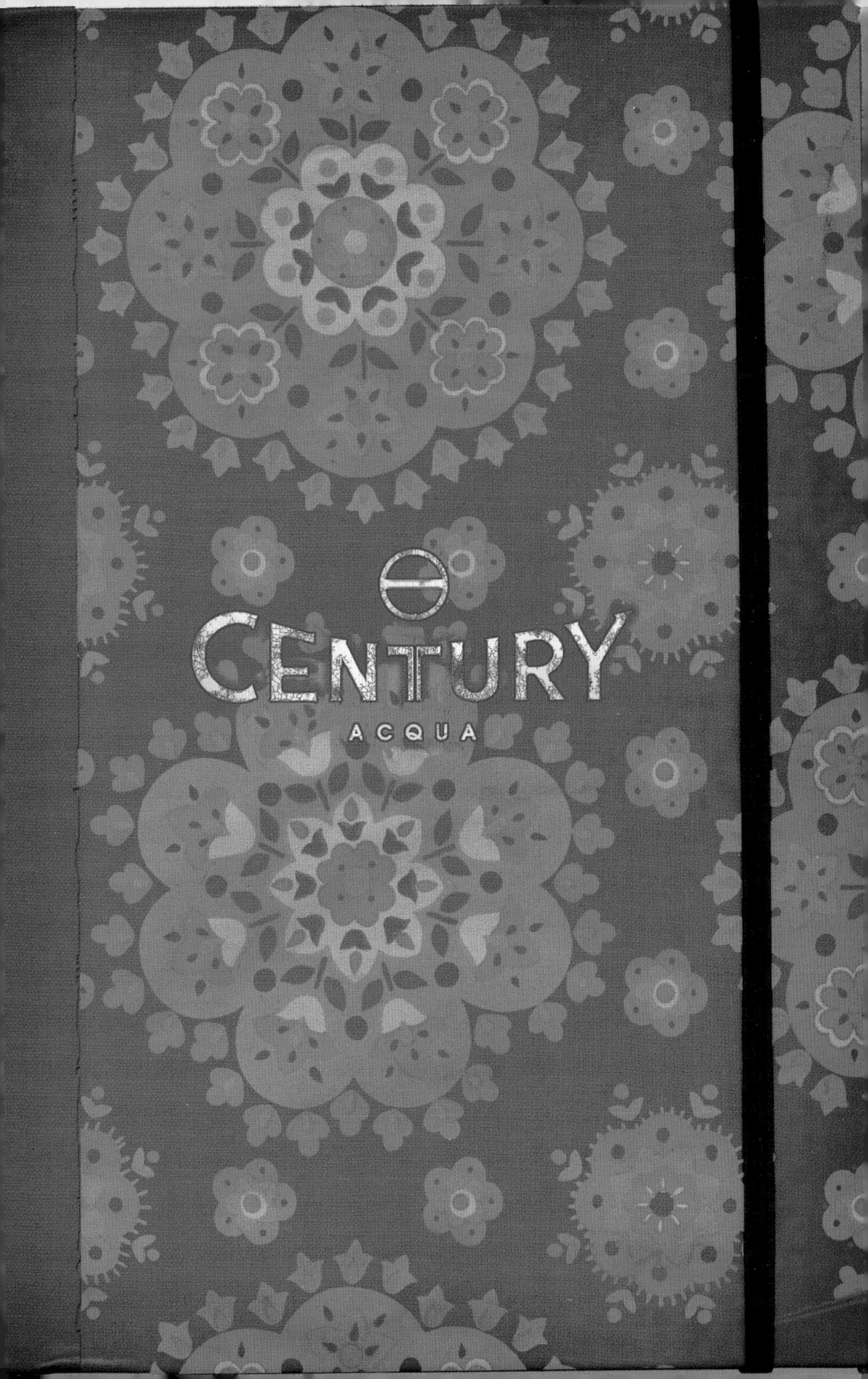
CENTURY
ACQUA

L. Melodia
Trans-Siberian
ry Park
rld Map
astiglione
Shanghai

MISSING

LINDA MELODIA

AVETE VISTO
QUESTA DONNA?

CHIAMATE: Eletta 06 78695

5

6

7

8

L. Melodia
'ry Park
Trans-Siberian
? China
Arrival in Shanghai

rld Map

astiglione

Shanghai

9

10
The Hongkong and Shanghai Banking Corporation

Promises to pay the bearer
on demand at its Office here

TEN DOLLARS

HONGKONG 1st JANUARY 1992

By order of the Board of Directors

GENERAL MANAGER

BI031064   BI031064

拾圓

香港上海滙豐銀行

10

10

PROV.

SCHUREI
Zizichar

130

ARCTIC OCEAN

Providenya

Anadyr

0   300   600 km

Murmansk

Kaliningrad

Vyborg Petrozavodsk

Saint Arkhangelsk

Petersburg

Magadan

Petropavlovsk-
Kamchatskiy

Nizhniy Novgorod

★ MOSCOW

Noril'sk

Yakutsk

Kazan'

Yekaterinburg

SIBERIA

Rostov

Chelyabinsk

Sea of
Okhotsk

NORTH
PACIFIC
OCEAN

Volgograd

Tunguska Event

Omsk

Khabarovsk

Astrakhan

KURIL
ISLANDS

Kholmsk

Nevelsk

JAPAN

Krasnoyarsk

Novosibirsk

Irkutsk

Lake Baikal

Nakhodka

Vostochnyy

Vladivostok

KAZAKHSTAN

CHINA

N. KOR.

11

全景导游图　CENTURY PARK

(Work Passage)
Gate 2

Jinxiu Rd

Jinxiu Rd

Century Avenue

Gate 1

Metro Line 2

Candoe Rd

Folk Village

Shbahua Rd

Ouyuan Rd

Nature Reserve

Wenying Bridge

Yunfan Bridge
Wobo Bridge

Yuzhu Bridge

Menghu Bridge

Jiazhan Bridge

Penghe Bridge

Quay

Bright Lake

Wutong Avenue

Friendship Tree

Gate 5
(Close Down)

Amenity Grass

Hongjin Bridge

Anlu Bridge

Yinhe Bridge

Gate 8
(Close down)

Zhangjiebang

Huamu Rd

Gate 6
(Work Passage)

Yingke Bridge

Huamu Rd

Gate 7

Metro Line 2

疏林	SPARSE FOREST
草坪	LAWN
湖泊	LAKE
道路	ROAD
桥梁	BRIDGE
景点	LANDMARK

N

12

19

13

15

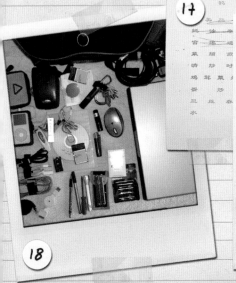

18

17

19

PASSPORT

United States
of America

20

Union européenne
République française

PASSEPORT

21

uropéenne
ue française

PORT

FRIDTJOF
NANSEN
LAND

O C E A N

KARA SEA

BARENTS SEA

LAPTEV SEA

U N I T E D   R E P U B L I C S

UNITED
REPUBLICS

C H I N A

BRITISH COMMONWEALTH OF NATIONS

INDIES

CENTURY

WORLD MAP

. A., with the coöperation of the Democracies of Latin-America, the British Commonwealth of
and the Union of Soviet Socialist Republics, assumes world leadership for the establishment of a
New World Moral Order
for permanent peace, freedom, justice, security and world reconstruction.

23

24

25

P. MATEO RICCI ITALIANO, DE LA COMPAÑIA DE JESUS INSIGNE MATEMATICO, Y PRIMERO QUE EVANGELIZO EN PEKIN. HIZOLE EL EMPERADOR MANDARIN Y RE

26

27

G.Castiglione
Hyatt/Bonomi/S-61

Shanghai

28

29

30

31

33

34

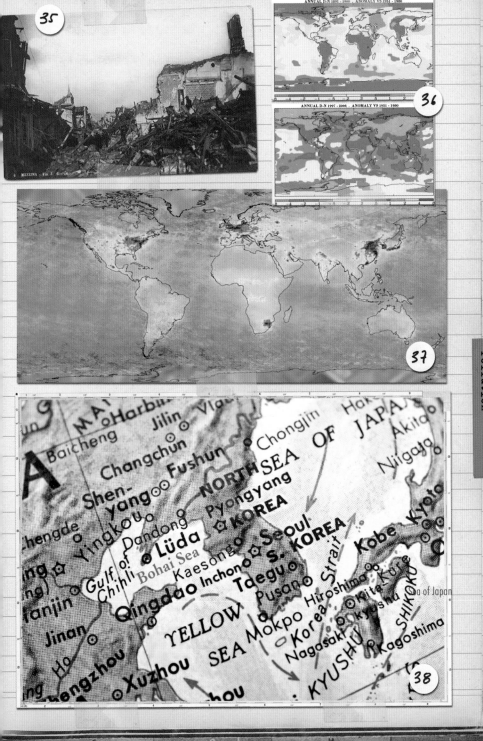

35

ANNUAL D-N 1891 - 1900 . ANOMALY VS 1951 - 1980

ANNUAL D-N 1997 - 2006 . ANOMALY VS 1951 - 1980

6 MESSINA - Via S. Giacomo

37

Shanghai
Pollution

Sea of Japan

MAI
Harbin
Baicheng   Jilin
Changchun   Fushun   Chongjin   Hok
Shen-   NORTH SEA OF JAPAN   Akita
yang   Vladi
Chengde   Yingkou   Dandong   Pyongyang   KOREA   Niigata
Lüda   KOREA   Seoul   S. KOREA
Bohai Sea   Kaesong   Inchon   Taegu   Kobe   Kyoto
Tianjin   Gulf of   Chihli   Qingdao   Pusan   Strait   Hiroshima   Kita
Jinan   YELLOW   Mokpo   Korea   Kyushu   SHIKOKU
Ho   SEA   Nagasaki   Kagoshima
wengzhou   Xuzhou   KYUSHU
hou

INDEX

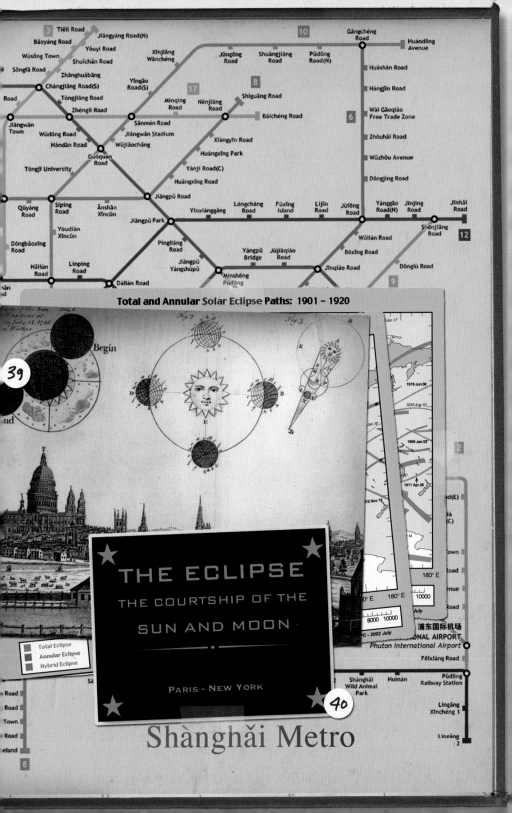

The instructions for getting out of the room traveled slowly through the night. And Harvey replied.

On. On. On.

"Okay."

In the darkness of the room, the boy opens his backpack, which was searched at the airport in New York and later by Hermit Devil's security team. He pulls out his shaving kit, takes out his toothbrush and twists its head. The sharp tip of a screwdriver appears among the bristles. Harvey puts it on the bed. Then he uncaps the tube of toothpaste and squeezes its bottom end. Hidden beneath a small layer of toothpaste is a tiny yet powerful flashlight.

The boy sits down on the bed and undoes his shoelaces: they're made of the same material as Mahler's violin bow. Razor-sharp threads.

He reaches into his sweater sleeves and tears out the linings, which are shaped into two perfectly fitting gloves. He puts them on.

Then he goes into the bathroom and detaches the plastic curtain from the shower rod. He brings it into the main room and spreads it out on the floor right below the small, square thermostat. He folds it into two insulating layers and steps onto it with his shoes. He studies the device in front of him. He loosens its four screws with his toothbrush, removes the cover from the little box and shines his toothpaste-tube flashlight into it. Inside the thermostat is a notched disk, a tiny glass tube with mercury in it, a green wire, a red wire, a blue wire. Mahler told him to clip the blue one. He loops a shoelace around the blue wire and tugs on it. The lights in the room go out for a second.

And the lock on the door goes *clack*.

* * *

The lights come back on a second later, but Harvey has already pulled the door toward him. He puts on his backpack and hurries out.

Once he's in the hallway, he checks his watch. He has just under twenty minutes.

He listens. A constant, ominous hum fills the air.

He peers around. The floor is made of sturdy teak. Overhead, in the corner, the red blinking light of a security camera. From what Mahler told him, it rotates to film the hallway every forty seconds. Harvey ducks back into the room a moment before the camera turns his way, then waits for it to return to its place and runs out again. He has forty seconds to reach a white door that should be somewhere on the opposite wall.

Thirty seconds. Twenty.

Beside the door is a keypad. Harvey knows the code. And he types it in.

8 . . . 2 . . . 6 . . . 8 . . .

He casts a final glance at the security camera.

Ten seconds.

. . . 6

The lock clicks open. Harvey hurries out the door, closes it behind him and starts going down the service stairs in Heremit Devil's building.

He goes down cautiously, careful not to make the slightest noise.

There aren't supposed to be any surveillance cameras here, but Harvey checks for them anyway. With every other flight of stairs, he counts down, keeping track of what floor he's reached, because there aren't any signs indicating the skyscraper's various levels.

Once he's reached what should be the ground floor, he goes down another half flight of stairs. A service door should be on the left.

Instead, he sees a keypad halfway up the two-tone wall. Harvey punches in the access code and a small section of the wall slides open along an invisible track.

On the other side is a passageway with a ceiling so low that he needs to crawl through it. On the far end, a second door with a coded lock.

Clack!

Harvey peeks outside. Nighttime. Darkness. A simple external metal cage in a narrow cement atrium. A tangle of rumbling pipes that plunge down belowground and disappear through a grate overhead. No access panel on the outside.

Harvey carefully keeps the door propped open with his foot. Then he leans out and whistles.

Three times.

He lets a minute go by and whistles again.

The pipes belch out hot steam. They hum, puff, hiss. Underground machinery lets out echoed thuds.

Suddenly, he spots a shadow passing over the grate ten meters overhead.

Harvey hides in the passageway, holding the door open a crack. The shadow slides under the grate, clips a snap hook to one of the metal cables running along the pipes and dangles in the void.

Harvey opens the door a little wider.

The shadow begins to slide down, the thick, heavy soles of his boots letting off sparks. When he's less than a meter away from the cage, he unclips himself and crouches down beside Harvey.

"You okay?" he asks.

The boy nods.

"Think you can handle going back up there?" The shadow looks at the passageway leading to the service stairs. He's brought along the violin case.

Again, Harvey nods. "We need to go up to the top floor of the building."

"It's not the top floor," Jacob Mahler corrects him, slipping into the passageway.

24

THE PLAN

○

IN THE NINTH-STORY APARTMENT ON THE CORNER OF LUJIAZUI Park, Elettra, Mistral, Ermete and Sheng have no idea what to do.

Mistral sends her mother a message saying everything is fine, no need to worry. "In any case, we can't stay here," she murmurs. "Mahler told us to leave within two hours."

"And to push the red button."

They look apprehensively at the tangle of wires on the floor.

"The red button and . . . boom!" Ermete mimes, holding up some wires attached to a black box that's been leaned up against the wall.

Elettra paces the room. "I'm going after them," she says.

"Where?"

"The skyscraper."

"And do what, once you get there? Ask for permission to go inside? 'Hello, my name is Elettra. Is Mr. Devil here? Check your list. I should have an appointment.'"

"Harvey's in there."

"He went there on purpose. They had a plan," Mistral says.

"Did they let any of you in on it?" Ermete asks. "Or did the two of them make an agreement without telling us anything?"

They all shake their heads.

Elettra pounds her fist on the table. "Why didn't he warn us?"

"Because we wouldn't have let him get captured just so he could get our things back."

Ermete nods vigorously. "Nice idea, though. If Harvey and Jacob's plan works, we'll have the tops and everything else back," he says. Then, while the kids are talking things over, he takes out the ancient map of the Chaldeans and rests it on the table. On the outside, it looks like a box covered with initials and signatures carved in the wood. Once it's open, it reveals its surface, marked with whorls and grooves, like deep fingerprints. One of its four corners is missing. "I say we try using the map," the engineer suggests, scratching his head, which is almost completely bald.

"But Harvey isn't here," Elettra points out.

"Let's try it anyway," Ermete insists.

"But what map do we put on top of it?" Mistral asks.

Sheng takes the Shanghai tourist map and spreads it out on the ancient wooden artifact. Then he reaches into the backpack, finds the last top they have left and puts it on the table. "Who's going to cast it?"

Indecision.

"I'll do it, then," Sheng decides after a moment.

He grabs the top, rests it on the center of the map and flicks it between his fingers. The oracle of the heart begins to whirl around, running along the ancient lines carved in the wood. It races through the area with the skyscrapers, crosses the river near the tourist ferries and heads toward the English Bund, the French

Concession and veers off to the streets that border the Old City, the most ancient area of Shanghai.

"Good top," Sheng says when it comes to a halt on a small rectangle surrounded by a jumble of narrow streets. At that spot is one of the red circles Sheng and Ermete drew during their search for the city's oldest buildings.

"What is that place?" Ermete asks.

"These green parts are the Yuyuan Garden," Sheng says, picking up the top. "And this little square here inside the garden is Huxinting, the mid-lake pavilion. It's the city's oldest teahouse."

"How old?" the engineer asks.

"A couple centuries, I think." Sheng concentrates, trying to recall what he learned in school. "From what I remember, the gardens were built by Emperor Qianlong of the Qing dynasty somewhere around the seventeen hundreds. Then, a century later, the place was turned into a restaurant by a group of cotton traders, and it stayed that way."

Elettra snatches up the top and casts it. "The problem is that every time you use it, the top stops in a different place," she says, remembering her attempts to find her aunt.

The top starts whirling around again. It quickly leaves the Old City and slows down near the skyscrapers in Pudong. It stops right on top of the black glass skyscraper where Jacob Mahler and Harvey are.

"Could it be," the French girl murmurs, "that the heart top simply follows the heart of the person who casts it?"

Two ghosts are climbing the service stairs in the Century Park skyscraper. They move without making a sound. The first one has

155

gray hair and is carrying a violin case. The second, in jeans and a sweater, has the steady pace and breathing of a trained athlete.

They don't say a word during the whole climb. Sixty-three floors. Forty-two steps between one floor and the next. Two thousand, six hundred and forty-six steps in all. A climb that could paralyze anyone's legs.

But not Jacob Mahler's.

And not Harvey Miller's.

On the second-to-top floor, the stairs end. The killer stops beside a small, white door. Harvey is panting and his thigh muscles are burning.

Jacob punches a code into the keypad. It's a different code, much longer than the others.

"I just hope that over the last few months," he whispers, "he hasn't changed it."

Once he's punched in the last of the twenty-three digits, the door opens with a whoosh. Behind Jacob, Harvey heaves a sigh of relief.

No one's in the office. It's dark. Rain begins to fall, ticking against the windowpanes.

Jacob Mahler strides over to the desk. He seems calm, as if he's certain there's no form of surveillance in the room.

And no imminent danger.

With amazing swiftness, he slips all the objects on the desk into Harvey's backpack and says, "Go on, get going."

Harvey is stunned. He figured they would leave together. "What about you?"

"I need to wait for an old friend." Mahler smiles.

Harvey slips his backpack onto his shoulders. "Thanks, Jacob."

The killer doesn't reply. He doesn't smile. He appears to be at a loss for words. No one has ever said thank you to him before.

"Take the gold elevator, if you want," he says quietly. "It isn't on the building's surveillance system. Stop on the first floor, go down half a flight of stairs and climb up to the grate you saw me come down through. You'll end up in a square courtyard. When the searchlights cross each other in the middle, count to fifteen. Then run across it. They won't spot you. Go up the stairs and open the gate to Century Park. Two private guards were there, but I took care of them."

Harvey walks over to Heremit Devil's private elevator. He presses the gold call button, waits a few seconds, and the door opens.

Trickles of water streak the windows.

"See you around," he says, disappearing.

Inside the office, Mahler holds up his hand.

The window of the ninth-story apartment in Lujiazui Park is also streaked with tears.

"Rain," Sheng says. "Just what we needed."

He rests his palm against the glass and follows the trickles of water, which branch off around his fingers. What the others are saying is muffled, distant to his ears. He's so tired that he could fall asleep right there, standing, his hand pressed against the glass. If only he wasn't afraid of dreaming about that freaking island again. And all that water.

He shuts his eyes and opens them again when he hears Ermete shout, "We gotta go, Sheng!"

The boy blinks, trying to snap out of it. He's cold. And the instant he realizes it, it's as though the entire room becomes a massive slab of ice. Outside, he sees the city lights distorted by the rain. Circles of streetlamps, glistening asphalt, clusters of dark leaves. The front steps look like the white keys on a piano.

Someone's there on the steps. Someone peering up.

Sheng jerks his hand away from the glass as if it was scorching hot.

On the rain-drenched steps is the boy in the number 89 jersey. Who's staring at the window.

A rustle, and Mistral is standing next to Sheng. "Sheng, we need to go. Hey, what's wrong?"

"It's that boy again."

"What boy?"

"He's down on the steps, staring at me."

Mistral smiles sheepishly. Then she gives a frightened start. "Sheng!" she cries. "Your eyes are yellow again!"

Heremit Devil's gold elevator plunges to the first floor. The yellow numbers flash by one after the other in a furious countdown. Harvey gulps, scared despite himself. He's huddled up in the corner opposite the door, watching the numbers plummet.

The elevator descends as if it was screaming.

Or maybe something inside his head is screaming. That strange call he heard in Heremit's office. He squeezes back into the corner even harder, shivering from the sudden cold. And the farther down the elevator goes, the more he feels the temperature drop.

And the farther down it goes, Harvey thinks, *the louder I hear it.* . . .

First floor. The door opens.

A call.

Harvey staggers over the threshold.

It isn't exactly a call. It's a voice.

Harvey . . . Harvey . . . Please . . . come here . . . come here. . . .

In the hallway, he sees the blinking light of the surveillance camera in the corner. Once again, he has forty seconds to reach the service stairs, go down half a flight, punch in the code and get out of there.

But that call . . . So clear, so close, so insistent. Like the one Harvey hears whenever he passes by Ground Zero in New York. Like the voices from the subway that led him into the maze of roots: voices from the Earth.

They're calling him.

Forty seconds, Harvey thinks, *and I'll be out of this building.*

He hesitates and stares at the elevator's gold panel. Below, there's another floor.

The call is coming from belowground.

It's the Earth asking him to go down there.

Harvey steps back into the elevator and pushes the last button.

He huddles in the corner opposite the door.

The elevator goes down a floor.

And then another.

It's cold.

Heremit Devil wakes up with a start.

He touches his cheeks and finds they're damp. He gropes for the light switch on the bedside table and flicks it. He looks around. The tiny bed he sleeps in is unwrinkled, as if he hasn't been lying on it. The door to the stairs that lead up to his old office on the top floor is closed. As is the door to the hallway and the bathroom.

Everything is in order. Everything is just as it should be.

He was dreaming. Once again, he was just dreaming.

The park. The playground. The trees.

The excavation site. The top. And then . . .

He was only dreaming.

Even still, he can barely breathe. The small, square window is streaked with rain.

It was raining that day, too, Heremit Devil thinks.

That blasted day.

He isn't tired anymore. In a matter of a few hours it'll be morning. Nik Knife will have taken care of Mademoiselle Cybel. And the kids will have arrived, too.

Ah, yes. All four of the kids.

Including the one from Shanghai.

Then he'll understand.

Of course.

Suddenly, everything will be clear.

Heremit Devil gets up, puts on a dressing gown, steps into the bathroom to rinse his face with mineralized water, opens the little door leading into the long hallway covered with drawings and inscriptions in a childish hand, and reaches his office, the room where he's spent most of his life. At least since that blasted day when he decided never again to step foot on the top floor.

Standing in the doorway, the man realizes at once that someone has been in the room. He smells their scent even before he notices that nothing is left on his desk.

The rain grows stronger.

"Hello, Heremit," an emotionless voice says. A violin bow glimmers in the darkness. "Did you get a good last night of sleep?"

Inside the apartment on the corner of Lujiazui Park, a cell phone rings. Elettra's cell phone.

Sheng pulls himself away from the window and staggers toward the door. His eyes are yellow.

He covers them with his hand. They don't ache. And he's seeing normally. So what's the anomaly?

Elettra's cell phone continues to ring, but no one answers it.

With every step, Sheng feels like he's passing out. Or swimming in a sea of dark water.

"I don't feel very good," he murmurs.

"Sit down here," someone says. Mistral, maybe. "You need to get some sleep."

Yes, it's Mistral beside him. She's beautiful.

"You don't see anyone on the steps, do you?" Sheng asks her.

The girl shakes her head.

"And you didn't see the museum guard at the Louvre, either, right?"

"Sheng . . ." Mistral rests her hand on his shoulder.

He squeezes it. "I love you," he says, smiling. And the instant he says it, something grips him inside. A pang of fear. The fear of being rejected. Of being wrong, out of place. Of being useless.

Elettra's cell phone is still ringing. Sheng lets go of Mistral's hand. "But he's there! He exists!" he shouts, exasperated. "I'm not crazy!"

Driven by sudden rage, he bolts to his feet and runs over to the

161

apartment door. He throws it open and leaves before the others can stop him.

"Sheng!" someone calls out. Mistral, maybe.

But he's already running down the stairs.

Elettra's finally found her phone.

She answers it. "Harvey? Where are you?"

"I went downstairs, Elettra."

"Downstairs where? Are you okay?"

"I'm downstairs, below the skyscraper. You wouldn't understand . . . and I don't have time to explain. The line's breaking up."

"What are you still doing there? Get out!"

"Let me talk! I followed the voices, okay? They made me come down here so I could warn you guys. It's all here! But you need to leave, and fast!"

"What are you talking about?"

"Heremit Devil had them excavate below the building," Harvey says. "There's a big pit. There are pipes . . . lights. A stairway leading down. There are statues, an ancient wall and that . . . that wooden thing."

"What wooden thing?"

"I don't know yet. It looks like . . . a monster. That's where the call was coming from. It told me to go see—"

"Harvey? Who was calling you?"

"The whole room, Elettra. Below the building's foundations. I didn't understand it. At first I thought it was just a voice, but then—"

"Harvey!"

"I really want to see you."

"So do I! I'm coming to get you!"

162

"No! Leave! You have to . . . you have to tell the others to leave town! There's no point looking for anything in Shanghai! He's already found it! Now I'm getting out of here and—"

A bang. And Harvey's voice goes silent.

"Harvey, what's happening?"

Silence.

Static.

Elettra presses the phone to her ear, listening carefully. The line breaks up. Then Harvey's voice again. He's panting. "I need to move, Elettra. Someone came downstairs. I'm going to try—hide. I don't know if I'll be able to call you again."

"Har—"

"Leave town, right away!—no point—"

Static. Harvey panting.

"Someone came out of the elevator. . . . Nine Fingers . . . Elettra!"

Another bang, this time louder.

Then nothing.

In the apartment, the door is still open.

They hear Sheng's footsteps on the stairs.

Mistral is in the doorway, calling to him.

Elettra throws her phone on the ground. "No! Harvey! No!"

"Hey!" Ermete exclaims. "Would you mind explaining what—"

"This can't be happening!" Elettra shouts, running to the door.

Mistral grabs her arm and holds her back. "Wait! Where are you going?"

She breaks free. "I'm going to save my boyfriend!"

"Hey!" Ermete cuts in, this time more determined. "Hold it! Are you out of your mind?"

But the Italian girl's eyes are shooting flames. The signal lamp in the middle of the room suddenly switches on.

"Elettra! Calm down, okay?" Ermete says, knowing where this is leading.

Elettra's gaze is fixed on Mistral.

"I'm going with you," the French girl says, although her friend hasn't asked her anything.

"Hey!" Ermete says for the third time, seeing that he's been left all alone. "Oh, these kids with powers . . . They're unbearable!"

He picks up everything he can from the table and rushes out, slamming the door behind him.

Then he opens it, presses the red button and shuts it again.

25

THE ADULTS

THE HOTEL IS SMALL BUT COMFORTABLE. IRENE AND THE GYPSY woman look around, thinking different things. To Irene, it's a temporary accommodation, fine for one night. For the gypsy woman, on the other hand, it's the first time in years that she'll be sleeping in a real bed. She steps into the bathroom, turns on the shower and stands there staring at the running water.

Lingering in the doorway to the hall, Fernando shoots a look at the old woman. "Are you sure this is a good idea?"

"Positive," Irene replies.

"And her?" Fernando asks, pointing in the gypsy woman's direction.

"We can trust her. She's on our side."

"Frankly, Irene, I don't see how you can be so sure. . . ."

"The power of intuition," the elderly woman replies, wheeling her chair up to the window. "Would you help me with these curtains?"

Fernando walks over beside her and opens them.

Outside, in the distance, is Tiberina Island, in the middle of the Tiber River. When she sees it, Irene grows even calmer. "Perfect," she says.

"The power of intuition?" Fernando starts up again. "What does intuition have to do with it?"

In the bathroom, the gypsy woman turns off the shower and begins to open all the little packages of soap and shower caps.

"It's fundamental," Irene replies. "Unless you're willing to listen to your instinct and do what it tells you to, you aren't willing to live life to the fullest."

Fernando puffs. "But that has nothing to do with . . ." He points toward the bathroom.

"Ah, but it does." Irene smiles. She clearly doesn't want to explain further. She takes Fernando's hand and says, "Go on, now."

Elettra's father looks around, embarrassed. "I'm not sure I should leave you here alone."

"I'm not alone. Besides"—Irene checks her watch—"you need to get going if you want to catch the plane for Shanghai."

"I'm only on the waiting list," Fernando says.

"Then all you have to do is wait," Irene concludes. "Go on! I'll be safe here."

"How did it go?" Quilleran asks Mrs. Miller when he sees her walk out of the local police station.

The woman is clutching a bundle of papers, official documents. "Fine, I suppose."

She's just reported being threatened by Egon Nose and his thugs. "They said they'd assign a police car to patrol our house."

"Perfect," the Indian replies. "But still . . ."

166

Mrs. Miller nods, guessing what he's about to say. "You're right. I'll stay somewhere else tonight anyway."

Quilleran touches the brim of his hat. "I'll stop by to check, too, just to be sure."

Mrs. Miller distractedly shuffles through the police report.

"Did you call your husband?" Quilleran asks.

"Yes."

"Has your son arrived?"

"Not yet," she says. "I think his flight was delayed."

The Indian nods, a grim look on his face. "Everything will be just fine, you'll see."

"Why are you helping us?" Mrs. Miller blurts out. "I mean, are you working for someone?"

The giant Indian shakes his head. "Oh, no. I work for myself. And for my city."

"I don't understand. . . ."

"Let's put it this way, ma'am: some people need to be forced to do things. Others just do it because they feel like it. They know it's the right thing to do."

"And you're one of them."

"I think so."

"But that doesn't explain why you're helping us. Why you're doing something for the Miller family, for my son."

"I've been waiting for your son for many years," Quilleran says. "Your son is an important person."

Mrs. Miller's ears perk up.

"And something important is about to happen. For the world."

"What?"

"We don't know, exactly. But it's near. Very near."

"*We* don't know? Who else is there, aside from you?"

"I think there are people like me in every city, people who love the place they live and sense that something is about to happen."

"I don't understand you, Mr. Quilleran. In fact, you're frightening me."

"Don't be frightened. I'm just trying to say that every place in the world is looked after by people who love it, who want to protect it. Here's my point: I think all these people have been warned."

"Warned about what?"

"That the world is about to change, ma'am. And that your son is one of the people who is going to change it."

"You'd better not get off the ship," Paul Magareva warns Professor Miller.

"I need to go to the embassy," Harvey's father replies, anxious. "My son was on the evening Air China flight and he never showed up. Something happened to him at the airport, but they won't tell me anything over the phone!"

Paul Magareva leans over the deck railing and points at the long, cement dock. The ship is moored to it with heavy chains. "The thing is, something strange is going on down on the dock."

"Like what?"

"People asking questions. The cook told me there are men asking about you."

"About me? How could that be?"

"I don't know, but do you think it might have something to do with your son? And your wife's phone call?"

Professor Miller peers out at the crowded, bustling port. "Who's asking the questions?"

"They're staying out of sight, in the shadows over there," Paul Magareva says in a low voice, "and they aren't from the police or Air China or the immigration office. I'm no expert, but I'd say they're shady characters. It's like they're waiting for you to step foot in Shanghai to—"

"Make me disappear?"

"Or, in any case, to force you to go with them."

George Miller is furious. "What on earth is going on, anyway?"

"Give me the documents for your son. I'll take them to the embassy for you."

"What about Harvey?"

"He's a big kid. He'll manage."

26
THE ESCAPE

Warm, heavy, relentless rain falls from the sky.

Ermete looks around, furious. He feels the raindrops thumping against his skull, seeping in everywhere, into his shirt, his pants cuffs, his socks.

Out of the corner of his eye, he spots Sheng running toward Century Park. Mistral and Elettra are running in the opposite direction.

"Where do you guys think you're going?" the engineer hollers.

But they don't even turn back to look at him.

Ermete can't follow all of them. He needs to decide.

He thinks it over for a split second and runs after Sheng. "Hey, yellow eyes! Wait up!"

The boy crosses the street without even looking. Two cars glistening with rain zoom past, just inches away from him.

Ermete dodges the puddles and races after him, trying to keep up. He crosses the street and horns blare. He calls out to Sheng again.

But Sheng keeps running. He turns down a dark alley, where it's impossible to see what's underfoot. The rain forms cones of golden light around the streetlamps and below a neon sign depicting a red dragon.

"Dammit!" the engineer exclaims, fuming. "When I get my hands on you, Sheng, I'm going to make you pay for all this running!"

Sheng is already at the far end of the alley and is getting ready to cross four lanes of traffic separated by a grassy divider with a row of scrubby trees. On the other side, an asphalted parking lot with orange lampposts and the gate to Century Park, which is closed.

Sheng crosses the street and reaches the tall gate, where he stops and seems to be deciding what to do next.

Then he starts climbing.

"Sheng!" Ermete shouts from across the street. "Are you insane?" He steps forward and is struck by a blinding white light and a blaring horn. He leaps back, frightened, and yells in Italian at the driver who almost ran him over.

Ermete counts to three and dashes between the cars. "Sorry!" he shouts, ignoring their honks.

He leaps onto the divider, a moment's respite, and crosses the remaining two lanes. When he reaches the parking lot on the other side, he feels like he's been miraculously saved.

"Sheng!" he calls out. "If you think I'm climbing over that gate, you can forget it!"

He's wet. Sopping wet from the warm rain.

"You hear me, Sheng?"

Sheng stops climbing and hangs there, clutching the top of the gate.

"Get down from there right now!" the engineer continues with the best furious uncle tone he can manage.

The gate suddenly grows dark. A multitude of insects bursts up from the park like an explosion. A dark swarm of wings, antennas and little legs seems to lunge toward the boy and engulf him. Twenty paces away, Ermete gapes and backs up. The swarm of insects surrounds both the gate and Sheng and pours into the parking lot.

"Aaaaaah!" Ermete screams. He swallows one, two, twenty mosquitoes. He spits them out, closes his mouth and throws himself to the ground, letting the horror wash past him and fly away. He hears horns blaring. Screeching. Tires skidding over the wet asphalt.

It lasts two, three, four seconds at most. Then the flood of insects—the invasion of grasshoppers, mosquitoes or whatever they are—drifts away from the parking lot.

Ermete finds himself curled up in a ball. He looks around and can't believe his eyes. Dead insects on the ground. Others wriggling in the puddles. He drags himself to his feet, staggering. Sheng has fallen to the ground.

"Hey!" Ermete calls out. He pats himself down and, to his surprise, notices he's unharmed. "It's over! They're gone! Are you all right? Sheng!"

He runs over to him. It starts to rain harder. Thousands of needles crashing down against the asphalt.

"Sheng?"

Sheng opens his eyes. They're blue again.

Ermete sighs. "You okay?"

"Mistral . . . ," Sheng whispers.

"What's that?"

On the ground, Sheng points at Heremit Devil's skyscraper. "Mistral summoned them. . . ."

Suddenly, the mirrored glass and steel building lights up like a sinister Christmas tree. Like a sixty-four-story-tall warning sign.

"Oh, man!" Ermete exclaims. "Oh man, oh man, oh man!"

"Answer," Jacob Mahler says in the office on the skyscraper's second-to-top floor.

Heremit Devil's phone is ringing.

"Or would you rather I do it?"

Heremit is on the opposite side of the desk. He shakes his head. "You? Here? How can it be?"

"Same codes as last year. The doors still open."

"How can you be here . . . alive?"

"I'm a man of many surprises, Heremit."

The phone continues to ring.

"Answer."

The building's owner slowly walks up to the desk. "You'll never get out of here alive," he hisses.

Mahler raises his violin. "Neither will you."

Heremit Devil clutches the receiver, his hand not revealing the slightest tremor. "Heremit," he says, as always:

As he listens, he switches on monitor number four. Black-and-white image, surveillance camera. Underground level. Corridor B. Nik Knife is in front of the monitor. He's holding Harvey to his left, a dagger pointed at his throat.

Mahler slowly lowers his bow.

Heremit narrows his eyes maliciously. "Bring him here," he

finally says. "Your friend has arrived in hell's kitchen," he whispers to Mahler.

Jacob doesn't say a word. He's quickly assessing what to do. He didn't anticipate that Nik Knife might capture Harvey.

Thump.

Thump.

Thump.

Something more solid than rain starts beating against the windows.

Insects. Swarms of crazed insects hurling themselves against the windowpanes as if they could shatter them.

Heremit Devil frowns, troubled. He switches on monitor number one. Main entrance. Two girls are walking up the street, a cloud of insects following them. Zoom in on the face of the first girl. Tall, thin, bobbed hair. She's singing.

"You may be right, Heremit," Jacob whispers, rising to his feet slowly, "but it seems he didn't come alone."

On the street, Elettra raises her hands.

And a blinding burst of light shuts down all the cameras.

SECOND STASIMON

"Vladimir?"

"Irene! Where have you been? I tried calling you, but—"

"I'm at a friend's. Did you feel that?"

"Yes, it was like . . . like suddenly waking up. Who caused it?"

"At least three of them. Together."

"Three?"

"Energy, harmony, memory . . . Elettra, Mistral and Harvey suddenly burst out. The time has come. This is it! They're ready!"

"We aren't ready! We're still missing . . . hope."

"He'll make it, too."

"It's almost as if Sheng is refusing to do his part."

"It wasn't supposed to be him. He wasn't ready."

"And he didn't have the same power as the other boy!"

"Maybe we should find a way to help him. If we felt the jolt, the others must've felt it, too. The ones who knew."

"Yes, it's possible."

"We need to warn them. And unite our voices to awaken Sheng."

27

THE AWAKENING

"Sheng! Sheng!" Ermete calls out. "Would you wake up?"

Sheng moves his head on the pillow from one side to the other before opening his eyes.

He's in a room he doesn't recognize. Electric light. A shuttered window with a strange glow filtering through it. Ermete is standing next to him.

"Finally!" he grumbles.

"Where am I?"

"Who knows?" the engineer replies. "I brought you to the first hotel I could find. On my back!"

"But . . ." Sheng sits up. "What time is it?"

"Six-thirty in the morning."

Sheng shakes his head. "I was having a strange dream. . . . There were lots of people. The antiques dealer, Elettra's aunt and even . . . the gypsy woman from Rome . . . and Quilleran the postman, and the guard from the Louvre museum. Then there was some kind of monk with a graying beard. They were all talking to me at the same time. But I don't remember what they were saying." Sheng concentrates. "Wait . . . now . . . now I remember. They were saying, 'Be brave. Look at the things others can't see.'"

Ermete steps away from the bed, sighing. He grabs the pair of pants draped over the back of a chair and starts to dry them with a tiny whirring hair dryer.

"The boy!" Sheng exclaims, remembering. "I was following that boy in the jersey!"

"I have no idea what you were doing."

"I got to the park and then . . . then the insects appeared!" Sheng jumps up from the bed. "Mistral! Elettra! Where—"

"Stop your brain right there, my friend," Ermete says, pointing the hair dryer at him. "There's nothing you can do about it. And you can't go there."

"Go where?"

The engineer steps over to a window and pulls back the curtain, letting in a pale light that filters through the dense clouds. Heavy, vibrant rain oozes from the sky like icing. And at the end of the leaden view is a black skyscraper.

Heremit Devil's skyscraper.

Below, the police cars' blue beacons fill the street with flashing lights. Above, two helicopters point their searchlights at the mirrored windows and circle the building like giant, crazed bees searching for the entrance to their hive.

"What happened?"

"It's been like this for hours," Ermete replies. "The police cordoned off the whole area. Nobody goes in and nobody comes out. No one's answering their cell phones anymore. Not Harvey, not Mistral, not Elettra. In three words: I don't know. But whatever happened, it's big. They talked about it on TV not long ago. The only captions in English read SKYSCRAPER ATTACK. CHINESE MAFIA PAYBACK?"

"I—I . . . ," Sheng stammers, without adding anything else. He stares at the building flooded with lights, trying to overcome his fear. "I should be there with them."

"Great idea," Ermete grumbles. "Great idea, really." He switches off the hair dryer and tosses it on the floor. "I don't know what you guys are thinking of doing, but as far as I know, you aren't superheroes yet. In any case, you aren't there with them. You're here with me."

"And what are we doing here?"

"I should be asking you that," Ermete shoots back. "For example, would you mind telling me why you decided to climb up that gate to the park?"

Sheng rubs his eyes and sits on the edge of the bed.

"My headache was driving me crazy," he says. "I couldn't take it anymore. And when I saw that boy staring at me from the steps, I thought I'd completely lost it. So I decided to go talk to him so I could understand."

"There was no boy, Sheng."

"Yes, there was!" he protests. "And when he saw I was heading his way, he ran off!"

"So yesterday you wanted to talk to an imaginary boy that only you can see?"

"Exactly."

Ermete shakes his head. He remembers Sheng running, but he's absolutely certain there was no boy in front of him, running away.

"And then"—Sheng spreads open his arms—"when I was

178

climbing up the park gate . . . he disappeared . . . and the insects showed up."

"You said Mistral did that," Ermete reminds him.

"I figured they were there because of her. Like in Paris, when she summoned the bees."

Ermete clearly remembers how, not long after the insects appeared, Heremit Devil's skyscraper lit up in a burst of blinding light. He tells Sheng.

"Elettra was furious. She got a call from Harvey. . . ." Ermete can't exactly reconstruct what they said during their call. All he knows is that right after that, the two girls headed off for the skyscraper.

While the engineer talks, Sheng keeps thinking about what he dreamed.

Be brave enough to see what others can't see.

"What if I was simply brave enough?" he exclaims.

"What?"

"I swear I really saw that boy. Maybe . . . I was brave enough to see him."

"Mistral was shouting that your eyes were yellow."

"Like during the blackout in Rome!" Sheng continues, electrified. "That's when my eyes turned yellow for the first time. Nobody could see a thing, but I could, like it was broad daylight."

"That doesn't—"

"And then at the museum in Paris! I was talking to a guard that Mistral couldn't see. Maybe it's my eyes that . . . How do they look now?"

"They're blue."

"They need to turn yellow. Maybe they turn yellow in

dangerous situations. Or maybe I'm the one that needs to . . . command them."

"We could ask Elettra's aunt."

Sheng shakes his head. "There's no time for that. We need to find out what happened to the others."

"Be my guest." He smirks, pointing at the skyscraper. "Go over there and ask him."

Sheng starts to throw on his clothes. "We need to do something for them, and fast! We can't wait another second!"

"You want to go to the skyscraper?"

"No, I want to follow the clues and find the Shanghai object," the boy says. "Elettra, Harvey and Mistral did their part. Now it's up to me. I'm the fourth and final element: water."

Ermete holds up the dripping clothes. "If you want water, just go outside."

"That's exactly what I'm going to do." Sheng finishes putting on his wet clothes, holding back a shiver. "You coming with me?"

"Where?"

"To the place the heart top suggested."

A humid dawn, trickling and heavy with mist, rises over the city.

The air is still, the rain slicing through it. Colorful umbrellas blossom on the streets, and Sheng and Ermete need to push their way through the crowd. They've just come out from the metro station in Sheng's neighborhood, a few blocks away from the Small Peach Garden Mosque.

"Everything's fine, Mom," the boy says into his cell phone.

He snaps it shut at the first cry of desperation.

"Next time, send her a fax," the engineer suggests.

The Yuyuan Garden is closed. At the main entrance, a sign in two languages says it opens at eight-thirty.

"One hour to go," Ermete says.

"We can't wait an hour," Sheng decides, walking along the perimeter of the garden. His determination stems from the only idea he's come up with to help Harvey, Elettra and Mistral: find the Shanghai object as fast as he can and hand it over to Heremit Devil in exchange for his friends.

When Sheng reaches the corner of Anren Lu and Fuyou Lu, he climbs up the wall without thinking twice. It takes only a minute. He jumps down on the other side, rolls over on the ground, gets back up covered with mud and damp leaves and calls out to Ermete, "Wait for me out there! I'm Chinese. I can pretend I work as an errand boy for them, but you . . ."

"Go on, go ahead," the engineer encourages him. "I'll find someplace dry and have a cup of coffee."

Mist rises from the ground of the Yuyuan Garden. Beneath the rain, it pools together like a blanket of fog. The raindrops form winding rivulets in the earth and, as they fall, hide the unattractive profiles of the cement buildings all around it. As he makes his way deeper into the garden, even the city's noises seem to disappear. Sheng walks down the paths and over small wooden bridges, skirting ponds where giant carp swim. Bamboo stalks sag in dripping clusters. Lotus blossoms quiver. The only things peeking through the gray fog that shrouds everything are the pavilions' white walls and the shapes of wooden dragons, which look like they're leaping out from a dream. The corrugated rooftops on the red-lacquered wooden pagodas sparkle with legend.

When Sheng reaches the Ten Thousand Flower Pavilion, he's left gaping in awe. He stops in front of a tree, its trunk massive, its branches trickling with rain. It's like a four-century-old wise man with pearls falling from his open arms.

"The city's great tree . . . ," Sheng whispers, touching its trunk. It's a ginkgo biloba, one of the world's most ancient trees, the same species whose seeds they found inside the Star of Stone.

The tree seems to confirm his hunch.

Sheng starts running again, his heart racing faster and faster.

Be brave enough to see what others can't see.

The emperor's teahouse pavilion is in the middle of a lake and is reached by crossing nine bridges built to keep out evil spirits. The pagoda is still dark, but a side door is ajar. Sheng walks in.

Without the throngs of tourists and their cameras, the old pagoda appears in all its magical charm, with its curved wood and dragon profiles. The picture windows that overlook the green lake fill the silent interior with shafts of gray light.

Sheng takes a deep breath and concentrates. He needs to find something that it's important to find. He walks across the creaking floor and closes his eyes for a moment. It's like going back through the centuries, back to when Shanghai was just a little fishermen's village on the big, winding river.

But the illusion lasts only a few seconds.

"Hey! We're still closed!" an old waiter says, his voice shrill. "What are you doing here?"

"I don't know," Sheng admits, looking at him. The waiter has come out from behind a giant candelabrum. The rain is pounding against the windows, but to Sheng it's like a drumroll. He smiles, flashing his gums. "That sounds nice, doesn't it?"

The waiter seems surprised by his remark. He walks over to Sheng as if his feet weren't even touching the ground and returns his smile. "You haven't answered my question, young man."

"Well, all I know is that I need to find something, and I'm convinced it's somewhere in this pagoda. But I don't know what it is, exactly."

"Very interesting . . . ," the waiter replies, his long silk robe rustling. "And why are you so sure it's here?"

"Because a toy top told me," Sheng replies calmly. "And because I dreamed about it."

"A toy and a dream. You are guided by great certainty. . . ."

"I don't know of any better guide."

"I don't believe there is one." The man looks around. "If this thing really is here, what do you plan on doing once you've recognized it?"

"I'll try to figure out why it let itself be recognized."

The man checks the big clock behind the counter that separates the tea room from the kitchen. "And do you think you'll manage to do all that in an hour's time?"

One hour later, the gates of the Yuyuan Garden are opened. Sheng runs out, dripping wet. He looks for Ermete where they split up and finds him at a small outdoor café not far away, leafing through the English edition of *Shanghai Daily*.

"Hey! Seen this?" the engineer asks, folding the paper and sticking the day's latest news under Sheng's nose.

"We've gotta move!" Sheng exclaims, even more excited. "I found it, Ermete!"

"What?"

"The clue! In the teahouse there was a big Chinese painting hanging right in the middle of the pavilion. It's always been there! Right in front of everybody's eyes in the most touristy place in the whole city, but it's like nobody ever saw it before!"

"Painting? What painting?"

"Picture this: four kids with different-color clothes on the back of a big dragon. A water dragon. A blue one."

"You mean one of those big, wingless snakes with horse snouts that you Chinese call dragons?"

"I mean the most powerful dragon of all dragons, with us four on it!"

"What do you mean, *us* four?"

"Listen! The boy sitting on the dragon's tail is holding some sort of stone egg. The girl in front of him has a mirror. The third one, a long, white mantle decorated with golden scales . . ."

"Stone, mirror, veil . . . and the fourth?"

"The fourth is holding the dragon's reins and making it fly toward a star that's shining over the sea."

"Wow!" Ermete says.

Sheng goes on. "Wait, there's more. A Jesuit priest painted it in the seventeen hundreds."

"A Jesuit priest? In the seventeen hundreds?"

"You got it! His name was Giuseppe Castiglione."

Ermete gapes. "How do you know that?"

"The waiter told me."

"A Jesuit from the seventeen hundreds who was a painter in China? Whoa!"

"The waiter says that if I want to find out more, I should ask the Shanghai Jesuits," Sheng goes on. "He says they've got a massive library and that they might help us."

"Do you know where it is?"

"We need to take the metro to Xujiahui, but that's no problem. The problem is getting in: from what the waiter told me, the library isn't open to the public, and it's got strange opening hours."

"Jesuits, huh?" Ermete murmurs. "I went to a Jesuit school. Let's see. . . . What time is it in Italy right now?" He makes a quick calculation. "It's early, but . . ."

The engineer dials a number.

"What are you doing?"

"Calling my mom. Meanwhile, lead the way to the metro."

"Are you insane? At this hour, she'll still be sleeping!"

"So? You want to get into a Jesuit library? I'll get you into a Jesuit library." Ermete waits for the phone to start ringing. "Haven't I mentioned I was an altar boy in all the churches in Rome? I've got connections. Important connections. And it looks like the time has come to use them!"

28
THE LIBRARY

◯

THE CHURCH IS CALLED ST. IGNATIUS CATHEDRAL, NAMED AFTER the founder of the order of Jesuits: St. Ignatius of Loyola.

It's a stately red church with two tapered bell towers. A large white Christ stands over the entrance with statues of the four evangelists to his sides. The library is next to the church in an old building that seems protected by a giant, age-old tree.

"A ginkgo biloba," Sheng cheers when he sees it. It can't be a coincidence: he's following a trail with deep roots.

Standing in the doorway to the library is a small priest. He has an oval, geometrical face, gold-rimmed glasses and a short salt-and-pepper beard.

Ermete and Sheng cross the courtyard, dashing toward him and what is now useless shelter from the rain.

"It's very kind of you to let us in!" Ermete says, almost shouting as he climbs the stairs that lead to the door.

"It's a pleasure, Dr. De Panfilis. The cardinal told me you'd be coming."

A simple, warm handshake.

When the priest turns to him, Sheng realizes he's seen the man before: he's one of the people who spoke to him in his dream last night. Along with the gypsy woman from Rome, the mailman from New York and the museum guard from Paris.

"Father Corrado," the man introduces himself.

"Sheng," the boy replies, shaking his hand just as cordially. *Here's the Shanghai guardian*, he thinks, grateful.

"Welcome to the Zi-Ka-Wei Library." The priest smiles. "Also known as the *Reservata Bibliotheca, Biblioteca de Mission, Bibliotheca Major, Xujiahui Tianzhutang Cangshulou* or, more simply, the Great Library."

Once the introductions have been made, Father Corrado leads them into the building. "The cardinal told me you were coming to do research. What is it you need, exactly?"

Ermete points at Sheng. "He's the expert."

As the boy briefly describes the painting, Father Corrado nods more and more gravely. "That's rather unusual, I must say. And where is it you saw the painting?"

"It's hanging in the teahouse in the Yuyuan Garden."

"Is it?"

"Do you know of this Giuseppe Castiglione?" Ermete asks.

The Jesuit smiles. "Naturally. Who doesn't know of Giuseppe Castiglione?"

"Of course . . . Who doesn't?" Ermete mumbles, joking.

"Giuseppe came to Shanghai when the great Qianlong was emperor, the one who had the garden and teahouse built. In those times, relations between the Jesuits and China were excellent and offered a mutually beneficial cultural exchange. Giuseppe was such a wonderful painter that he soon became the court painter for the emperor, who preferred him over many Chinese artists. In China, he went by the name of Lang Shining."

As he speaks, Father Corrado delves farther into the old library.

"I didn't know there were Jesuits in China," Ermete says.

"Few people do. And yet, I believe we were the first Westerners to establish solid relations with the empire. We had a court delegation starting in the sixteenth century. We were the ones who reformed their calendar. We were also the first to translate the Chinese language into letters that could be understood in Europe."

"So it's your fault there are four different street signs for every road?" Ermete jokes.

Father Corrado smiles. "If you want to put it that way, yes. In any case, our presence wasn't always appreciated. But despite many difficulties, we've managed to preserve these books, which are now one of the most important collections in the country. Especially for those who want to track down information about children riding a dragon, which otherwise would be impossible to find."

The Chinese books section they've just walked into has red lacquer bookcases and occupies a long hallway leading into five side rooms with white wooden lofts around the upper shelves.

"There were six rooms once," Father Corrado says with regret, "and the number wasn't by chance: the library was a perfect copy of the Ming dynasty's Tian Yi Ge private library and the perfect balance between sky and earth, between horizontal and vertical.

But due to the metro line construction, the last room became part of the sidewalk outside."

"Naturally," Ermete says under his breath, pretending to understand what the man just said.

Father Corrado stops by the door to the fifth room. "This section is called Cang Jing Lou, meaning—"

"A building for a book collection," Sheng translates.

"And it looks like there are lots of books," Ermete says with admiration. "There must be at least . . . what, a hundred thousand?"

"Oh! We've never cataloged all of them, particularly the Chinese ones. Still, we think that, newspapers included, there might be over five hundred thousand. Subdivided into thirty-six main categories and two hundred eighty-six subcategories. Or perhaps I should say thirty-seven main categories and two hundred eighty-five subcategories."

Father Corrado looks at the two with a hint of a complicity. "That is, if you count the 'books-that-shouldn't-exist' category, which we keep on our . . . 'non-bookshelf.'"

He removes two massive leather-bound books from a lacquered shelf and presses on the back wall, making the painted panel slide open. Inside, in a small niche, are some old books. Father Corrado picks up a booklet bound with leather strings and holds it out to Sheng. Then he quickly slides the panel in place and puts back the two books, smiling. "Not even the men from the Communist Liberation Army found this when they decided to come here and burn all the books."

Sheng turns the leather volume over in his hands.

"What I've just given you is one of Giuseppe Castiglione's

journals, which he wrote the year he came to Shanghai and kindly left to our mission."

"A journal?" Ermete exclaims, peeking over Sheng's shoulder.

The priest leads them into a small, secluded room. "No one will disturb you here. The photocopier is down there, if you need it."

29
THE OFFICE

Two men go up to the top floor of Century Park's tall, black building. They've walked down a long hallway full of childish drawings, across a small bedroom, up a staircase and through an airtight door.

The first of the two men walks rigidly, his hands clasped behind his back. The second has short, gray hair and is clutching an old violin.

"You don't know what you're doing," Heremit Devil repeats obsessively.

Behind him, Jacob Mahler prods him with the violin bow. "It's over, Heremit. Don't you realize that?"

Helicopters are roaring outside the picture windows, trying to find out what's happening inside. News of the swarm of insects has traveled fast, as has news of the explosions on the lower floors. The skyscraper has been divided in two: in the office on the second-to-top floor, it's no longer possible to learn what's going on below. The security system's television screens have gone out, shutting down one by one.

The room on the top floor is almost completely bare. It's a

large office without furniture. The painting of a world map covers the entire floor. The two men are soon walking over its continents. Before the building's electrical system went dead, the map would produce a series of ticking noises, its tiny lights blinking on and off.

"Your old office," Jacob Mahler hisses. "How much longer did you think you could rule the world, hmm?"

"Why did you make me come up here?"

"Because I know how much you hate this room. This is where you were when they gave you the news, isn't it? When was it? Five years ago? Four?"

Heremit Devil's face turns ashen.

"It was devastating, wasn't it? Even for a heartless man like you."

Outside, sirens and bright beacons that look like Christmas lights. Heremit can't stand the uncertainty of not knowing what's going on below. And not knowing what Mahler intends to do.

"If you even try to lay a finger on me, Jacob, Nik will kill your little American friend."

"And how's he going to find out? Were you thinking of calling him?"

"He's on his way up."

"He'll go to your new office. He'll wonder where you are. And by the time he decides to come up here . . . I'll already be done."

"Done doing what, Jacob?"

The killer rests his bow on the violin strings. Rain lashes against the windowpanes, along with swarms of mosquitoes trying to get in.

The bow screeches against the strings, producing a shrill note. Heremit Devil backs up, irritated. "What are you doing?"

The violin produces a second and a third note, which reverberate against the infrangible walls like a wave of razor blades. Some of the otherwise indestructible windowpanes crack imperceptibly. Then the cracks grow longer and the glass finally shatters in a cascade of shards.

"It's time to let in a little air," Jacob whispers as the rain, insects and wind burst into the hermit devil's former office.

Gunshots. That's what Elettra and Mistral hear whistling over their heads.

"Get down!" Elettra shouts, diving to the floor.

Mistral stops singing, and the moment she does, the insects fly off every which way, slipping into every office, opening, room.

People are shouting. More gunshots. The two girls are bellydown on the ground inside Heremit Devil's building, in what seems to be a massive restaurant.

Up to this point, they've encountered few obstacles: Elettra short-circuited all the doors and detectors they came across while Mistral caused panic and confusion with her swarms of grasshoppers, mosquitoes, flies and dragonflies.

They did everything they could to try to get down to the underground level, but they didn't find a single staircase, so they climbed one instead and looked around. And now the security guards, after their initial disorientation, have sprung into action.

"This way!" Elettra shouts, crawling between the tables.

"Where are we going?"

Mosquitoes, flies, dragonflies are everywhere. Their buzzing fills the air.

"To the elevators!"

They run, hunched over, as other gunshots shatter the nearby aquariums.

"Summon the insects!" Elettra shouts when they reach a long hallway that provides no cover.

Mistral starts singing again and, as if enchanted, a buzzing black mantle forms around her and swarms into the hallway.

The two friends dive into the first available elevator. The only underground level is one with a parking lot. Elettra presses the button. The elevator plunges down.

Underground parking lot. Cement. Cars with tinted windows.

Is this where Harvey called her from?

Elettra looks around, frantic.

"Get out!" she shouts to Mistral. Then she rests her hands on the control panel, concentrates a second and lets her anger explode.

The gold elevator lurches to a halt halfway between the fifty-third and fifty-fourth floors. Nik Knife presses the button several times, but nothing happens. The lights go out, replaced by the glow of the emergency lights.

"You'd better let me go," Harvey says, next to him.

With two swift moves, Nik Knife flings open a hatch in the ceiling, pulls himself up out of the car and stands on its roof. He's less than a meter away from the doors to the fifty-fourth floor. He reaches them with a leap, takes out a long knife and wedges it into the crack between the doors.

Once they're open wide enough to get through, he jumps out and shouts to Harvey to follow him.

"Forget it!" the boy replies from inside the elevator.

A hiss.

Harvey feels a burning sensation in his arm and a moment later he sees that a knife has pinned the shoulder of his sweater to the elevator wall.

"Next time I aim at your arm!" Nik Knife shouts, above him.

30
THE JESUIT

ERMETE AND SHENG ARE SITTING AT A GNARLED WOODEN TABLE with old, handwritten registers stacked on it. Sheng unwinds the journal's strings and opens the little book, in which the ancient Jesuit painted illustrations.

"The dates might fit," Ermete murmurs, trembling with curiosity. "The seventeen hundreds is when they lost track of the Pact in Asia."

"Yeah," Sheng says, nodding, "but there's no telling whether it'll explain the clues we have: a box of coins and a red lacquer tile with four knives on it."

The pages are numbered with a square red stamp, and the first ones contain no writing—just large watercolor illustrations and sketches in black ink: a bird with red plumage, two horses, a man brandishing a long bamboo spear.

Then, on page four, the first annotations begin, but Sheng discovers he can't read them. "I think they're in Italian."

The engineer examines the Jesuit's small, cramped handwriting.

"It's more Latin than Italian . . . but that's fine, too. 'Draw-

196

ings and notes by Giuseppe Castiglione during his journey from Zhaoquing to Xujiahui, in the former home of Xu Guangqi, imperial court official and Christian brother.'" Ermete turns the page. There's a sketch of a large tree with mighty branches. "Sheng, what are we looking for in this journal, anyway?"

"I'm not exactly sure."

On page six, Giuseppe makes a note of the stops along his journey and adds small illustrations that look more like reminders or sketches for other drawings than anything else. Ermete scans down the text, reading a word here and a word there.

"We risk spending all day on this," he says a quarter of an hour later.

Sheng stares at the journal's brightly colored pictures and meticulous penmanship. "Let me see. . . ." He starts to flip through the pages.

Then, suddenly, he stops. He's found a miniature copy of the painting he saw at the teahouse: the four kids riding a dragon and the star sparkling over a cobalt-blue sea.

"What does it say here?" he asks Ermete.

"'The four Sages ride the Sea Dragon,'" the engineer reads.

On the next page is the sketch of a fleet of ships sailing toward the same sea.

"And here?" Sheng asks, pointing at a paragraph.

"'Zheng He's fleet leaves the ports of China to follow the Sages of the Dragon,'" Ermete translates. "What's written next isn't clear. He crossed out a line. It looks like, 'It will be destroyed, because one cannot follow the Sea Dragon . . . without a heart.'"

Ermete nervously turns the page. The next drawing depicts a comet shining above a tiny isle. The comet's tail is blue, like the dragon in the first illustration. Beside the star is the constellation Ursa Major. In front of the island, a ship with a dragon on its prow. "'The ship and the Sea Dragon reach Penglang Island in the Bohai Sea, the dwelling of the eight immortal Sages.'"

Then, his voice brimming with emotion, he goes on. "'Legend has it that the island rises up out of the water only once every hundred years. . . .'"

"Yes!" Sheng exclaims. "What about here?" he asks, pointing at a line written in smaller handwriting.

"'Only the Sea Dragon knows its location . . . and only the four Sages have the gifts needed to awaken the dragon.'"

"Looks like we found it."

Ermete turns the page and finds a drawing of two men at the intersection of two rivers. One man is pointing at the water. The second is hunched over a wooden instrument.

"Look at what he's doing," Sheng whispers, breathless.

"He's casting a top . . . on the map!" the engineer exclaims. Then he reads aloud, "'The name China is said to derive from the Persian *chini*, with which the ancient Chaldeans would indicate these religions.'"

"The Chaldeans came here?"

"Seems so," Ermete says.

The next page is blank. Ermete flips back through the journal, returning to the page with the four kids riding the dragon. The page before it contains a rough sketch and an annotation. "'The legend of the island of the Penglang Sages as it was told to me by Hsu Kwang-ch'i, our friend and pupil, to whom it was told by the Sage Chi-Han-Ho, who in turn learned it from his master.'"

"Master . . . master . . . master . . . ," Sheng murmurs. "Here's the trail of information that was lost."

"And now that we know about it?" Ermete asks.

"Seems clear to me: we need to find the Sea Dragon," Sheng replies. "Only the four Sages can reawaken it."

"With the gifts . . ."

"Yeah. Mirror, star, veil and—"

"Once it's reawakened, the dragon will show us how to get to Penglang," Ermete continues, "an island that surfaces only once every hundred years. Sounds easy." He rolls his eyes.

"A dragon . . . ," Sheng whispers.

"Which may well be right over our heads," a voice says, surprising them.

Ermete and Sheng spin around. It was Father Corrado who spoke. "Forgive me for listening in on a part of your conversation. But as you can imagine, I'm familiar with the legend of that island. And I believe it's an astronomical legend. The dragon he speaks of, you see, is near Ursa Major. Therefore, it could be the constellation Draco, which in ancient times was the constellation in which the northern polestar was located. And which pointed north."

Ermete clasps his hands behind his head, puzzled.

Father Corrado continues. "Some thousands of years ago, the North Star wasn't our Polaris, which is found in Ursa Minor's tail, but the star Thuban in the constellation of Draco. The Dragon— or the Serpent, as we call it here in the East—is a very long constellation that contains all twelve signs of the zodiac in its tail. The Dragon is tied in with all the zodiacal signs. To us Catholics, it's the inescapable temptation of evil. But to those who study the heavens, it has a different significance: by studying how it moves in the sky, they can predict solar and lunar eclipses, which always occur in either its head or its tail. That's why there's a popular saying among astronomers that goes, 'The dragon causes eclipses.' And also, 'The dragon ate the sun.' A moment ago, you were speaking of the Chaldeans. . . ."

"Yeah," Sheng says, "the journal says they came all the way to Shanghai in ancient times."

"That's likely. Their Magi visited a good deal of the known world. In any case, the Chaldeans understood the stars and eclipses better than anyone else. Thanks to them, the great Greek scholar Thales of Miletus predicted the May 585 BC eclipse, which took place right on schedule."

Father Corrado stares at the library's two guests, who are surprised by his knowledge of astronomy. "There's one last thing I can tell you: the word *dragon* derives from the Greek word *derkesthai*, which means 'to see.' And one must be very brave to ride a dragon. And to see."

Father Corrado is staring straight at Sheng, whose jaw drops in astonishment.

Be brave enough to see things others can't see, Sheng thinks. *Be brave enough to reawaken the dragon.*

And to follow it to the island of the immortal Sages.

His heart is racing. He finally understands what he needs to do. Turning to Ermete, he says, "I know where it is."

As soon as Sheng and Ermete leave, Father Corrado puts away the old journal, deep in thought. He's never shown it to anyone before. And no one has ever shown up asking to see it. The journal hasn't left that bookcase for at least two hundred years.

When everything is back in its place, Father Corrado walks over to the metro and squeezes into a packed train heading for Huangpi Nan Lu. Once he arrives, he heads toward the Old City. Twenty minutes later, he shakes the rain off his umbrella on the wooden terrace of the Yuyuan Garden teahouse. He looks around, curious, searching for the old waiter and the painting by Giuseppe Castiglione that the boy claims to have seen.

Naturally, neither of them is there. Father Corrado nods, as if this was confirmation of what he already assumed. "Hope has eyes of gold . . . ," he murmurs.

"What's that?" a young waiter asks.

"It takes eyes of gold to see others' dreams clearly. And yet, they're right here before everyone's eyes."

31
THE CAR

"*DASVIDANIYA! DASVIDANIYA!*" THE PEOPLE IN THE TRAIN CHEER WHEN it slows down, approaching a tiny, secluded station in the middle of the Siberian taiga.

Linda Melodia shakes everyone's hand and looks around, satisfied. In a matter of hours she transformed the filthy-dirty Soviet train car into a sparkling little jewel. All the clothes are neatly folded in the luggage racks, the shoes lined up in the back, clean and polished. The floor was wiped down with a rag doused in alcohol, the trash collected in a bag in the bathroom. Quite a feat, which all cleverly began when she properly folded the clothes of the woman sitting next to her and little by little turned into an activity for the entire train car. At first Linda had acted alone, putting away an overcoat here and a sweater there. Then the other women followed her lead, laughing at first, but gradually more convinced and determined as the task of tidying the car proceeded. After one hour, Linda was giving orders to a team of fifteen sprightly Russian women, who magically understood her every command. And by the end of the second hour, even the most skeptical of the travelers, forced to give up their smelly cigars, had to admit that traveling in such clean surroundings was like traveling in first class.

"Oh, no, thank you, I couldn't!" Linda is saying to one of the chess players, who insists she accept his half-full bottle of vodka.

She has also firmly declined two marriage proposals.

When the train whistles and comes to a halt, Linda Melodia picks up her travel bag and, waving goodbye triumphantly, steps onto the platform. Farther down, a porter has already unloaded her large suitcase, but the pavement is so uneven that its wheels won't turn.

"Oh, heavens!" the woman exclaims, looking around.

The station, whose name she no longer remembers, is dirty, full of people coming and going . . . and horse-drawn carts. She hasn't seen horse-drawn carts and wagons for years.

"Your shoes!" she cries, noticing a man boarding her train car, his soles dripping with mud. The man stares at her, not understanding, and Linda shrugs. She hopes her apprentices will keep him from setting foot inside in such a state.

Linda sighs and grabs her suitcase. She hands some coins to the porter, who stayed to keep an eye on it, and begins to drag it out of the station. The plastic wheels become two little plows in the dirt path beside the sidewalk, making her sweat proverbial buckets.

By the time she's reached the deserted area on the other side of the station, Linda is panting. She reaches into her pocket and pulls out the slip of paper with her travel plans. She's already crossed off the first ten lines, leaving only the last one: HIRE A CAR AND DRIVER FOR TUNGUSKA.

"Very well," the woman decides, still determined to solve every problem as soon as possible.

She looks around.

Apart from the station, there isn't even a house. Just a flat, desolate clearing of low grass and shrubs with horses grazing on it. As she's debating which direction to go in, a black car comes bouncing along toward her.

"Miss Melodia?" a man asks, getting out of the backseat. A fine example of an older gentleman, refined and elegant.

"Yes," Linda replies. "Who are you?"

"My name is Vladimir. I am a friend of your sister."

"I believe you're mistaken. As I recently discovered, I don't have any sisters."

The man smiles.

"Forgive me, but I do believe you're the one who's mistaken. From what I can gather, you have at least one. In any event, I might have been a friend of the sister whom you've lost."

Linda frowns. "You speak in quite an eloquent manner, sir."

"That's because of my work. I deal in old things. And I speak in an old manner."

"Well, whatever the case," Linda mumbles, "why are you here?"

"Your sister—that is, the person you believed to be your sister—informed me that you were coming and I thought it would be nice if someone came to the station to welcome you."

"That's very kind, of course, but—"

"I would like to take you to see someone who can tell you the things you would like to know. The ones for which you came all the way here."

"But I need to go to—"

"Tunguska. Yes, I know."

"Oh," Linda says, taken aback. "How do you know that?"

"Sometimes even people who deal in old things know the latest news. Would you care to get in, or would you rather stay out here in the cold?" Vladimir smiles at her.

32

THE PARK

○

SHIJI PARK METRO STATION.

Green line, number two.

Century Park stop.

Sheng comes out with Ermete following. They've bought two light blue plastic raincoats that make them look like strange, poorly packaged fish.

"Would you try to be a little clearer?" Ermete asks Sheng for the umpteenth time.

"I need to find that boy!" Sheng shouts.

"What about the coins? The lacquer tile?"

"I don't know," he says, "but those clues aren't as important as the boy is. I can feel it!"

Ermete doesn't reply. True, it isn't very clear how they can find a dragon that might be a constellation by using a cookie tin, some old coins and a lacquer tile. Or even the Veil of Isis and Mistral's notebooks, which they've been carrying around in the backpack all day long. "But even if we find it," he says, "what then?"

"If we find what?"

"The dragon."

"We trade both it and the Veil of Isis for Mistral, Elettra and Harvey," Sheng says. "That way, he'll have all four objects and we'll be safe and sound. Then we can forget about this whole thing once and for all. Nobody's forcing us to see it through to the end, right? Our masters didn't, and nothing happened."

"Except a meteorite in Siberia and an earthquake in Messina," Ermete reminds him.

Sheng bites his lip and looks up. A helicopter is still circling the black skyscraper on the other side of the park.

"How are you planning to let Heremit Devil know you want to make a trade, anyway?" Ermete asks.

"We go back to the Grand Hyatt, find the guy with the bull's-eye tattooed on his head and make our offer."

They walk into the park. To the left, a big lake. To the right, a roller-skating rink, benches. Trees. And other, smaller lakes.

"You must be kidding," Ermete says after a while.

"Kidding about what?"

"It's not a good idea, handing over the objects now that we've figured out what they're for."

"Which would be . . . ?"

"The objects are the offerings to reawaken the Sea Dragon, which, when ridden by the four young Sages, will show the location of Penglang Island or whatever the heck it's called."

"Yeah, it's simple," Sheng jokes. "It's just a shame we don't know what the Sea Dragon is or how it can point out the route to an island we aren't even sure exists. And on top of that, we don't know what's on the island or why we should even go there in the first place."

But I do know, Sheng thinks. Because he's been dreaming

about it for a year now: he dreams of him and his friends struggling to get out of a jungle and diving into the sea. Swimming over to the island. And, once on the beach, being greeted by a woman whose face is hidden behind a veil.

"The chance to reach it comes only once every hundred years," Ermete says, "and you're the one who has to take them there."

"Huh?"

"In the Jesuit's drawing, Harvey is sitting on the dragon's tail, holding the Star of Stone. Then come Elettra and Mistral. While you . . . you have the dragon's reins in your hands! Whatever the dragon is, you're holding the reins now."

"Why does it have to be so complicated?" Sheng grumbles, exasperated. "I—I don't understand anything anymore."

"Let's try going over everything we've discovered, then."

"The map of the Chaldeans," Sheng begins.

"A map handed down from Marco Polo to Christopher Columbus, which was designed to help mankind make decisions, and which at this point is supposed to help you solve the mystery."

"And who are we?"

"The four chosen ones."

"Chosen by who?"

"By the four Sages who came before you. The ones who used to have the tops and tried using them the last time the island rose out of the water, but failed."

"How many tops are there in all?"

"We've had six of them. The tops mimic the stars spinning through the universe. The map is a representation of our world. Each top contains a question, and whenever one of them is cast, it makes a prophesy."

"Why did it all begin in Rome?"

"We don't know. Zoe was the one who chose it. Maybe because they had to start with fire."

"Fire: Elettra, Mithra, Prometheus and the Ring of Fire," Sheng says.

"Elettra uses the energy surrounding her. Mithra is a divinity of Chaldean origins, rediscovered in Rome as a sun god. His priests kept well-guarded secrets."

"Like the cult of the goddess Isis, in Paris."

"Isis shares the same origins as Mithra, even though she's an Egyptian divinity. If he was the sun, she's the moon, which always has a dark side. In fact, she's also the goddess of Nature, who loves to hide."

"The stars: Ursa Major, the North Star, the Star of Isis, Draco," Sheng continues.

"That's easy. The sun, the moon . . . and finally the stars. As they spin through the universe, they mark the passing of time and orientation. They're directions for those who know how to read them."

"And the Star of Stone?"

"It was a meteorite. A falling star."

"And the Dendera calendar at the Louvre museum?"

"A sign of the connection among the ancient religions, the cult of nature and the notion that mankind is bound by a pact. If we keep asking questions, nature will give us the answers . . . as long as we understand their meaning."

"Do you think there actually is a meaning?"

"You can bet there is. And I think it's . . . feeling like we're part of a master plan."

"So what's the Pact, then?"

"It's a possibility, I think. It's the moment when you can reach something it would be impossible to reach at other moments. Maybe it's an island that pops up out of the waves once every hundred years."

"And why is it so important?"

This time, Ermete is silent. Then he says, "For the same reason Heremit Devil wants to get there before us."

The two are standing on a path in Century Park, talking in the rain, which shows no sign of letting up. Then they walk toward the center of the park, looking for Sheng's mysterious friend.

Sheng grabs Ermete's arm.

"It's him."

"Him who?"

"The boy."

Under the blanket of rain, at the edge of the man-made lake, is the boy in the number 89 jersey. His wet hair sticks to his forehead. His face is pale, his eyes big and dark.

"You can't see him, can you?"

Ermete sees an old woman dressed in red who's walking a dog that sports a little sweater in the same color, a jogging fanatic who's running down the paved path, splashing up puddles, and no one else.

"Sheng," he says. "Your eyes . . ."

The boy motions for him to be quiet. "I know, I know. . . . They've turned yellow." He takes a step toward the lake. The boy is stock-still at the water's edge, staring at him.

Sheng raises his hand in a greeting.

The boy raises his own.

"Stay here," Sheng tells Ermete.

"What are you going to do?"

"I'm going to talk to him."

The engineer shakes his head.

Sheng slowly walks toward the lake. He even tries to smile, although his heart's pounding like crazy.

Be brave. Be brave.

He's afraid the other boy is going to get scared and run away, like he did last night.

It takes him four long minutes to reach the lake. Then he steps off the path, crosses over the wet lawn and stops in front of him.

The boy is soaking wet, but it's as if the rain was passing through him.

"Hi," Sheng says.

"Hi."

"Sorry about yesterday."

"Me too. I was scared. . . ."

"I just wanted to talk to you. My name's Sheng."

"I know," the boy says.

"But how?"

"I was looking for you for a long time."

"Looking for me? Following me is more like it."

"I didn't know how else to . . . help you."

"You want to help me?"

The boy nods. The rain is pouring down around them, slow and warm. It makes ripples in the water. Intersecting lines.

Unpredictable paths, like the ones carved on the map of the Chaldeans.

"What is it you want to help me do?" Sheng asks.

"I know what you're looking for. You want the Pearl of the Sea Dragon."

"The Pearl of the Sea Dragon . . . ," Sheng repeats. "Yeah . . . that's what I'm looking for."

"I know where it is," says the boy in the number 89 jersey. He points at the center of Century Park's man-made lake.

"In the lake?"

The boy shakes his head. Tiny raindrops fall all around him. His hair is fine, sparse and fragile.

"It's dark down there. But there's a way in. You need to hold your breath. For a really long time. And you can make it."

Sheng nods. "But I can't swim."

"You don't need to swim. You just need to follow me."

Sheng feels like his heart is about to leap out of his chest. He wades a few steps into the lake. The water is the same color as the gray sky and his feet seem to disappear below it. It isn't deep. It's just murky.

"Wait," Sheng adds. He points at Ermete, who's standing at the top of the rise, the backpack on his back. "So what do we need the coins for, or the tile with the knives . . . and the other things we found?"

"Oh, I don't know about those," the boy answers. "All I know is where to find the Pearl of the Sea Dragon. And the dragon, of course."

"But how do you know that?"

"I used to dream about it every night."

"I have the same dream every night, too."

"I know, Sheng. You dream about the island."

"How do you know that?"

"Because I dreamed about it, too. But only a few times. I wasn't . . . powerful enough." The boy touches Sheng's forehead with his fingertip. "That's why you can see me. Because you see dreams, like I do."

"Are you a dream?"

"I'm Hi-Nau."

From the top of the rise, Ermete watches Sheng walk toward the lake, stop for a few seconds and point in his direction. Then the Chinese boy moves a few steps closer to the water.

"Hey!" the engineer exclaims. "What are you doing?" He takes a few steps forward. Sheng is still standing at the edge of the lake, as if deciding whether or not to dive in.

"No way. He wouldn't actually—"

Sheng dives into the lake.

"Oh, man, no!" the engineer shouts. "He's lost his mind!"

He starts running toward the lake, slips on the slick asphalt and scrambles back up. "Sheng! Sheng!" he shouts. "Get out of there right now!"

It's raining harder and harder. Just then, a helicopter roars over the park.

Ermete waves his arms. "Help! Help! Come back! He fell into the lake! Sheng fell into the lake!"

But the helicopter zooms away, heading toward the dark outline of Heremit Devil's skyscraper.

Ermete reaches the lake. He looks down at the gray water

speckled with rain. He dumps the backpack on the ground, rips off one shoe and then the other one, then his plastic raincoat. He leaves everything on the shore and grumbles, "You and your imaginary friend . . . You'll pay for this! As sure as my name's Ermete De—"

The words die in his throat when Sheng pops out of the water a few meters away from him, dripping wet.

"Hey, Ermete," he says. "You don't need to know how to swim." He points at something below the surface. "Bring the backpack," he says.

33
THE HOSTAGE

INSECTS, WIND, RAIN. SHARDS OF GLASS ON THE FLOOR WITH THE four continents painted on it. The roar of the helicopters. At the top of the black skyscraper, two shadows. One holding a violin.

"Go on! Walk!" Jacob Mahler shouts.

Heremit Devil bursts out laughing. "Walk, Jacob? To go where?"

Mahler points at the shattered picture windows with his bow. "Take your pick. . . ."

"Do you really believe you can force me to jump?"

"What better death could there be for someone who builds skyscrapers?"

Hesitant, Heremit backs up a step. Mosquitoes are everywhere and he has to shoo them away with both hands. "We can talk about this, Jacob."

The violin lets out off-pitch chords. "Talk all you want. Meanwhile, walk!"

"I never gave orders for you to be killed."

"Oh, no? Then how did Nose's women find me?"

Heremit backs up even farther. Shards of glass crunch beneath his shoes. "It was the Italian. That Vinile . . . He wanted revenge for losing his man, Little Lynch. He said you were the one who killed him."

"That's not true!" Jacob Mahler shouts, making his bow dance across the violin. Little Lynch died when Professor Van Der Berger's apartment building collapsed, crushed by the rubble and his own colossal weight.

Heremit Devil is less than a meter from the abyss now. His back is soaked with rain. "Do you really mean to do this to me, Jacob?" he asks, feeling his panic rising steadily.

He's lost control.

He's lost control of everything.

"I'm not doing anything," the killer replies.

"Stop it!" Heremit shrieks. His stony face has suddenly turned into the face of a spoiled child whose parents have just denied him something.

"I can't, Heremit," Jacob Mahler replies, cradling his violin. "This isn't a game anymore."

He forces the man back another step.

"I'll give you everything!" Heremit says, trying again. "Everything I discovered! I'll let the kids go!"

"I'm not here for them." Jacob Mahler raises his shiny metal bow. "I'm here for me."

Then everything happens in a flash. Mahler perks up his ears and darts to the side as fast as a falcon. A knife whizzes right through the spot where his back was an instant ago, passes centimeters away from Heremit's arm and flies out of the building, vanishing.

216

Heremit Devil falls to the ground. Jacob rolls over on the floor twice and leaps up.

Nik Knife is standing in the doorway.

And he isn't alone.

"Put down the violin," the knife thrower orders, holding Harvey in front of him, "and I will not cut his throat."

Jacob Mahler slowly does as he says.

"Very good . . ." Nik Knife steps into the room. "Now let's go call the girls, shall we?"

Jacob Mahler thinks, *Base jump.*

34

THE WATER

It's impossible to make out anything through the lake's murky water. It's like floating in grayness. You need to grope your way around.

A meter below the surface is the opening to a duct: a steel pipe just big enough to slip into. Once they're inside of it, the gray water becomes black and they need to move quickly, pushing themselves forward with their hands and feet. There isn't a current. It's still, stagnant water.

It's warm, the same tropical temperature as rainwater. Water that's far from refreshing.

Sheng leads the way. Ermete follows close behind him. They move through the duct like two giant, awkward crabs, thrusting their feet against the inside of the pipe. In the dark.

You need to be really brave, Sheng thinks, *to do something like this.*

You need to be insane, Ermete thinks, trying not to think at all.

Because after the first thirty seconds in the darkness, the pipe narrows. While at first they could swim through it by moving their hands and arms, now they need to tuck them against their sides and push themselves along with only their tiptoes.

The backpack is in front of them, in the lead, like a figurehead. Or like one of those battering rams they once used to knock down castle doors.

Right after the bottleneck, the pipe begins to descend, and as the descent sharpens, so does the feeling they're falling into a trap. They can't turn around and they can't go back. They can only continue along in the darkness, hoping they have enough breath.

A minute has gone by.

And at that point, the pipe narrows a second time. Now the backpack is stuck and Sheng needs to push it through. For Ermete, who's bringing up the rear, the slowdown is becoming terrible. Gripped with panic, he coughs.

Coughing, he inhales water.

Inhaling the water, he feels his panic rise. But he forces himself to calm down, because his head is throbbing and he knows his lungs are out of oxygen. Sheng has stopped, so he reaches out into the darkness, grabs what feels like Sheng's foot and shoves it. His friend slips forward and Ermete tries to catch up with him. But he bangs into a metal wall. On all sides, there's only metal. The duct has come to an end.

Ermete spins around like a screw and looks up. He sees a circle of gray light and in the circle he sees the shadow of a hand reaching down into the water.

The engineer grabs it.

And lets himself be pulled out.

Ermete sputters, coughing the water out of his lungs.

Beside him, Sheng is doubled over on his knees, exhausted.

The engineer rolls over on the ground, coughs a few more times and asks, "Where are we?"

"I don't know," Sheng answers, peering around. "It looks like a cave. But from what I know, there aren't any caves here in Shanghai. . . ."

"We're under the park," Ermete murmurs, raising his arms to feel around for a ceiling. His hands brush against a smooth cement wall to the side of the pipe they just came out of. "This place is man-made."

He takes a few uncertain steps, trying to figure out how big their surroundings are. The ground is covered with a few centimeters of flowing water. They hear cascades up ahead, in the darkness.

"It seems like some kind of maintenance tunnel," he says.

"There are pipes in the ceiling," Sheng adds, "and water's coming out of them, up there!"

"How do you know that?"

"I can see them," the boy answers. "Let me go first."

They make their way along, single file, and reach the corner of the cement wall. Now there are at least ten centimeters of water on the ground. Once they turn the corner, even Ermete starts to make out a dim glow. A shaft of light. Or a low-voltage fluorescent tube forgotten by whoever built the place. Now he can also see the pipes Sheng mentioned.

Water outlets along the cement walls spew rainwater, which

pools together on the ground and flows over to the duct they came in through.

"It's a rainwater reservoir that feeds into the lake," Ermete realizes.

Sheng looks up. The passageway they're walking through is at least four meters tall. "This place probably fills all the way up during the rainy season."

"Oh, great! And when's the rainy season?"

"Right now," Sheng says in a quiet voice, wading through the water.

As they continue along in the only possible direction, the cement passageway grows chillier. And the water on the ground becomes freezing.

"Nothing better than a tropical cold," Ermete grumbles, coughing. "Where are we going, anyway?"

"I don't know, Ermete."

"Don't you have some imaginary friend you could ask?"

"Not funny."

"You know what else isn't funny? Walking down a rainwater drainpipe in the dark, and for no good reason."

"You can go back, if you want."

"Ooh, nice one! Did you go to the same stand-up comedy school as Harvey? Welcome to our planet: bitter youth."

Ermete grumbles to himself for the next dozen steps.

Then he asks, "Now what?"

Sheng has halted in front of him.

". . . what? . . . what?" a strange echo repeats.

"Don't push," Sheng whispers, letting Ermete see why he stopped.

"Oh, no!" the engineer exclaims.

". . . no! . . . no!"

They're on the edge of a large, round reservoir as wide as an Olympic swimming pool. The ceiling is twenty meters overhead, the grates of a dozen manholes positioned around it in a circle, like the hours on a clockface. The dim light is coming in through the manholes, along with streams of rainwater. On the reservoir's gray cement walls are the openings of pipes in different sizes, marked with numbers written in black characters, and metal rings that look like they haven't been touched for years. Water is flowing into the reservoir through the pipes' dark mouths. Some of them only seep thin, yellowish sewage, while water spews copiously from others. The murky water in the reservoir below is rippling and churning from the constant intake coming from all directions.

The water is a few centimeters below the level in the passageway they just stepped out of.

"Man," Ermete whispers. "Now how do we get out of here?"

"I'm not so sure we need to get out," Sheng replies, looking around. He studies the ducts' wide openings, the numbers, the crumbling gray cement, the strange iron rings, the manholes in the ceiling and finally the metal rungs of a ladder leading up on the opposite side of the reservoir.

"We need to go there!" he says, pointing at the wall.

"Up that ladder?"

"No." Sheng points at a rather large opening next to it, half a meter above the surface of the water. It's marked with a two-digit number. "We need to go through that duct."

"Why that one?"

"Because it's duct number eighty-nine," Sheng answers, as if it was obvious.

"On my three!" Ermete shouts from the underground reservoir. Cupping Sheng's right foot in his hands, he starts counting slowly. "One . . . two . . . three!"

He boosts his friend up, grunting from the effort. Sheng springs up, grabs hold of the lower rim of duct number 89 and hangs there.

Meanwhile, Ermete sinks down under the whirling water in the reservoir and quickly tries to resurface. By the time he does, Sheng has already hoisted himself into the duct and has turned around to reach out his hand.

Ermete grabs it.

"On three! One . . . two . . . three!"

Ermete jumps as high as he can and, at the same time, feels himself being pulled up. He grabs hold of the edge of the duct with his free hand and drags himself up.

Sheng turns around and leads the way.

Duct number 89 is around half a meter tall, just enough to crawl through. It slopes upward and is relatively dry. More than damp, it's cold. Freezing cold.

After a few minutes of this slow advance, when the light from the manholes disappears, the two can finally stand up and start walking through the darkness again.

"It ends here," Sheng says after a dozen or so meters.

Ermete bumps into him. "What do you mean, it ends here?" he asks.

"There's a grate."

"Open it."

Clunk! Clunk! Clunk!

"It won't open."

"Let's try it together. Make room."

"Easier said than done."

"Hand me the backpack."

Sheng presses his back against the wall and tries to let Ermete through. In seconds, they're stuck, the tips of their noses touching.

"Oh, would you—look at—this mess . . . ," the engineer grunts into Sheng's face. Then he grabs the grate with both hands and shoves on it.

Beside him, Sheng does the same.

Clunk! Clunk! Clank!

"We're doing it," the engineer cheers when he hears the last noise. "C'mon!"

A few more shoves and the grate gives way, tumbling down on the other side with a deafening clatter.

Ermete is the first one to roll out. He ends up in a strange underground hall lit by a row of fluorescent lights high overhead. Sheng follows him in.

They're sopping wet, dirty and grimy.

"First possibility," Ermete observes, trying to make out their surroundings. "We're in a giant's freezer."

"The second?"

"We've wandered onto a movie set at a studio that makes catastrophe movies. You know, Pompeii, the Trojan War. . . ."

They wander through the strange place, feeling like they're in the middle of an archeological excavation site. Slowly but surely as they proceed, they see metal walkways arranged at different heights over an old stone pavement, the remains of small walls and more massive walls that section the underground hall into smaller rooms, some crumbling pillars, and, in the back, a larger wall covered with thousands of blue mosaic tiles.

In front of it, the remains of two giant statues facing each other. Both of them appear human. The one on the left, which is better preserved, is a woman whose arm is stretched out in the act of giving a blessing. The other one, destroyed from the knees up, seems to have been a man. Between the two statues is a third carved figure, its strange, dark, hunched, spiral shape covered with scales.

The backpack slung over his shoulder, Sheng walks up to the strange collection of artifacts. Ermete follows him. On the surviving walls around them are the remains of large, strange masks that are similar to the gargoyles on Gothic churches but look far more ancient. Claws, beaks and monster faces leer down from a ceiling that has only partially withstood the test of time. In the uneven paving stones is a series of circular holes that look like little wells. Now that they're closer, Sheng notices that the statue on the left really is a woman, her face covered by a veil.

"It can't be . . . ," he whispers, holding back a wave of shivers.

The woman wears a long gown, a tunic covered with stylized depictions of all the world's animals. What remains of her arm is raised in front of her.

"Isis . . . ," Ermete whispers beside him, dripping. "The goddess of Nature."

The twin statue facing her has only one foot and a male leg carved into the rock.

"And my bet is that this one's Mithra, who was born from stone."

But both of them are left speechless when they look at the third statue, the one between the other two: seen from behind, it looks like a monster crouched over, ready to pounce.

"And this one?" Ermete asks.

"I think it's . . . the Sea Dragon," Sheng says, his eyes completely flooded with gold.

35
THE SEER

TUNGUSKA IS THE NAME OF A SCARCELY INHABITED VALLEY. THE
little village that Vladimir takes Linda Melodia to is a group of
low houses clustered together as if huddled up against the cold.
They have conical wooden rooftops.

All around the village are slopes that grow wilder and more
savage in the distance, dotted with sparse patches of evergreens
and bogs.

"This way," Vladimir says, leading Linda Melodia up the
town's only road: a winding dirt path that passes by the doors of
the various houses.

Under the almost-white sky, the village's only colors are the
gray of the stone and the dark brown of the tree trunks in the
roofs.

The elderly antiques dealer from New York stops in front of a
whitewashed house, the last one in the village. Drawn in red and
black around the door are pictures of stylized animals. Vladimir
waits for Linda to catch up with him, knocks and goes in, his long
back hunched over.

Indoors, the house looks like the inside of a tent: the walls are very thick—almost forty centimeters—and they lead into a single, round room with furniture pushed up against its sides. A bed, an old military stove, a credenza, a dilapidated sink hidden behind some curtains. Containers in all shapes and sizes, vases, tins, wineskins, woven baskets, rucksacks lie on the ground. The floor is covered with overlapping rugs. The stuffy, musty air smells like burnt cardamom and incense.

"Come . . . come in . . . ," says the elderly woman who sits cross-legged in a pool of amber light in the center of the room.

Vladimir motions for Linda to take off her shoes and leave them in a niche in the wall before stepping onto the carpeted floor. As she does so, she sniffs the air and peers around, horrified. Nevertheless, she follows the man onto the rugs.

She stares in awe at the drapes in colorful fabrics hung from the conical ceiling, swaying like strands of multicolored seaweed. And for a long moment she has the sensation she's swimming through the air, which is thick and brims with memories.

With her every step across the soft rugs, the objects scattered around her seem to take on a meaning, almost as if it was possible to glimpse a precise pattern, an idea, a story in all that disorder.

There are strange wooden masks that peer out from the shadows, metal jewelry hand-wrought on long-forgotten anvils. There are silver trinkets hung from strands of silk, ritual footwear in bright, showy colors. There are pages of herbariums that contain flowers unseen for centuries and crude malachite crystals that glow like silent embers. There's a gold nugget that looks like a forbidden fruit, lace fringe that looks like embroidered frost. And in the center of that circle of enchantments sits a small, frail woman with a wizened face, her skin withered in a thousand wrinkles, enough to cover two faces just like hers. Hidden within its folds are two amber-colored eyes, one of which points all the way to the side. Far from beautiful, the woman's face is oddly reassuring. And when Linda looks at her for the first time, her only sensation is one of absolute peace.

"Welcome, Linda," the Seer says, holding out her hand, her fingers bent and gnarled by time.

Linda shakes it gently.

"Do sit down," the old woman continues. "You too, Vladimir. You can stay here with us."

As Linda sits down beside her, she feels like she's in the center of the world. She feels as if everything of any importance is right here in their presence, or will come to pass at any moment.

And it's a strange sensation to have in this remote village in Siberia, which isn't even on the map.

"I know you've had a long journey, Linda," the Seer says, folding her hands in her lap.

Elettra's aunt nods. "Yes, actually. It was weeks before I decided to come here. First I had to find the courage. This is the first time I've ever traveled alone."

She smiles, as if she finds it completely natural to open up like this to a stranger.

Linda looks for the right words to describe how it feels. After a lifetime spent organizing other people's lives—looking after her two sisters; her nephew, Fernando, especially after first his mother, then his wife, passed away—the hotel, her train journey across half of Europe and just as much of Asia is an experience that is both terrifying and wonderful. It makes her feel alive. More alive than she's felt for many years now.

"And it's very nice," she tells the Seer, relieved.

Then she looks around, bewildered. She raises her hand to her mouth, realizing only now that she's been speaking in Italian.

"But . . . you understand me! And I understand you!"

Vladimir exchanges glances with the Seer, who makes a vague gesture with her hands, leaving Linda in doubt one instant longer.

Then the old woman begins to explain. "They call me the Seer because of my eye, this one . . . and because I'm very, very old. I'm two hundred and twelve years old now. But I've never been particularly good at seeing things. Others are far better at that than me. My power is with words. I've always been able to speak to anyone and make myself understood. It doesn't matter if we're perfect strangers or what part of the world we're in. All we need to do is talk."

Linda stiffens, but only for a second.

"My master was the one who helped me discover this power of mine. Before I met him, I'd never left my village and I couldn't even imagine there were languages other than our dialect. But when my master arrived, he taught me many things. He was already very old then. He came from the City of Wind, a place beyond the steppes and the mountains and the desolate fields of grain. His name was Nicholas. But everyone called him the Alchemist. It was he who brought me the tops. And he spoke to me of a long line of Sages that had been around since ancient times and had powers like mine. It was 1802 when I met him, and soon

230

afterward I used the tops to answer the questions he left unanswered."

Linda would like to ask something, but she decides to wait.

"Naturally, I didn't find the answers I wanted. However, I discovered there was another gift that Nature had decided to grant me: while the other women aged visibly, I stayed young far longer than they did. And because my appearance didn't change, the others began to believe I was some sort of enchantress. Or witch. And to some extent, that's what I was." The Seer pauses before going on. "In 1906, a hundred years after I met my master and was given the tops, I left the village to do what the Alchemist had asked me to do: find my successors. I had only vague instructions on how to go about it, and no knowledge of the world. Just like you. One of the people I needed to find was a little girl in Messina, Sicily. Her name was Irene."

The Seer holds up her palms, as if to keep Linda from interrupting.

And so, Linda listens to the woman's calm, measured voice as she tells of how, in 1907, the Pact was handed down to four children, who as of that moment stopped aging.

"A few months later, everything here changed. A valley not far away from where you are now was devastated by a powerful explosion that destroyed everything, flattened the trees and scorched the earth. They thought the world had come to an end. But the world, fortunately, continued to exist. I returned home, believing that the catastrophe had somehow been my fault. Years later, the four children I had found in just as many cities around the world came to visit me. They came here, just like now," the

Seer says, pointing at Vladimir, "to ask questions I didn't have the answers to."

"What I'd like to know," Linda speaks up, "and the reason why I've come all the way here—"

"I realize what you want to know," the Seer says, "and if you don't have time to listen to the whole story, I'll tell you right away: you and your sister are my grandchildren. My daughter's daughters."

The simplicity and straightforwardness of her statement strikes Linda like a whiplash, but she limits herself to raising a hand and saying, "You're . . . my grandmother?"

"When Irene returned the second time, after World War II, the village had been devastated. Every province in Siberia had been reduced to starvation. Soldiers were everywhere. And along with the soldiers were foolish statesmen, Bolshevik visionaries who believed they could structure everything following the ideals of their strange, distant centralized state. I don't mean to tell you the history of the Soviet Union after the war. What I mean to tell you is that in those years, my daughter had two wonderful baby girls. One of them, older by a year, was named Linda."

Linda Melodia brushes the back of her hand over her eyes and finds they're soaked with tears. "What . . . what was my mother's name?"

"Olga," the Seer replies. "When Irene came here, together with Vladimir and Alfred—Zoe hadn't obtained the visas she needed for the journey and remained in Europe—your mother begged her to take care of her daughters. She thought they wouldn't have a future here in the village. Particularly the younger one, who had a persistent cough."

Through her tears, Linda nods. "She always did have weak lungs."

"We all felt that if we sent them away to live in Italy, they would be better off than they would if they stayed here. And that's what we did."

Linda is sobbing uncontrollably now. Vladimir would like to offer her a handkerchief, but the Seer stops him. "Give her time to let it out, now that she has nothing else to discover."

"And now?" Linda asks when she's done crying. "What should I do now?"

The Seer smiles, taking her hand. "What all of us here need to do . . ." She reaches out to Vladimir and rests both their hands on her knees. "We have a dragon to reawaken."

36

THE DRAGON

○

THE SEA DRAGON IS AT LEAST FIVE METERS LONG AND TWO ME-
ters high.

It's a mighty serpent carved in wood and is as dark as night.
Its bristly body is covered with shell-like scales. It rests on its
back paws and its front ones are pulled back, like a feline ready
to lash out with its claws. Its boxy head has massive teeth and
round eyes, with bulging eyebrows and long, coiled whiskers.
One of its two eye sockets is empty, while the other one still
holds a radiant sapphire. A second precious gem rests on its back,
between its shoulder blades at the base of its neck. It's a large,
gray pearl.

The creature is depicted as if it's about to pounce toward the
back wall, the one covered with blue mosaic tiles.

Ermete and Sheng walk around it, examining it from every
angle. And they uselessly try to figure out the meaning behind
the arrangement of the extraordinary room's various features:
the path on the floor with round holes in it, the two statues, the
wooden dragon in the middle, the blue wall, like ones found in
ancient Babylonian temples.

Overwhelmed, Sheng sits down on the ground, his eyes glued to the dragon's lazy eye. Golden specks fill his pupils like minuscule nuggets.

"The gold letters . . . ," he suddenly murmurs.

Still soaked to the skin, Ermete feels cold shivers run down him from head to toe. "What's that, Sheng?"

"Mistral told us there were strange gold letters in the Veil of Isis."

"Something like that, yeah. Her mom said that in X-rays, they look like Chinese characters or cuneiform letters. Whatever they are, we didn't have time to read them." Pulling his clothes around his body more snugly in the useless attempt to warm himself, he exclaims, "It's like the North Pole in here! Somebody's pumping ice-cold air into the place. Don't you hear that noise?"

Sitting on the ground beside him, Sheng bursts out laughing.

"What's so f-funny?" Ermete stammers. "Don't you think it's cold in here?"

But Sheng doesn't answer. He laughs. And he keeps laughing, raising his hand apologetically. "*Hao!* Ermete, I'm not laughing at you! Sorry! But yeah, it's freezing!"

"Then what's so funny?"

"I figured it out," Sheng says, standing up. "It's like those shows my dad used to put on for me when I was little."

Ermete sneezes. "What is it you figured out?" he asks, sniffling.

"These are just . . . Chinese shadows," the boy continues. "The objects . . . the offerings to the Sea Dragon . . . Look!"

Sheng steps over to the first hole in the floor. He measures it with his eye and says, "Imagine slipping the Star of Stone into one of these holes."

235

"Okay . . . What then?"

Sheng smiles. "Next, fill it with paper and light a fire inside it." He looks overhead. "See that ugly mask on the ceiling?"

"Keep going. . . ."

"It looks like it was designed to hold a rope. Tie a rope to its beak and hang the Ring of Fire over the flame. The mirror reflects the light . . . in this direction."

Now Sheng is standing in the space between the statues of Isis and Mithra.

"Look at Isis. She's holding out her arm. Let's imagine the other statue doing the same thing. Like they're holding something up. Hang the Veil of Isis between them and what do you get?"

"A curtain," Ermete replies. Then he exclaims, "No! You've made a projection! The light from the fire passes over the dragon, then onto the curtain . . . and it hits that wall with the blue mosaic, casting . . ."

"A Chinese shadow play," Sheng concludes.

Ermete studies the blue-tiled wall and guesses the final piece in the puzzle. "That wall isn't a wall . . . it's the sea!"

"Exactly," Sheng says, nodding. "And I'm convinced that the letters on the Veil of Isis combined with the dragon's shadow cast a projection on the sea that'll show us how to find . . ."

"The island."

A long silence follows as the two let the importance of their discovery sink in.

Suddenly, a burst of applause fills the room. The cruel, mocking noise echoes through the ice-cold underground level.

Ermete and Sheng look up and see a man smirking at them from above.

It's Heremit Devil.

"Nice work," the man hisses, still applauding. "Excellent work."

Then he adds sadistically, "And welcome to my home."

37

HI-NAU

HEREMIT DEVIL SLOWLY DESCENDS A STAIRCASE CARVED INTO THE dark side of the underground hall. As he does, he says, "Excellent, young man. A remarkable job, truly . . ."

Behind him appears the Chinese man with the shaved head, the one Sheng and Ermete saw at the Grand Hyatt. And he isn't alone: he's leading a team of security men dressed in black.

When Heremit reaches them, he still has a faint smile on his face. "I can finally put a face to a name, Sheng," he hisses, keeping a certain distance from the two of them. "If you only knew how long I've been looking for you! I couldn't find out what your name was. It was a well-kept secret, it seems."

"Let us go, Mr. Devil," Sheng replies, a tinge of disappointment in his voice, "and I promise you'll never hear my name again!"

"Does that go for your friends as well?"

Heremit Devil gestures to his men, who lead Harvey, Elettra and Mistral down the stairs, bound and gagged. Next, they bring Jacob Mahler, who's unconscious.

"What did you do to them?" Sheng says, almost shouting, when he sees his friends staggering down the stairs.

Harvey's ears are filled with softened wax. Mistral's mouth is bound so she can't move her lips. Elettra is bundled up in a complex outfit of blue bindings that make it almost impossible for her to walk.

Heremit Devil waits until they're beside him and then explains, "What did I do to them? Nothing. I defended myself, that's all. Your American friend said he could hear strange voices, so I thought I'd spare him that. I think it's best to keep the pretty French girl from singing, given that she has the unpleasant habit of attracting horrible insects with her voice. As for your electrifying friend from Rome, I decided to contain her vitality with a dress made of polyester and porcelain."

"You turned her into a capacitor!" Ermete exclaims, realizing Elettra has been electrically isolated.

Heremit Devil shoots him a piercing glare. "You never keep quiet, do you, Mr. De Panfilis?"

Ermete stares at Jacob Mahler, who's been dumped to the ground at their feet and lies there, unconscious. But Heremit Devil doesn't offer a word of explanation about the killer. He turns to look at Sheng again and continues. "Your friends tried to attack me, Sheng. But as you can see, their attack failed. I am very angry with them. But with you . . . things are different. You've given me the best-possible explanation of how this Dragon Hall works. The archeologist studied it for years, inch by inch. A waste of time. While you, young man, understood everything there was to understand in minutes."

Sheng looks at his friends and clenches his teeth, unsure what to do.

Heremit Devil slowly takes off his glasses. "And it's strange, indeed, given that you shouldn't even be here. Given that you aren't one of the four . . . chosen ones."

"What are you talking about?"

Heremit looks back and gestures to Nik Knife, who rips the gag off Elettra's mouth.

"Don't believe him!" the girl shouts instantly. "Don't believe a single word he tells you!"

"Go on," Heremit Devil invites her. "Why don't you explain to Sheng that the real chosen one was replaced at the last minute?"

Sheng's lip starts to tremble. "Who told you that?"

"He's lying!" Elettra shouts again. "He's lying! You were chosen, just like we were!"

"The chosen one from Shanghai was a boy called Hi-Nau," Heremit Devil says coldly. "A boy with extraordinary powers. A boy who could see things others couldn't even imagine. He saw other people's dreams walking around like real people. But Hi-Nau was a tormented child. Because the dreams he saw during the day were often terrible. But the dreams kept on speaking to him, and they were terrible because they were his father's dreams. And so one day Hi-Nau went to his father and asked him why he had dreams like that, asked him if he really was a person who killed other people."

Sheng stays silent, as if petrified.

"And the father answered yes, he was a man who killed other people. And that was how the father lost him." Heremit Devil whirls around to stare at the black dragon that's ready to leap out at the blue mosaic wall. "Hi-Nau discovered this place. He dreamed of it the night before he died and called it the Magi Hall. He was eight years old."

An icy silence descends on the Magi Hall. The only sound

240

is the air conditioner, which continues to pump freezing-cold air into the underground level.

"Hi-Nau was my son," Heremit Devil concludes, after a seemingly endless pause. "And he didn't make it. He'd always been very ill, but I always believed that somehow he would live longer. I thought his 'power' would save him. Instead, it consumed him. He died in his sleep on the second-to-top floor of this building, at the end of the hallway he'd covered with drawings. He was still wearing his favorite shirt. When it happened, I was on the top floor, where I conducted my business. A place I've rarely returned to." The hermit devil clasps his hands together so tightly that his knuckles turn pale. "Ever since that night, I've wanted to understand what was hidden down here below the building. What this room meant. And why my son had the gift of seeing those things. The gift that made me lose him forever."

"Number eighty-nine," Sheng says.

Heremit Devil spins around. "What?"

"Your son's favorite shirt had the number eighty-nine on it."

"How do you—"

"He was the one who led me here. I can see him. I see other people's dreams, too. And you dream about him every night."

Heremit Devil stares at Sheng with tiger eyes, his fists clenched. Then he walks away.

He orders his men to bind and gag both the boy and Ermete. And to bring him the objects that are on his desk.

It's time to awaken the dragon.

They place the Star of Stone in the fourth of the seven visible holes in the floor of the hall. They fill it with paper soaked in alcohol and set fire to it. They hang the Ring of Fire over the Star. Spread out in front of the lapis lazuli wall, the Veil of Isis casts a series of dotted lines and golden shadows that, combined with others present on the wall, form a coastline and an immediately legible sentence.

Now enlarged on the mosaic, the Veil of Isis is both a map of time and a geographical chart. The writing indicates the year, month and date on which Penglang Island will emerge from the waters of the ocean. The gold line along its lower edge is the coastline. And the dragon's shadow seems to start from there to reach a specific point: the location of the Pearl of the Sea.

All of this is discovered little by little by Heremit Devil's team. The kids watch, impassive, as his men proceed to translate the calendar and calculate the island's exact position. Ermete watches their every step, moving his lips as if he was taking part, too. Sitting off to the side in grim silence, Heremit Devil waits. His stony stare is broken only by an uncontrollable tic in his left eye. His one concern is that someone might hear his heart pounding furiously.

In the end, when the code is broken, they put out the fire, cover the mirror, drape the veil over the statue of Isis like a gown, remove the pearl from the dragon's shoulder blades. Then the four objects are handed to Heremit Devil.

Nik Knife gives him his report. "According to our calculations, sir, the island should already be visible. It is four hundred and eighty kilometers north by northeast of here. If I leave now, I can reach it in under two hours."

The tic in Heremit Devil's left eye grows stronger. "Have the helicopter prepared."

Nik Knife makes a little bow and turns to walk away.

Heremit Devil clenches his teeth before he manages to add, "Have them prepare a place for me as well."

Nik Knife hesitates. He thinks he heard wrong. Since he started working for Heremit Devil, the man hasn't left the building once.

But it's only a matter of an instant. "Very well, sir," he murmurs, disappearing into the shadows.

38

THE PRISONERS

FANTASTIC, JUST FANTASTIC, ERMETE THINKS AN HOUR LATER. *Exactly the kind of fate I always imagined.*

He jabs his tongue against the tape that seals his mouth shut, feels the glue that's saturated his lips. He looks around. He's tied to the wall of the rainwater reservoir that he and Sheng passed through only a few hours ago. Overhead, he sees the gray light of the sky over Shanghai dripping down into the reservoir through the manholes. Below, the level of the murky water rises steadily, with streams of water pouring into it from the many ducts.

He tries to wriggle free from his ropes, but it's no use. Heremit Devil's men did an excellent job. His hands, arms and shoulders are tightly bound to the iron rings on the cement wall, leaving him no chance of moving. The coil upon coil of rope wound around him look like a silk cocoon. But he isn't destined to turn into a butterfly. His end will be that of a drowned rat. With the dirty water slowly rising at his feet.

The engineer senses a movement beside him. He cranes his head to look.

Jacob Mahler is tied up to his right, but the man isn't moving. He has the swollen face of someone who's been beaten to a pulp. His head is slumped down onto his shoulder and his body is limp in the harness of ropes and tape.

To Ermete's left is the giant Mademoiselle Cybel. A network of ropes twice as thick as his own are keeping her suspended over the surface of the water.

The woman still wears the same dress she had on when she walked out of Heremit Devil's office. She's the one who's been squirming, trying to break free, for almost half an hour now. It's like watching an elephant writhe around in a whale net.

There are better chances of the whole cement wall collapsing, Ermete thinks, *than this woman managing to get out of those ropes.*

He looks up at the manholes again. If only he could call out for help!

Cascades of murky water are crashing down around him. If it keeps raining this hard, Jacob will be submerged in the water in under an hour. Then it'll be Ermete's turn. And, finally, Mademoiselle Cybel's. Otherwise they'll die more slowly, from hunger and thirst.

The engineer continues to jab his tongue against the tape in useless attempts to get it off his mouth.

Then the reservoir walls begin to tremble and he stops.

They're leaving, thinks Ermete.

A massive shadow swoops over the manholes, the shadow of a Sikorsky S-61, a medium/heavy-lift naval rescue chopper. Ermete has used it dozens of times in his role-playing games with friends. Eight tons of warfare helicopter with twin General Electric T58-GE10 turbines, five-blade main rotor, 16.69 meters long and 5.13

meters high, a 1,000-kilometer range with a top speed of 267 kilometers per hour.

The Sea King.

The roar of the Sikorsky soon fades away and silence returns to the reservoir. Ermete senses more movement beside him, this time accompanied by the sound of flesh moving. Amazingly, Mademoiselle Cybel has managed to free her massive right leg from the ropes. And now she's continuing her movements of friction and traction, trying to free her other leg.

A *lingering death*, Ermete thinks.

That's all it is.

Then, unexpectedly, something hits the engineer. Mademoiselle Cybel's foot has struck him full in the face. The woman's head is turned in his direction and she's moving her eyes as if trying to communicate with him.

Cybel kicks him and rolls her eyes again. Ermete can't understand what she's trying to do.

She waves her foot with long, purple-polished toenails in front of his nose and a second later runs her toes over the ropes that are keeping her trapped.

Ermete soon starts to get it. Sharp toenails . . . Mademoiselle Cybel wants to use them to get the tape off his mouth so he can call for help through the manholes!

A ridiculous, exhausting, crazy plan. But maybe their only chance of getting out of there alive. Ermete nods. Then he stretches his neck out toward the woman and lets himself be struck by another massive kick, which knocks his head back against the cement wall.

This time, he feels the inside of his lip sting. He jabs his tongue against the tape and has the sensation his gag might have moved a fraction of an inch.

He stretches out his neck.

Again.

And again.

Meanwhile, the water below him continues to rise.

Nik Knife is at the controls of the Sikorsky S-61. The copilot is seated next to him, checking the instruments.

Behind them, in a black leather seat, an expressionless Hermit Devil wears a dark gray life vest over his impeccable Korean jacket. The man is rigidly clutching a handle, a seat belt strapped over his chest. All that's seen through the windows is the flat expanse of the ocean. A shimmering slab of slate. Gray everywhere, except for the long crests of the waves.

"Fog at twelve-six-six," Nik Knife says into his microphone, which is connected to the copilot's headphones.

The noise on board and the vibrations of the bulkheads prevent any other communication. The knife thrower slows down the engine and descends. Now, under the helicopter's belly, the uniform expanse of the waves becomes crystal-clear, revealing the shimmering backs of schools of silvery fish. A breathtaking sight that whizzes by at 212 kilometers an hour before Sheng, Harvey, Elettra and Mistral's eyes.

The four kids are sitting one beside the other, like parachutists ready to jump. They don't know what's going to become of them. And they don't know what's become of Ermete.

"I'm sorry," Sheng told the others when they were pushed on board.

247

"It wasn't your fault," Harvey told him.

The American boy looked at the two gagged girls. Elettra, in her insulating straitjacket, and Mistral, who had a long scratch on her neck. Signs of a pointless struggle.

We were outnumbered, he told himself. In his mind's eye, he could still see the top floor of the building, with gusts of rain and wind coming in through the shattered windows. The distant sounds from the street. The shouts of the service staff. The electrical circuits shorting out, letting off bursts of sparks. The elevators coming to a halt. The printers spewing out tons of paper, the hot tubs going berserk, the electric furnaces overheating. And insects everywhere, in their eyes, in their ears, in every room. Hopeless.

Totally hopeless.

"I should've been there, too," Sheng murmured, letting them strap a seat belt on him.

"Nobody should've been there," Harvey replied as the helicopter climbed into the air and left Shanghai behind it.

The sea disappears from sight as the helicopter flies into a thick bank of fog. The emergency lights go on. And there's nothing more to be seen.

"Slow down," Nik Knife says into the microphone. "Let's descend twenty meters." As they zoom along, the shuddering, whirling turbines rip the fog to shreds.

Heremit Devil stares straight ahead. Then he looks at the four chosen ones, his eyes lingering on Sheng, as if he wants to ask him something.

But he doesn't.

* * *

"I see it. One o'clock," Nik Knife says half an hour later. He points at a flashing green blip that has just appeared on the radar. All around them, fog. Thick, dense, mysterious fog. "Twelve kilometers. Approaching. Ten."

Heremit Devil leans forward to rest his hand on the pilot's seat. "How big is it?" he asks.

"It looks like an atoll. Seven, eight hundred meters in diameter at most. We will begin to descend."

The Sikorsky's nose dips forward and the helicopter drops down almost to sea level. Looking outside, Sheng has the sensation he can almost hear the waves churning. The fog thins out and offers a trace of visibility. It's like an empty gap between two walls: gray fog above, dark water below.

"There," Nik Knife says, pointing to the right.

Far off on the horizon, the fog thickens into a storm. A gray curtain indicates the line of the rain, which seems to hide everything else from sight. Sudden bolts of lightning streak from the sky to crash down into the sea. And in the middle of that raging sea, between heaven and earth, the darker line of an island.

Penglang.

The island of the eight immortals.

The helicopter reaches it in just a few minutes and flies over it once: it's small, not much bigger than a soccer stadium in hard black rock, covered with calcareous concretions, slick seaweed and shells. Glistening rivulets of dark, brackish water stream out from its jagged hollows and flow back into the sea. The frothy ocean waves crash down against its rocky sides. The island is like a giant turtle shell rising up in the middle of the sea. On the turtle's back are strange rocks that look like spires, sticking out of it like little harpoons.

"Sir," the copilot says, pointing at the instruments, "the compass has gone haywire."

Nik Knife flies over the atoll a second time, descending even farther.

Everyone is asking themselves the same question: how can the island rise up from and sink back down into the waves every hundred years? It's a rare phenomenon, but not impossible. Harvey's father could explain that in 1963, a series of volcanic eruptions off the southern coast of Iceland created Surtsey Island, which still exists today. Then there's Ferdinandea, an island that appeared between Sicily and Pantelleria in a matter of days in 1831 and disappeared a few months later. In the Venetian Lagoon, the isles of Caltrazio, Centranica and Ammianella appear and disappear as the tides command. But none of these phantom islands have the same wild, primordial allure as Penglang: magnetic rock capable of interfering with the helicopter's instruments. Volcanic, furious, contorted. Neither birds nor other animals are in sight; just a few fish flopping around as they try to escape the pools of water in which they've been trapped.

On their third trip over the island, the chopper's blades raise up sprays of froth. And the strange rocky formations that look like harpoons prove to be something even eerier.

They're statues. Ancient profiles of divinities, sovereigns, queens, heroes, giants, goddesses that have been worn away by the water, encrusted with mollusk shells, adorned with stoles and cloaks of seaweed. Statues that were carved into the island's living rock and now, centuries later, sparkle in the sunshine, eroded and silent.

But still standing. The statues of the immortal inhabitants of Penglang.

"Take us down! Land!" Heremit Devil snaps at the pilot, pointing at the rocky black island, his hand trembling.

The nine-fingered man shakes his head vigorously. "There is no room!" he replies. "Besides, the island has a strong magnetic field! The rotor is not responding as it should and—"

"Then open the cargo door and lower me down!"

"Sir, it is dangerous!"

"Lower me down, I said!"

Nik Knife points at the helicopter's gas gauge. The tank is almost half-empty. "Another time, sir! We can come back! We do not have much fuel left. In order to make it back to Shanghai—"

"I don't care about getting back to Shanghai! I want to go down onto that blasted island!"

Nik Knife consults with the copilot. "Twenty minutes, sir!" the copilot says. "Twenty minutes, no more. Then we'll need to leave or we won't make it back!"

"Twenty minutes," Heremit Devil repeats. "Fine."

The lord of the black skyscraper unbuckles his seat belt with shaking hands. His left eye is almost constantly shut now.

Nik Knife leaves the commands to the copilot, slips on the backpack containing all the objects that belonged to the kids and makes his way into the rear section of the helicopter. He clips a snap hook onto Heremit Devil's life vest and attaches it to a line that's connected to the hoist on the Sikorsky's belly.

"Well, then, we will go down, sir!" he says, shouting so that he'll be heard over the roar of the rotors. "Are you certain?"

"Open the door!"

A blast of ice-cold air mixed with a spray of water sweeps over the side of the helicopter. The copilot corrects their angle, passing over the island for the fourth time.

"I will lower you down now," Nik Knife says. "When you reach the ground, unhook yourself here and here!"

Heremit Devil's eyes slowly drink up the mystery of the volcanic rock. He feels ruthless euphoria running through his veins, making his temples throb and his hands go numb. A mix of panic and terror, of omnipotence and grandeur. Heremit Devil takes three steps toward the door and reaches the edge, his legs as heavy as bricks.

"Them too!" he shouts as he prepares to lower himself down the line. "I want them to come, too!"

Nik Knife tries to protest, but the man doesn't give him the chance. His fourth step is into thin air. Then the hoist slowly starts to lower him toward the place he's been trying to track down for five years.

The place others have kept secret for six thousand years.

The moment she's dangling in the void, her hands free, Mistral rips the gag off her mouth and breathes in the damp air, which is pungent and salty. Harvey and Sheng are already on the ground, six meters below her. Elettra is peering out of the cargo door, beside Nik Knife. Mistral breathes in hungrily as the wind stirs her hair. When she's only a meter off the ground, Harvey and Sheng help her, unclipping the line and leaving it free to go back up to the helicopter.

"It's beautiful!" Sheng exclaims, his voice filled with a strange exhilaration. "It's a beautiful island!"

Mistral looks around, thinking the exact opposite. Penglang is dark, harsh, slimy and pummeled by waves coming from every direction. Beyond the edge of the rocks, the seafloor seems to drop straight down, becoming an abyss of black water.

Heremit Devil is a few steps away from them, his hair blowing in the wind. His left eye shut. Hands in his pockets. His body moving awkwardly.

He's afraid, Mistral thinks, looking at him. *For a man who's never left his building, the sight of such a wild, primitive island must be quite a shock.*

Mistral shades her eyes with her hand and watches Elettra's descent. A few seconds later, the Italian girl touches down and unclips herself. The kids hug, holding each other tight. They're together again.

Nik Knife comes down last, and the moment he reaches the ground, he checks his watch. "Eighteen minutes!" he shouts to his boss as the helicopter flies off over the open sea.

The noise of the chopper blades fades away.

Leaving only the wind and waves.

And a barren island of black rock.

"So this is the objective behind everything?" shouts the man who's been pursuing them all this time. "A reef? Show me what we're looking for."

"We don't know what we're looking for," Harvey replies, the other three behind him. The four kids are standing close together, forming a sort of wall. They made it here together and they're going to stick together to the very end.

Heremit Devil laughs. But it's a nervous, hollow laugh. "I don't believe you!" he exclaims. "I don't believe that your masters didn't tell you what was on this island!"

"Why don't you tell us?" Elettra shoots back. Her hair is whirling in the wind.

"The archeologist didn't know!" Heremit Devil shouts.

Nik Knife walks over to one of the statues sticking out of the rock. It looks like a man with bare legs and sandals.

"None of them knew," Mistral says. She turns to the others, waiting for them to back her up. "We're the first ones to get here."

"I want an explanation!" Heremit threatens. "We didn't come all this way for nothing! I want to know what gave my son his power!"

Sheng takes a step forward, his palm raised in a peaceful gesture. "The truth is, none of us knows why everything led here, Heremit. But . . . maybe . . . maybe there's a reason we all ended up here."

Sheng is right. The kids feel a vibration here on the island. It's as if their hearts are bigger. Their heads more receptive. Their eyes sharp, their ears attentive, their noses and throats more sensitive than they've ever been before.

Heremit Devil looks around suspiciously. He doesn't feel any of these vibrations. He only has a desperate desire to understand. To find something. To take it with him.

"You have fifteen minutes," he says, stepping aside. "Give me the answer I'm looking for . . . or I'll leave you here."

The kids begin to explore the rocks.

Apart from the statues, there's no sign that humans have ever been on the island.

Harvey rests his hands on the ground and listens.

"What do you hear?"

"The sea. And voices. They're faint. Far away. Really far away. I . . . I can't make out a single word of it."

Mistral continues to watch Heremit. He's walked up to the edge of the rocks, where he lets the spray from the waves wash over him. Near him, Nik Knife is constantly checking his watch.

"Let's think this through," Elettra says. "How long has it been since anyone stepped foot on this island?"

"Our masters never made it this far."

"Neither did the ones before them."

"And we don't know what happened before that. But we can bet nobody's been here for at least . . . two hundred years?"

"One, two, three . . . ," Elettra starts to count. "And seven. Seven statues. Just like . . ."

"The days of the week," Harvey says.

"The tops," Mistral says.

"The Jesuit said something about eight immortals," Sheng remembers.

The statues are featureless figures, worn and eroded.

Sheng studies how they're arranged. "These four . . . make a sort of rectangle."

"With a handle . . . formed by these other three statues," Elettra says, following his logic.

"Seven statues, seven stars," Harvey concludes. "Yeah, you're right. The statues are positioned like Ursa Major!"

"What does Ursa Major point to?" Elettra asks.

"It always revolves around the North Star."

"Six thousand years ago, the North Star didn't point north," Sheng says. "Six thousand years ago, north was marked by a star in the constellation Draco. . . ."

"To find the North Star, you need to triple the short side of the Dipper . . . in this direction. One . . . two . . ." Harvey begins to take long strides over the rocks.

When he sees them walking away, Heremit Devil turns and motions to Nik Knife.

"Eleven . . . and twelve!" Harvey exclaims, stopping between the island's slick black stones.

"See anything?"

The boy looks around. Rocks, rocks, rocks. And a pool of brackish water. He sinks his hands into the icy water and finds that the stone below has a different texture.

"Come help me!" he shouts to the others.

Nik Knife starts running.

The four kids kneel down and scoop out the water with their hands as fast as they can, revealing a stone circle that looks like the base of a statue. It's a meter in diameter and thirty centimeters tall. The outer circumference of the base is protected by a copper ring. Harvey digs his foot into the rock and pries it up. Below it, carved all around the base are seven round holes.

"It looks like a submarine hatch," Elettra murmurs.

"A door?" Harvey wonders.

Sheng sits down on the wet rock. "Okay, but how do we open it?" He points at the seven holes around it. He smiles faintly, turns to Nik Knife, who's a few paces away from them, and waves him over.

"What do you want from him?" Elettra whispers.

"I need the tops," Sheng replies.

Heremit Devil joins them, too, and Nik Knife shows him the strange round base. When the man nods, the knife thrower takes the tops out of the backpack one by one. When the tops are inserted into the round holes, they slide into place and their metal tips interlock with an ancient mechanism. Heremit personally inserts his own top, the one with the skull on it.

Then Harvey tries pushing on the base, but nothing happens. He asks for help from the others. Even from Nik Knife.

"C'mon!"

"It's moving!"

With a groan, the stone base slides aside, revealing a complex notched mechanism that kept it clasped to the surrounding rock with an airtight seal.

It really is a rudimentary hatch.

And now there's a stairway leading down into the darkness.

The knife thrower looks at his watch and then at the helicopter, which is little more than a speck on the horizon. "Ten minutes!" he exclaims, worried.

39

BELOW

"CECILE?" FERNANDO MELODIA ASKS FALTERINGLY INTO THE GOLD phone at the Grand Hyatt.

"Fernando?" Mistral's mother asks, surprised.

She spent a sleepless night hoping to hear from her daughter. She was expecting something more reassuring than the simple text she received after their escape from the hotel.

Meanwhile, Cecile followed the instructions from the man with the baseball cap, that Jacob Mahler she first met in Paris. She couldn't sleep, aware that what was going on was no longer a simple treasure hunt.

Someone was sitting in the hotel lobby, spying on her.

"You need to go down to the lobby," Jacob Mahler ordered her. "Make sure you're dressed up and that people notice you, but don't look at anybody. Order room service. For three people. Raise your voice so others can hear you. Speak in French."

Cecile had to convince the man keeping tabs on her that she intended to spend the whole night in the room. Then she switched on the television in Elettra's room, turning up the volume so it could be heard from the hallway.

Cecile waited a whole night without sleeping. She kept up the ruse the next day: breakfast for three from room service. Lunch. She went down to the reception desk to order it, and when she was heading back upstairs, she tried to peek through the elevator doors to observe the other guests sitting in the lobby, reading the paper. She hoped to discover which of them might be the mysterious spy they had to avoid.

These are the thoughts whirling through Cecile's mind the moment she recognizes Fernando's voice.

"Are you all right, Cecile?" Elettra's father asks her.

"Yes, of course. Where are you?"

"Below you."

A wave of relief sweeps over the young perfume designer's face.

"I'm in the lobby," the man specifies.

Fernando is there, in Shanghai, just a few floors away. "What are you doing in the lobby?"

"I came to help you. How are things going? The kids?"

"Come upstairs. Room four-oh-five."

Minutes later, to their own surprise, Cecile Blanchard and Fernando Melodia are in each other's arms. Fernando tells her he made the mistake of taking the world's fastest train, spending almost two hours to reach the Grand Hyatt. He hasn't made a reservation and there aren't any rooms available. But he's planning on sleeping in Elettra's room next door.

"We've had problems," Cecile finally says. She tells him about the man called Jacob Mahler and his escape with the girls.

"A guy about this tall . . . with gray hair?" Fernando asks, still holding Cecile in his arms, with less and less embarrassment.

259

"You know him?"

"I fought him," he replies with understandable exaggeration.

His words have an instant effect: Cecile feels she has a real man beside her and buries her face even deeper into Fernando's sweater.

"I haven't held anyone like this," he suddenly says, "since Elettra's mother passed away."

These words also have an instant effect: Cecile pulls away from him and comes up with a series of nonexistent problems and unnecessary justifications. "Oh, Fernando, I'm sorry, it's just that I—I didn't mean to, but—but I don't really know what—"

Then she opens her eyes wide, surprised.

Fernando Melodia is kissing her.

Then they tell each other everything they have to tell, from the discovery of the golden patterns in the Veil of Isis to Aunt Irene's role in the whole situation. Behind the river, the sun sets, if it ever came out, and the rain dies down.

The two parents check their cell phones. No calls. No messages.

"Maybe we should go out," Fernando suggests.

She's at a loss. "What if the kids call?"

"Then they call. They're called mobile phones because they're mobile."

"Mahler said we were being watched, and that we might be followed."

Fernando takes Cecile's hands in his own and squeezes them gently. "Let's let them follow us, then."

* * *

After changing their minds a hundred times, Fernando and Cecile decide to leave on foot.

They step out onto the damp sidewalk the moment the street-lights and signs begin to light up. They walk along the river and past shops, turn down a side street and walk back up the blocks among the skyscrapers, their necks craned skyward. They watch as helicopters scan the streets with their big, white searchlights. They see police cars pass by, lights flashing and sirens blaring. Their hearts in their mouths and knots in their stomachs, they follow them.

They enter Century Park at seven forty-five, a quarter of an hour before the gates will be closed for the night.

On the other end of the park, helicopters are circling around a black glass and steel skyscraper and another nearby building, whose top floor is engulfed in smoke.

"A fire. Or a gas leak," Fernando guesses. He doesn't realize it, but he's staring at Jacob Mahler's former home.

He has no way of knowing that someone from Heremit Devil's security team opened a door that was better left shut.

The two stand there for a long time, staring at the lights and listening to the helicopters.

"What did you say?" Cecile asks him.

"I didn't say anything."

She looks around and asks, "Down where?"

"Down where what?"

"Didn't you say 'Down here'?"

"No, I didn't say anything. . . ."

Then Fernando also hears someone shouting. It's a distant

voice, but it sounds so close. And it's asking for help. In Italian, of all things.

"Help! Can anybody hear me? Help! I'm down here! Down here!" the stranger shouts with a desperate tone.

Following the faint voice, Fernando and Cecile walk over to a playground bordered by a ring of manholes. The voice is coming from below them.

Fernando kneels down and presses his face up against the metal grate, but he can't see anything.

Then the voice from below the manhole shouts, "Fernando!"

"Ermete?" Elettra's father asks, stunned. "Is that you?"

"Come down here! We're about to drown!" shouts the engineer.

Mademoiselle Cybel has managed to remove the gag from his mouth.

40
THE SECRET

○

THE FIRST ONE TO GO DOWN THE STAIRS IS HARVEY. THERE ARE only twelve steps, which lead into a large, sloping, low-ceilinged chamber carved into the rock.

"It's dry," he says.

"What do you see?"

The only source of light is the narrow opening he just came down through.

"Nothing," he replies.

"Move," Heremit Devil says from behind them. He goes down the stairs and stands beside Harvey. He switches on a flashlight and shines it around. Sheng, Mistral and Elettra follow him, escorted by Nik Knife.

"So this is it?" the man mutters. "This is the secret?"

The dim light illuminates walls covered with writings, carved stone panels, a metal tripod that looks like a torch holder and other stone slabs lying on the ground.

"Who knows what this room is for?"

Nik Knife checks his watch. Nine minutes until the helicopter returns.

Elettra feels her fingers sizzling with energy, despite the insulating outfit she's still wearing. She spreads open her hands. "Light," she says.

And twelve metal torches are instantly ablaze.

When the room lights up, Heremit Devil staggers, frightened.

"How did you do that?" he shrieks.

Then he looks around, astonished. The chamber now looks much larger than it seemed. It's almost three meters high and the sloping floor leads into a long, spiral passageway that winds down into the rock. On the walls are torches and large vases with stylized trees painted on them. Inside the vases are handfuls of seeds that look just like the ones they found in the underground realms of New York. Slabs of carved stone are on the ground, leaned up against the bare walls. But farther down the passageway, the walls are covered with inscriptions and engravings. Plaques in different materials covered with writings, the most recent ones in Western characters and in a totally unexpected language.

"Spanish?" Heremit Devil asks aloud, walking over to the most recent panel to read it.

JUAN CABOTO, PER ENCÀRREC DE LA CORONA ANGLESA, DESEMBARCA A TERRANOVA (1499)

The panel beside it is in Chinese. On it is the account of Zheng He's fleet leaving the ports of China to explore the world many years before Christopher Columbus's discovery of America.

Peering around and glancing at the writings, the little group makes its way down the spiral passage, Heremit Devil at a restrained pace, the kids almost running. The farther down they go, the more ancient the plaques are. And the languages keep changing, moving from Chinese to Arabic, from Hebrew to Russian.

Farther down.

Latin. Greek.

Even farther down.

Hieroglyphs. Cuneiform alphabet.

It's like going back in time through the history of the world's languages. Heremit Devil looks around, astonished.

At the umpteenth turn, the passageway comes to an end at a wall covered with an intricate mosaic. In the center of the mosaic is the sun. And the eleven rings around it are the uniform orbits of the planets in the solar system. A twelfth planet's ring is completely out of phase compared to the others: a long ellipsis tapered on its far ends.

Resting on a small altar on the floor in front of the wall is a crudely carved stone.

While the others are looking around, trying to make sense of their surroundings, Sheng is looking around as if the chamber was filled with people. And for him, it really is: standing before the stone slabs are people of all different nationalities and from all different eras. Navigators, mandarins, knights, court officials, priests, legionaries, scribes, desert nomads, tribal shamans. Passing before his golden eyes are guns, lances, chariots, coats of arms, warhorses. Passing by are ideas and dreams from different times and different countries, which have remained there, filling the chamber with images for those who are able to see them.

"They're our . . . ancestors," the boy whispers, captivated by the flurry of visions. He steps closer to the walls and touches them. "And this is their diary."

Carved into the rock in the long, spiral chamber are mankind's ideas, feats and explorations. It's a diary of stone, added to every hundred years by different people with different alphabets.

Sheng sways on his feet as he touches the millennia-old stone slabs. "This was done by the Sages who came before us," he says.

"The words of the Sages?" Heremit Devil screams. "That's all that's hidden inside this island? Crumbling old writings?"

"Don't you understand?" Sheng exclaims.

"What is there to understand?"

"It's all here!" Sheng says, continuing to dream as he brushes his hand over the hieroglyphs next to him. "Look! This one is about the construction of the first pyramid! It wasn't a tomb! And they didn't use slaves! But . . . of course, it's so simple!"

Heremit grabs him violently by the shirt. "What's so simple?"

Sheng closes his golden eyes. When he opens them, they're blue again. Everything has disappeared. The dreams have vanished. "You made them go away . . . ," he murmurs.

Heremit lets go of him, furious. He sees Nik Knife standing behind the two girls and Harvey leaning over the stone in front of the mosaic. "And what's that?"

"Stop," Elettra says, planting herself between him and her boyfriend.

"St-stop?" Heremit stammers, stunned that a girl would dare give him orders.

Elettra claws the air like a wounded cat and her gesture is so unexpected that Heremit Devil backs up. Nik Knife rests his hands on the daggers tucked into his belt, but when Heremit motions for him to stand still, he withdraws into the shadows, seething.

"What is that?" Heremit asks again.

"It might be an answer," Harvey says, looking at him.

Harvey rests both hands on the stone and listens.

He stays there for a long time, in silence. Then, slowly, he relaxes.

"This stone fell to Earth when mankind didn't exist here yet," he says. "It fell along with thousands of other meteorites. It came from the orbit of a planet called Nibiru, which passed by thousands of years ago, leaving behind a shower of stellar material. Some of the stones burned up in the atmosphere. Others fell into the seas. Still others smashed open against the rocks. One, which was too large to fall, was trapped in the Earth's orbit and became its only satellite: the Moon. The wandering planet passed by our planet many other times. During one of its last crossings, it found people expecting it. People who'd told others about its passing. People who believed they descended from it, like angels raining down from the heavens. People who saw Nibiru passing the last time believed they were the fruit of its eternal wanderings and returns. They thought they were stellar seeds that had fallen to this world."

"When did that happen?" Mistral asked, crouching down in front of Harvey.

"I don't know, exactly . . . ," the boy murmurs, taking his hands off the stone. "A long time ago."

"In the time of the Chaldeans," Sheng says, staring at something or someone in the middle of the room. "They were the ones who were expecting it to pass by."

"How do you know that?" Elettra asks.

"I don't know," Sheng replies, pointing at the empty space in front of him. "But I can see it."

"What can you see?"

Sheng's eyes are gold again. "It's a man. He has a beard, and his hair is woven into little braids. He's wearing a quiver full of arrows and a gown with the stars drawn on it."

"Where is he?" Harvey asks.

"In front of you. Next to the mosaic. And he's looking straight at me."

Harvey stands up and rests both hands on the wall. "He says he's one of the first Magi," he begins, "and that he lived when the Earth was different from what it's like today. The North Pole and South Pole were reversed. The sun set in the east and rose in the west."

Beside him, Sheng nods, describing to the others what he's seeing. "He's making a gesture, like he's turning a ball upside down. And he's pointing at the strange orbit in the mosaic, the one that's different from the other planets in the solar system. That's Nibiru's path."

"He says that the last time it passed by," Harvey continues, "its passing caused unprecedented cataclysms. The Earth turned over and was engulfed by water. All the world's populations speak of the flood."

Sheng and Harvey lapse into silence. In the shadows, Heremit Devil's eyes burn like embers.

"What's he telling you now?" Mistral asks with a tiny voice.

"He's saying how the Magi studied Nibiru's passing and calculated how long it would take it to return," Harvey says. "They made sure their calculations and discoveries could be passed on. To do that, they entrusted a small group of scholars with the task of handing down the secret from generation to generation so the secret of the wandering planet would always be protected and mankind could prepare for its return."

"The Pact?" Mistral murmurs, looking at the others.

"Along with the secret of the wandering planet, the Magi passed down the biggest secret of all: the whole universe is alive . . . and it follows the four fundamental laws of the universe."

"What are they?" Elettra whispers.

"He says they apply to everything in the universe, big and small. Other men have studied them and have given them names like mathematics, genetics, physics, quantum mechanics . . . but they're actually four very simple things: harmony, energy, memory and hope, or to use another word: dreams."

In the underground chamber, they can hear the sea now. Nik Knife whispers something in Heremit Devil's ear. Then he moves back a few steps.

Warned by the man that only he can see, Sheng notices. "He looks scared," he says.

Harvey nods. "He is. Nibiru's coming back. It's headed toward us. And this isn't a good time for it to come back. On the Earth, the four laws have been seriously put to the test. The planet's harmony has been wounded, it's been robbed of its energy and its diamond memory has been diminished."

"Wait!" Elettra exclaims. "You mean diamonds are the Earth's memory?"

Harvey nods. "That's what he says. But he also says the most serious thing is that we're robbing it of its dreams."

"Our planet can dream?" Mistral asks, amazed.

"He says it does it all the time," Harvey continues. "It dreams of animals that appear in the woods. It dreams of men who explore its mysteries. It dreams of songs it entrusts to the wind. It dreams of new tongues of ice and silences full of ideas. And it waits."

"Waits for what?"

"For Nibiru to return to the solar system and come back toward us." Suddenly, Harvey almost starts to tremble. "And when Nibiru approaches, the Earth will use its energy to speak to it, its memory to tell it what happened . . . and will tell it whether the dream is still possible."

"And then . . . ?"

"If the dream is possible, Nibiru will pass by and disappear into the universe, its tail aflame with asteroids, to return again after thousands and thousands of years. But if the dream isn't possible . . ."

Harvey hesitates.

Elettra steps closer to him. "What will happen?"

"Nibiru will establish a new harmony. It will flip the North Pole and South Pole, east and west, and wipe out mankind with a flood or a shower of meteorites. To start over again. Just like it did in the past and just like it will do again in the future."

"Does he say . . . when it's going to happen?"

Harvey waits a few seconds, pulls his hands away from the wall as if he felt a shock and buries himself in Elettra's arms.

"Enough!" Heremit Devil shouts, bursting in between them. "Enough of this nonsense!" He kicks the stone, making it tumble over to the mosaic wall. "I've spent far too long listening to your ramblings! You're trying to make a fool of me! There's no old man talking here!"

He lunges toward Elettra. "I waited five years to come here! And now I want the power! I want your energy, little girl! And I want to summon the animals!" he screams, shoving Mistral to the ground. "Where's the power of this great secret?" he continues. "Where's the secret? I can't see a thing! I can't hear a thing! I want something concrete!"

He pounds his fist against a stone slab, panting.

"I don't want to hear about a nonexistent planet and the dreams of the Earth. I don't want to hear how many thousands of years ago all this was written. I don't believe you. I'll never believe you. What you're saying is impossible. But I saw the torches light up . . . I saw the swarms of insects, so I know there's something . . . something that I want, too!"

From the shadows of the passageway leading up, Nik Knife warns him, "The helicopter is here! We must leave! Immediately!"

But nobody moves.

In the underground chamber, the five stare at each other. Behind them, Nik Knife starts counting down. "Fifty-nine . . . fifty-eight . . ."

"Talk," Heremit Devil orders.

"We have nothing to say," Elettra replies.

"Talk! Or else I'll leave you here!"

"Forty-nine . . . forty-eight . . . ," Nik Knife continues relentlessly.

"You're going to leave us here anyway," Harvey says, leaning against the mosaic, "no matter what we do."

"You'll die! The island will sink down into the ocean!"

"Yeah, could be," Harvey says, shrugging. "So what?"

"What point will there have been in coming all the way here? And your powers? And my son's powers?"

"I don't have any powers," Harvey shoots back, looking the man straight in the eyes. Then he decides to risk it all. "I made up everything I said."

"That's not true! You—you heard it!"

"Heard what? The stone?"

Heremit Devil searches his pockets frantically. He pulls out a gun, raises it. "The truth! I want the truth! Why you kids? And what power is there on this island?"

"The greatest power of all," Sheng replies. "The power of knowing."

Harvey takes a step toward Heremit. "Where we come from, who we are, where we're going and why we should do it . . . those are the answers you've been looking for. We come from memory, we're harmony, we're moving toward hope . . . and all this be-cause the entire universe is pure energy."

"But what's different about the four of you . . . and my son? Why isn't he here? Why didn't he make it? Why—why don't I feel anything?"

"Thirty seconds, sir," Nik Knife says.

Mistral leans back against the wall and slides down to the ground. Her eyes are full of tears and she shakes her head weakly. "I knew it would end like this. . . ."

272

Heremit Devil stares at them one by one. "Would somebody answer me?"

"Twenty . . . nineteen . . . eighteen . . ."

"Why don't I feel anything?" the man asks again.

Harvey and Elettra stand there in front of him, hugging each other in silence.

"Would someone . . . answer me?"

"Twelve . . . eleven . . . ten . . ."

The lord of the black skyscraper raises his gun and points it first at Harvey, then at Elettra. At Sheng, at Mistral. His arm is rigid, tense. His hand trembling. Five years of waiting. A journey across the ocean. An incomprehensible island. And still nothing. No answers. Four completely meaningless words: energy, harmony, memory and hope. Those aren't answers. His hands are tingling. His head is throbbing. There's too much reality down there. Too much outside world. And no power. Nothing he hoped to find. After years of isolation, of disinfected air, of security teams, now, in the total uncertainty, in the total incomprehensibility of the world around him, Heremit Devil is losing his mind. He even thinks he can hear a voice whispering inside of him. A voice saying words that make no sense. Like a woodworm devouring him.

"Eight . . . seven . . . six . . . We must go, sir. . . . Five . . . four . . ."

Four. Four. Four.

At that number, Heremit Devil raises his gun, exasperated. His inhuman scream fills the entire underground chamber. "Nooooooo! Enough!"

He whirls toward Nik Knife and pulls the trigger.

* * *

When he hears the gunshot, Sheng thinks he's dead. Then, opening his eyes, he sees Heremit Devil standing there, facing the
other direction, and the knife thrower's lifeless body slumping to
the ground. A thin trail of smoke drifts up from the barrel of Heremit Devil's gun.

Mistral is beside Sheng, clutching his knee.

Harvey is standing perfectly still beside the mosaic, Elettra's
face buried in his shoulder. The stellar stone lies on the ground.
The sea roars outside the grotto. And the sound of the chopper
begins to fade away.

"A little . . . silence . . . ," Heremit Devil says, turning back
toward the kids. Now his face is a grimacing mask: his left eyelid
has started to tremble furiously again; his cheek is quivering; his
lip is curled, baring his gums.

Once again, the man waves his gun.

"Where . . . were we?"

Harvey, Elettra, Sheng and Mistral hold each other tight, discovering that the contact has a calming effect on them. Their fingers seek out the others' fingers, interlock, squeeze tight. If they've
gotten all this way just to die here in this grotto, then, they think,
it's better to die together.

Their gesture doesn't escape Heremit Devil's only watchful
eye.

The man waves his gun around and says, "You're four pathetic
little kids. Everyone lives alone. And everyone dies even more
alone. Hope? What nonsense."

He takes a step toward them and repeats, horribly transformed,
"Where . . . were we?"

274

Behind him, something moves. A metallic gleam appears between the knife thrower's four fingers. From the ground, with his last strength, Nik Knife hurls the dagger. The blade glimmers through the air. A dull thud, like an apple being split in two.

Heremit Devil cringes and his eyes grow wide with disbelief. He stiffens, tries to take another half step forward. But his hands freeze and the gun falls to the ground.

Harvey kicks it, sending it flying across the floor.

Heremit Devil coughs. Below his curled lip, his white, white teeth are streaked with red. He takes another half step forward. "Oh, yes . . . now . . . I remember . . . ," he gasps, staggering over to Harvey. "We were saying that I . . . don't feel . . . anything. I've never . . . felt . . . anything."

Still staring at Harvey, Heremit collapses into the boy's strong arms.

"Maybe this is the answer you were looking for," Harvey says, holding him up with very little effort. Heremit Devil's body is light, like a child's. It's fragile, without experience, scratches, grazes. A body that's never touched anything. That's never been lashed by the rain, by the icy winter wind. A body that's never been scorched by sunlight or parched with salty seawater. It hasn't sweated. It hasn't been licked by a dog, scratched by a cat, thrown from a horse's saddle. It hasn't danced, jumped, rejoiced. It's never felt anything.

"Yes," the lord of the black skyscraper whispers. "That is the answer."

With this, he dies, a strange smile of satisfaction on his lips.

* * *

Four figures climb the twelve stairs leading out of the grotto and step outside. They look around, stare at the island, an empty shell of black rock. The helicopter is a tiny white dot, a fly far away on the horizon.

The sea crashes down onto the rocky shores.

And apart from the roaring, churning waves, there's nothing and no one.

Just perfect silence.

41

THE SHIP

WHEN THE PHONE CALL ARRIVES, PROFESSOR MILLER IS HUNCHED over the documents he's been studying for months now. According to the data from the astronomical observatory in Pasadena, the most catastrophic theory of the location of a hypothetical Planet X headed through the solar system predicts the arrival somewhere between the years 2050 and 2110. Far enough in the future to not be his problem, Professor Miller thinks, but not far enough not to deal with it seriously.

But with every phone call he's made to his various astronomer colleagues, George Miller has received only sarcastic, vague or annoyed responses. No one is willing to believe that the statistical irregularities detected in the Atlantic Ocean might be due to an anomalous gravitational attraction. Like one caused by a large black body in the outer solar system heading our way. But where, exactly?

Professor Miller has calculated an angle between Planet X's orbit and Earth's ecliptic orbit at around seventeen degrees . . . the same inclination as Pluto, the outermost planet in the solar system. And all this for what? To prove something to his colleagues?

Namely, that the climatic disturbances they've been encountering are nothing compared to what's in store for them?

A planet capable of changing the data on the tides of the Pacific when it's sixty years away from Earth could cause a serious catastrophe when it finally arrived.

"Arrived or returned?" Professor Miller wonders, slipping the tip of his pen between his lips.

As he's brooding over the possible sightings of this planet by scientists in ancient times, there's a knock on Professor Miller's door.

It's Paul Magareva, his colleague from the Polynesian Oceanographic Institute, who, as always, is in a good mood. "What if it's an island?" he asks, appearing in the doorway.

"If it's an island doing what?"

"An island popping up right in the middle of the Yellow Sea, or the Bohai."

"Volcanic eruption?"

"Maybe."

"Possible, but it would have to be a relatively large island."

"But the data would fit. No remote planet, no stellar phenomenon."

Professor Miller slumps back in his chair. Fascinating theory, but . . . "What kinds of seafloors are there in the area you're talking about?"

"Seafloors that no damn island could ever surface from, if you ask me."

George Miller looks at his colleague, grinning. "Then why are you telling me about it?"

"Maybe to make you worry less about some ghost planet heading our way." The man smiles. "Or maybe because there's a guy on the phone telling me I've got to believe him."

Paul Magareva holds the phone out to his colleague. "A guy with pretty lousy English . . . says he wants to talk to you."

Professor Miller frowns.

"Says he's a friend of your son's," Paul Magareva adds.

When Professor Miller hears Harvey's name, he bolts upright in his chair. He's been expecting him for two days now.

"Harvey? Finally!" he exclaims into the receiver. "We've contacted consulates halfway around the world!"

"It isn't Harvey!" someone says on the other end of the line.

"Who is this? Who's speaking?"

"Professor Miller! It's Ermete De Panfilis!"

The name is almost completely unknown to Professor Miller's analytic mind. *Almost* completely. The man glances at his colleague, who's still standing in the doorway. "Jog my memory. . . ."

"Are you still in Shanghai? On the ship?"

"Yes. Why do you ask?"

"Then you've absolutely got to head for the Yellow Sea, sir! Don't wait a minute longer! You need to go get your son! I'll explain everything on your way there."

42

THE KISS

"It might not be much of a contribution," Mistral tells
the others, looking at her notebooks, which are lined up on the
ground right after the last engraved panel, the one in Spanish.
"They aren't written in stone . . . but it's better than nothing."

Leaving Mistral's notebooks behind, they calmly climb out of
the chamber for the last time. They've put the stellar stone back
in its place and dragged Nik Knife and Heremit Devil's bodies
outside. They left them in a hollow in the rocks so they won't
have to see them whenever they look around. Sheng wanted to
throw them into the sea, but Elettra was against it. "When the
island sinks down again, the sea will take them anyway."

Before going outside, Harvey took four seeds from one of the
vases decorated with stylized trees. He figured he still needs the
two he has left, to plant them in Shanghai and Rome, and he'll
need four more seeds to set up the next Pact.

If they ever find a way to get off the island, that is.

Then the kids closed the base leading into the underground
chamber, picked up the seven tops, distractedly looked at the one

with the skull, which belonged first to Hi-Nau and later to Hermit Devil, and put back the copper disk protecting the old lock.

Only then did they sit down outside, in silence.

Their first thought is for Ermete.

"Who knows what happened to him," Elettra whispers.

"I say they didn't kill him," Sheng replies, hopeful. "And now that Heremit's dead . . ."

It's a nice thought, but nobody believes it.

Harvey gets some provisions from Nik Knife's backpack and hands them out to the others. Nobody's hungry, but they force themselves to eat anyway. Then they take out the Ring of Fire, the Star of Stone, the Veil of Isis and the Pearl of the Sea Dragon. They pass them around.

When he sees the Ring of Fire, Sheng laughs.

"What's so funny?"

"Nothing," the boy replies. "Remember Ermete, the first time we rang the bell at his place?"

The image of the engineer's bewildered face at the Regno del Dado flashes vividly through their minds. Only Mistral says nothing, staring at them. She wasn't there then.

"What about his disguises?"

Now even Mistral laughs wistfully.

They're laughing, but it's a bitter, pained laugh. Then Sheng stands up, grabs hold of imaginary handlebars and asks Elettra, "Who am I? *Vroom-vroom-vroom-vroom!*"

Elettra nudges his ankle with her foot. "Cut it out!" Then she turns to the others. "Did you know Sheng has never driven a motor scooter in his whole life?"

They talk about silly things, but they're all thinking of painful things. Ermete, the island, which sooner or later is going to sink, the secret of the planet that sooner or later will make its way back into the solar system.

"Harvey?" Elettra says.

"What?"

"Down there, when you took your hand off the wall," the girl continues, "we asked when the mysterious planet would come back. . . ."

Harvey nods. "Yeah."

"When will it?"

"Soon," he replies.

"Meaning?" Sheng says.

Harvey shrugs. "It'll pass by when we need to choose our successors."

"You mean a hundred years from now?"

"Sometime around then, yeah."

"So we've only got a hundred years to make the Earth dream again," Sheng says, turning to look at Mistral.

But she isn't beside him anymore.

The French girl has gotten up without making a noise and is walking over to the edge of the rocks.

Sheng mumbles something and follows her.

When he hears that the girl is singing softly, he slows down. Mistral notices him coming her way and stops.

"I didn't mean to bother you," Sheng says, embarrassed.

"You aren't bothering me."

"Keep singing," he encourages her. "If it's okay with you, I'll

282

stay here and listen. Because back there, well . . . you know what it's like. . . ."

They turn around. Elettra and Harvey are kissing.

"No," Mistral says. She smiles, looking at Sheng, unusually sassy. "To tell you the truth, I don't know what it's like."

"You mean . . . you mean that . . ."

"I mean you and I could kiss," Mistral says.

Sheng faces her, standing as straight as he can, but he still barely comes up to her shoulders. Mistral closes her eyes. Centimeters away from her face, Sheng keeps his open. Wide open. He stares at the French girl's graceful features, her small, thin nose, her bobbed hair blowing in the wind, her long cat-like eyelashes, her slender lips. If he's ever doubted he could really see other people's dreams, right now Sheng is absolutely positive: his big dream is right here in front of him. In flesh and blood.

But a second before he brushes his lips against Mistral's, Sheng freezes, as if paralyzed. Having kept his eyes open, he's spotted something moving on the horizon. A little dot. A little dot that's puffing out smoke.

"*Hao!*" he whispers.

Mistral opens her eyes, disappointed. "*Hao* what, Sheng?"

He takes her hand, turns her around and points at the little dot. "There's a ship down there."

43

THE PARTY

It's a strange October in Rome. There hasn't been a single day of rain yet.

Unpredictable climatic changes caused by the greenhouse effect, or mere coincidence? After the snow on New Year's, when a few journalists talked about a theoretical ice age, nobody knows what side to take anymore.

Sprawled out in a leather armchair he ordered through an Internet auction, Ermete De Panfilis switches off the television, disgusted. He's fed up with people who are all talk and no action.

If they really want to make a change, they need facts.

The Regno del Dado is closed. The roller shutter pulled down. The plastic tables still covered with board games full of colorful playing pieces.

Ermete yawns. Then he realizes it's time to leave. He stretches, picks up the keys to his motorcycle and hurries out.

He's thrilled it isn't raining in October. The motorcycle zips through the hot autumn air going at its top speed of ninety kilometers an hour, leaving the capital behind him. Then he makes his way along the Grande Raccordo Anulare heading toward Fiumicino Airport.

When he parks on the sidewalk outside the international arrivals area and steps inside, he sees that the flight from Shanghai has arrived right on time.

"Yet another surprise!" Ermete exclaims.

He's pulling a second helmet out of the sidecar's storage compartment when he sees Sheng, in jeans, a T-shirt and sneakers. The boy is holding a giant stack of fluttering papers.

"They lost my luggage!" he exclaims, furious.

Ermete seems relieved. "Whew! That's good," he says, handing him the second helmet. "It means we're still in Rome after all."

Having a conversation aboard a sidecar in the middle of traffic in the Italian capital is far from easy, but that's no reason not to try.

"News from home?" Ermete asks, hunched over the handlebars and zooming along.

"Nothing big, except that they finally managed to get their hands on the Devil family's accounting books."

"Great! So what happened?"

"The accountant gave them the figures and the proof they needed to expose all sorts of dirty dealings." Sheng laughs. "And to arrest other officials. Corrupt people on every level. Some of them agreed to explain how the family really made their fortune. And you won't believe this, but in the aftermath they found out what Heremit Devil's real name was. He was called John Smith."

Ermete turns to look at Sheng. "You're kidding me."

285

"No, I swear. That was his name. John Smith. A mixed family, Chinese and English, like Mahler told us. The devil was hiding behind the most ordinary name possible."

"And now that his empire's falling to pieces?"

"People are a lot more careful, and they might think twice the next time they want to authorize building a nine-lane super-highway that would be a total eyesore."

Ermete smiles. "Harmony," he says to himself, taking the exit for the city center.

The entrance of the Domus Quintilia is decorated with colorful paper festoons. Ermete parks his motorcycle in Piazza in Piscinula and, when the roar of the Ural engine dies down, he and Sheng hear music coming from the inner courtyard.

"Sounds like the party's already started. . . ."

"*Hao!*" Sheng exclaims, baring his gums. "Let's get going, then!"

The hotel courtyard is crowded with guests, and new faces can be seen among familiar ones. A strand of blinking white lights has been wound around the arches and down to the central well. On the far end, a table covered with red-and-white-checked cloths is piled high with treats and freshly uncorked bottles.

Ermete nudges Sheng and gestures at waiters in black tuxedo jackets and bow ties who are serving the guests. "You know where they found the catering?"

"No, where?"

Ermete points at what at first sight looked like a flowered tent but turns out to be a giant woman in a rustling silk gown.

"Mademoiselle Cybel de Paris."

"But isn't that dangerous?"

"Well, Sheng, after we got out of that hole of a reservoir," Ermete remembers, "you might just say we became good friends."

"Sheng!" Harvey says, leaning against a column a few steps away. "How's it going?"

The boy from New York has a strange bandage on his nose.

"*Hao!* Harvey!" Sheng smiles and shakes his hand. "Fine, thanks. I mean, except for my luggage. How about you?"

Harvey touches his nose. "Except for my nose . . . pretty good."

"What happened?"

"It broke. Finally."

"*Finally?*"

"If you practice boxing, it's bound to happen sooner or later. At least now I don't have to worry about it anymore."

"How did your folks take it?"

"Let's just say we made a compromise: if I want to go on boxing, I have to get tutoring and keep my grades up."

"And you agreed?"

As his answer, Harvey points at a corner of the courtyard. Olympia and two other people from the gym are there.

"You been here long?" Sheng asks.

"Got in yesterday. I planted my last seed here in Rome."

"Where?"

Harvey raises a finger to his lips to say it's a secret. "I'll tell you once it's grown."

"Ermete, do you know?" Sheng asks, but he finds that the engineer has slipped away without saying a word, so he turns back to Harvey. "Then will you tell me where you planted the one in Shanghai, too?"

"I promise."

Sheng spots Mrs. Miller on the other side of the courtyard, deep in conversation with Vladimir Askenazy.

"Come on," Harvey says, pushing his friend toward them. "You can say hi."

"Harvey!" the woman exclaims as though she hasn't seen her son in ages. "I didn't know you had a friend like Vladimir! What a delightful person. He has such wonderful taste!"

The boy grins. "Well, Sheng's a friend of mine, too," he jokes.

Vladimir shakes Sheng's hand and welcomes him. Harvey and Sheng leave him in Mrs. Miller's company and go over to the refreshments table.

"The others?"

"My dad's over there, talking to those big-shot professors," Harvey says. "He's instilling a bit of healthy environmental panic in all of them. Without overdoing it, naturally."

"Like by telling them that in a hundred years a planet's going to come wipe us off the face of the universe?"

"Something like that."

Among the various smiling faces in the courtyard, Sheng recognizes Cecile Blanchard, Mistral's mom, who's surrounded by Parisian friends from the world of fashion, as well as Madame Cocot, who wears a flashy dress with peacock feathers. The music teacher has cornered a smartly dressed, arrogant-looking man: François Ganglof from the Conservatoire de Paris.

As Sheng watches them, Fernando Melodia appears, carrying two flutes of champagne. He hands one to Cecile.

"Hmm . . . so how's it going between those two?" Sheng asks.

"Mistral and Elettra won't say much about it . . . but they seem to be getting along great," Harvey replies.

"Why, if it isn't *Alfred's nephew!*" Agatha chimes in, appearing behind Sheng. "How is everything?"

"*Hao!* Agatha!" Sheng is really surprised to see the elderly New York actress, who was Professor Van Der Berger's longtime love. "Nice to see you! I didn't think you'd be coming."

"Oh, I traveled in excellent company."

Sheng finds himself shaking a massive hand, which belongs to an equally giant man. After a moment's hesitation, Sheng smiles. "I almost didn't recognize you without your mailman's uniform on."

Quilleran winks at him and then, when Agatha turns to follow the scent of fresh canapés arriving, he trails behind her like a bodyguard.

Sheng suddenly thinks of Egon Nose and asks Harvey how things turned out with the owner of the nightclub Lucifer.

"Problem solved," Harvey replies. "One of his chauffeurs got into an accident while they were driving down Broadway. She wasn't hurt, but Egon . . ."

"I can't say I'll cry, but . . . how did it happen?"

Harvey's eyes become piercing. "It seems a crow flew in front of her car."

At the party, time flies, but Sheng doesn't see any trace of Elettra or Mistral. He's spotted Quilleran's Seneca friends and the gypsy woman with the gold earring, who wears a cheerful flowered apron and is carrying a tray full of hot ravioli.

"The girls?" he asks Harvey, tired of wandering around aimlessly.

"No sign of them," Harvey confirms, biting into a canapé.

Sheng leans against a column.

"Hello, son," his father says, taking him by surprise. "Did you have a good trip?"

"Yeah, Dad. Nice clothes," Sheng remarks, staring at his father's pea-green silk suit. "You could win the prize for the evening's worst outfit."

His father laughs. "Well, I might come in second. . . ."

In fact, a man standing off to the side in a dark corner of the courtyard is dressed in a mismatched suit, the pinstripes on the trousers and jacket in different colors. Sheng doesn't remember him, so he has to ask Ermete, who's passing by with a blond woman.

"That's the Siberian who gave us the heart top in Paris," the engineer says. "He doesn't speak a single word of French, English or Italian, but it looks like he's having fun."

A peal of unmistakable laughter makes Sheng turn to look at the door of the Domus Quintilia, and his heart skips a beat.

It's Mistral, dressed in a knee-length red and white outfit and black lace tights with a flower pattern. Her laugh announces the long-awaited entrance of the ladies of the house: the three Melodia women in sparkling sequins. The elderly Irene, in her wheelchair, wears a light gray gown, gray pearl earrings and a shawl draped over her lap. Linda, to her left, sports a short hairdo, dangling gemstone earrings and a very elegant snake-shaped bracelet. On the other side is Elettra, whose wild black hair hangs down over her shoulders. She's wearing a glittering lilac-colored tube dress with purple tights and ballerina flats.

Their entrance is a bit theatrical, but it wins applause from all the guests. Elettra, Linda and Irene look around like movie stars, going along with it. They reach the center of the courtyard and go their separate ways to mingle.

"Hello, my dear!" Elettra says with a coquettish tone, walking up to Harvey.

Her purple eye shadow sparkles, as does her red lip gloss.

"Isn't purple supposed to be bad luck?" Harvey says.

He turns to Sheng for backup, but his friend is gone. He's slipped through the other guests, carrying two glasses, and pops up right behind Mistral, who's saying hello to her mother's friends, Professor Ganglof and the other people in the Parisian delegation.

"Hi, Sheng!" the French girl says.

But before he can even hand her the glass, she introduces him to a blond boy, whom Sheng instantly finds detestable. "You remember Michel, don't you?"

"Actually, no." Sheng forces a smile.

"Of course you do! The organist from Saint-Germain-des-Prés in Paris!"

"Oh, right!" he exclaims, giving in. "But it's a little hard for me to shake his hand," he adds, looking at the glasses he's holding.

Mistral accepts a flute and makes Sheng give the other one to Michel.

Sheng notices something in Mistral's eyes, something he's never noticed before. A strange energy . . .

Whatever it is, they're interrupted by applause. People are trying to persuade Irene to make a speech.

The elderly woman finally gives in. "Oh, all right!" she

exclaims. "You want me to speak, so I'll speak: Thank you all for coming!"

She then pretends to roll herself away in her wheelchair. The guests' laughter makes her smile and stop. Her gray pearls gleam.

"Honestly!" she continues. "I don't have much more to tell you. All around me, I see the people dearest to my heart, along with others whom I met only tonight. I know they're here because they're all connected in some way by a common friendship . . . with an extraordinary person."

The courtyard falls silent. Unseen by the others, Fernando turns down the music.

"A special person who traveled, studied and read a great, great deal . . . all to pursue his big dream: to help us better understand the world we live in."

Sheng stares hard at Irene, trying to avoid looking at Mistral and the blond boy from Paris.

"And so . . . thank you, Alfred! God willing, we'll all get together from time to time, like tonight, to show our gratitude for everything you did for us and for giving us the chance to meet. And maybe to try to change the things that need changing, at least a little bit."

"To Alfred!" Fernando exclaims, raising his glass.

"To Alfred!" the others repeat, applauding.

Sheng sneaks away to avoid seeing Mistral and the blond French boy toast and sadly heads toward the dark archway leading outside.

For a moment, he has the impression he sees old Professor Van Der Berger coming in through the entrance, like a friend who's stopping by to say hello. The impression is so vivid that Sheng does a double take, but then he realizes he's wrong. The music is turned up again and the party goes on, but something in the courtyard is bothering him, making him feel the need to be alone for a while.

He goes out onto the street.

There, he sees another person, who's standing beside the door.

"Hello, Sheng."

It's a hard, inflexible voice. The voice of a shadow.

"Jacob . . . ," Sheng replies in a whisper.

Jacob Mahler is dressed in an elegant black-and-white herringbone overcoat with a fur-trimmed collar. He's holding the violin he used to take Professor Van Der Berger's life not far from here. It's a strange moment: the killer and the professor's friend standing face to face, both of them feeling awkward in their own way.

"There's something I'd like to do," Jacob Mahler says, breaking the silence, "but I need your help."

Sheng nods and, without saying a word, listens to what the shadow has to tell him.

"All right," he says, nodding, once the man's finished. He takes the musical score from the violinist's hands, turns to go back inside and then stops, realizing that this is a sort of final farewell. And he hasn't said goodbye.

But when he turns around, Jacob Mahler has already disappeared.

Sheng pushes his way through the guests, determined.

He sees Mistral, makes a beeline for her and tries to interrupt her conversation with the French organist. He has to say her name a couple of times and ends up pulling her away.

"Sheng! Do you have to be so pushy?"

"I think so," the boy replies, handing her the score Jacob Mahler gave him. "I need you to sing this."

Mistral glances at the sheet music. "What? Oh, no, are you crazy? I'd be ashamed!"

"You've got to do it."

"Sheng, cut it out! What is it, anyway?" The female chorus solo of Gustav Mahler's Symphony no. 2, called *The Resurrection.* "I've never sung this in my life!"

"The notes are there," Sheng insists. "Sing."

Seeing Mistral's hesitation, the boy calls out to everyone, "Your attention for a moment, please! We have a pleasant surprise! Mistral Blanchard would like to sing us a song."

"Sheng!" Mistral protests. "Have you lost your mind?"

But he doesn't even look her way. Instead, he repeats his announcement, tapping a spoon against a glass to quiet down the people who didn't hear him the first time. He asks Fernando to switch off the music, turns to Mistral and looks her straight in the eye.

"Please," he tells her, lowering his voice, "trust me."

Mistral stares at the faces of all the guests at the party. In particular, those of Madame Cocot and Professor Ganglof, who appear to be burning with curiosity. Her face flushed, she clutches the score and, in the two seconds that follow, wishes she knew the magic formula for disappearing.

"Brava!" Harvey and Elettra start cheering, to encourage her.

Mistral smiles and tries to spot them among all the faces, but she can't find them. Still, the ice has been broken.

She opens the score and begins to sing, her voice slowly growing louder. She discovers it's a sweet melody that flows with grace and power through the shadows of the courtyard and the string of blinking lights, rising up to the wooden balcony and the windows on the top floors, all the way to the four statues that peer down like owls.

Mistral sings a simple, perfect harmony, and as they listen, all those present have the feeling they already know the song, even if this is the first time they've ever heard it. And as her voice weaves its spell, they all gradually hear the mesmerizing notes of a violin joining it. But no matter how hard they look for the mysterious violinist, they can't see anyone playing. Not even a shadow of him, or a glimpse of his steely-gray hair.

Mistral allows the sound of the violin to pervade her and, to her own amazement, lets the shivers running down her spine give her energy, transforming them into voice. She continues to sing, with hope. And as she sings, somewhere deep in her heart, she ends up thinking that it isn't too late. People can change. Everything can change. The same instrument can be used to do evil or to do good. It depends on the mind of the person using it.

Mistral sings, accompanied by Jacob Mahler's violin. And for a few long moments, everything seems perfect.

When the song is over, the silence that follows is so intense that the little lights can be heard blinking on and off. Sheng discovers

he has tears in his eyes. He moves before anyone else does. Once
again, he leaves the courtyard of the Domus Quintilia.

And he finds an unexpected gift on the ground.

A case.

A violin.

And its razor-sharp bow.

Which will never be used again.

EPILOGUE

LATER THAT NIGHT, WHEN THE PARTY IN HONOR OF ALFRED VAN
Der Berger is over, Cybel's waiters clear the tables. And six people
are in the secret room right below them. They can hear the wait-
staff's footsteps and voices through the grate over the well, but,
protected by the basement's thick walls, they know they can talk
without being overheard.

"It's up to you now," Aunt Irene begins, looking at the four
kids. "Isn't that right, Vladimir?"

The antiques dealer nods. "Yes, it's up to you to agree to do it
or not."

"I accept," Elettra replies, her mind made up. "I like the idea
of aging slower than other people."

"One year for every four," Sheng says. "Being born on February twenty-ninth is cool! If I try hard, I could end up being four
hundred years old."

"It isn't as simple as that," Irene says. "The possibility of aging more slowly depends on the power within us . . . and on how
well Nature manages to help us pave the way for those who'll
come later."

"Look at what terrible shape I'm in after only a hundred and ten years," Vladimir jokes, sitting down on the edge of the desk.

The group laughs.

"Of course, we aren't giving ourselves an easy task," Mistral points out. Then, when everyone stares at her, she adds, "We need to hide the four objects in four cities again, choose our successors—"

"*Hao!*" Sheng exclaims, cutting her off. "There's something I always wanted to ask you guys: when the four of you chose us . . . I mean, them . . ."

"Sheng . . ."

Sheng smiles. "What did you choose first, the cities or us?"

"The cities were chosen by our masters and by their masters before them," Vladimir replies.

"Meaning?"

"Meaning, when the time comes, you'll know what to do. That's why you have the tops."

"A hundred years," Harvey says to the others. "I don't know if we can even imagine. . . ."

"A hundred years isn't long at all, you'll see," Aunt Irene chimes in with a smile. "Especially if we really want to change the way people think . . . and make our planet dream again."

"But . . . you aren't going to leave us all on our own, are you?" Sheng asks, sensing that they're drawing close to some kind of goodbye.

"In theory, when the pupils have become as good as—and better than—their teachers, it's best for the teachers to step aside," Vladimir replies.

"But there are still hundreds of things we don't know!" Elettra protests.

"Mithra, Isis, all those gods . . . ," Mistral says, beside her.

"And the Egyptian calendar," Sheng adds, "with all that stuff about the year with four eclipses . . ."

"Not to mention that wandering planet called Nibiru," Harvey concludes, "which should be coming back here in a hundred years or so."

The two elderly Sages look at each other, hesitant.

"Well?" Elettra insists. "If we accept the Pact, are you going to help us or aren't you?"

"If only Alfred were still here," Vladimir grumbles as he gets up from the table, almost angry. "He was the one who studied the Pact better than the rest of us. He understood the connection with the stars and the legends of the ancient Chaldeans. . . ."

"We've got Ermete for that," Sheng says. "Well? Why are you all staring at me? He might not be one of the four chosen ones or the four masters, but he knows more bizarre facts than the rest of us put together."

"Sheng is right," Mistral says. "We never would've managed to get anywhere without his help."

"Not to mention your mom's," Elettra tells Mistral.

"And my dad's, too," Harvey says. "Now that he's convinced he needs to do something to try and restore our planet's health, he's on our side. As long as we don't get him wrapped up in anything even remotely . . . supernatural."

"My father's got a bunch of discounts for airlines and hotels all around the world," Sheng adds. "If we need to travel the globe to hide a Ring of Fire or a Veil of Isis, that could always come in handy. . . ."

The others nod, convinced.

They make a nice team. One that's reckless and inconsistent, sure. Or maybe just unpredictable and brilliant.

Sheng lets out a loud yawn. "Guys, I really need to get some sleep now."

"Me too," Mistral says.

"Tired of chatting with your organ-playing friend?"

"Hey, Sheng?" Elettra breaks in. "You wouldn't happen to be jealous, would you?"

Sheng pretends to yawn a second time and gets up from his chair.

"Just a moment," Irene says, calling him back. "It's time for each of you to take custody of your object."

"Now?" Elettra grumbles. "Can't we do it tomorrow, Auntie?"

"It's better to do it right away. Where are they?"

"We put them all in here," Elettra replies, picking up Nik Knife's backpack from the ground.

A moment later, the Ring of Fire, the Star of Stone and the Pearl of the Sea Dragon are on the table.

"What about the Veil of Isis?" Mistral asks, noticing that her object is missing.

Elettra feels around the bottom of the backpack. "I don't understand," she mumbles. "I'm sure it was in here."

Then she's struck by a horrible doubt. "Harvey!"

"What?"

"When you got here, where did you put the backpack?"

"In your room. Why?"

"No! Aunt Linda!" Elettra cries, racing out of the underground room.

She crosses the hallway in a flash, dives into the elevator and jabs the buttons, punching in the secret combination to make it go back upstairs. She throws open the iron doors and bursts into her aunt's room.

"Auntie!" she cries.

Linda is sitting on the edge of the puff chair in front of her dressing table and is taking off her earrings. Despite the chill, her window is wide open, as if to air out the room.

"Elettra, dear!" she exclaims, glancing at the girl. "You're covered with dust! Have you been rolling around in the streets with the stray cats?"

"That's not funny!" Elettra snaps. "Where did you put the Veil of Isis?"

"The veil of what?"

Her makeup from the party still impeccable, the woman rests her second earring on the dressing table, lining it up with the first one.

Elettra insists. "It was in my room, in Harvey's backpack, and it was there until this afternoon when we went out to plant the tree!"

"Oh, of course!" Linda Melodia finally exclaims, perfectly calm. "You mean that old filthy-dirty sheet?"

"Auntie . . ."

"It's downstairs in the linen closet, washed and pressed."

"Oh, no . . . Auntie, no . . ."

"And scented with lavender!"

Elettra slumps against the door, shocked.

301

This is a catastrophe, she thinks. *A centuries-old relic has undergone Aunt Linda's antibacterial treatment. It might be totally useless now.*

But as a world of thoughts races around in her mind, she hears, through the open window and the well in the courtyard, the unmistakable sound of laughter.

"This is a joke, isn't it?" she asks, full of hope. "You guys are just playing a joke on me?"

Linda Melodia strokes Elettra's hair, smiling. "What if we were?"

CREDITS

© arturbo/iStockphoto.com (p. 5, photo 8).

© Stefan Ataman/iStockphoto.com (p. 3, photo 2).

© Iocopo Bruno (p. 4, photo 4; p. 4, photo 5; p. 5, photo 9; p. 6, photo 12; p. 6, photo 15; p. 7, photo 16; p. 7, photo 17; p. 7, photo 18; p. 7, photo 19; pp. 8–9, photo 22; p. 11, photo 27; p. 11, photo 28; p. 12, photo 32; p. 13, photo 36; p. 13, photo 37; p. 15, photo 40).

© Ricardo De Mattos/iStockphoto.com (p. 12, photo 33).

© Silke Dietze/iStockphoto.com (p. 4, photo 6).

© dra_schwartz/iStockphoto.com (p. 3, photo 1).

© Tarek El Sombo/iStockphoto.com (p. 7, photo 21).

GNU Free Documentation Licence (p. 5, photo 11).

© HultonArchive/iStockphoto.com (p. 15, photo 39).

© Juanmonino/iStockphoto.com (p. 13, photo 38).

Library of Congress (p. 3, photo 3).

© Bartlomiej Magierowski/iStockphoto.com (p. 12, photo 30).

© Naran/iStockphoto.com (p. 12, photo 34).

© Nikada/iStockphoto.com (p. 6, photo 14).

© photo168/iStockphoto.com (p. 5, photo 10).

ABOUT THE AUTHOR

PIERDOMENICO BACCALARIO was born in Acqui Terme, a beautiful little town in the Piedmont region of northern Italy. He grew up in the middle of the woods with his three dogs and his black bicycle.

He started writing in high school. When lessons got particularly boring, he'd pretend he was taking notes, but he was actually coming up with stories. He also met a group of friends who were crazy about role-playing games, and with them he invented and explored dozens of fantastic worlds.

He studied law at university but kept writing and began publishing novels. After he graduated, he also worked with museums and cultural projects, trying to make dusty old objects tell interesting stories. He began to travel and change horizons: Celle Ligure, Pisa, Rome, Verona . . .

He loves seeing new places and discovering new lifestyles, although, in the end, he always returns to the comfort of familiar ones.

1 1

THE CAFÉ

Jacob Mahler hands the taxi driver a slip of paper and says, "We feel like having a decent coffee."

Then, in silence, he waits for the car to make its way from Shanghai's south side to the French Concession. Passing by outside the window are congested streets, skyscrapers in iridescent colors, the characteristic bridge spanning the river with spiral ramps, anonymous cement buildings with all kinds of shops and, finally, the French residential quarter with its old colonial dwellings.

The taxi pulls up in front of the Bonomi Café, located in a villa from the early 1900s, with large, elegant rooms and little tables on the lawn. Immersed in the colossal city, it looks like the classic fairy home in the middle of the woods with a pointed red roof and sponge-cake doors.

Mahler gets out of the car without even looking around and walks up the path leading inside as if it was his own home.

"Hey!" grumbles Ermete, the last one left in the taxi. The engineer pulls out a wad of banknotes and tries to find out from the taxi driver how much they owe him. Then he runs inside

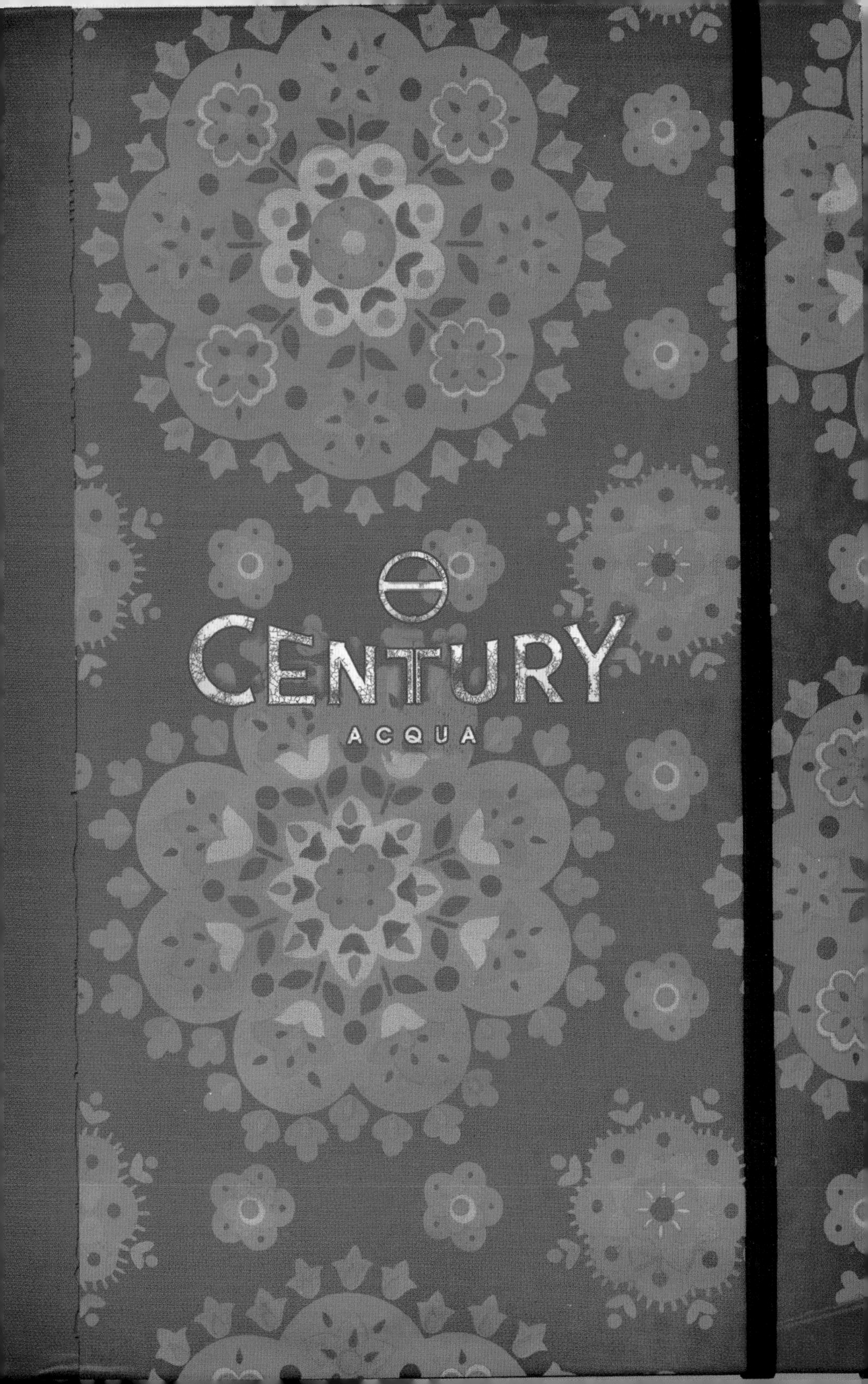
CENTURY
ACQUA

MISSING

LINDA MELODIA

AVETE VISTO QUESTA DONNA?

CHIAMARE: Elettra 06 78695

全景导游图　CENTURY PARK

12

Jinxiu Rd

Century Avenue

(Work Passage)
Gate 2

Jinxiu Rd

Fangdian Rd

Caihong Rd

Lushan Rd

Metro Line 2
Gate 1

Jinxiu Rd

Fork Village

Shibahua Rd

Huayao Rd N

Ouyuan Rd

Nature Reserve

Wenying Bridge

Yuzhu Bridge

(Close Down)
Gate 4

Yunfan Bridge

Wobo Bridge

Lügong Rd

Menghu Bridge

Jiezhan Bridge

Quay

Bright Lake

Fenghe Bridge

Wutong Avenue

Wutong Avenue

Friendship Tree

Huayao Rd S

Mini Golf
(Close Down)

Amphitr Grass

Hongjin Bridge

Gate 5
(Close Down)

Anliu Bridge

Huayao Rd S

Huamu Rd S

Yongan Rd

Gate 6
(Work Passage)

Linyin Rd

Zhanganbang

Huamu Rd

Gate 8
(Close down)

Yinhe Bridge

Yingke Bridge

Huamu Rd

Gate 7

Metro Line 2

疏林: SPARSE FOREST
草坪: LAWN
湖泊: LAKE
道路: ROAD
桥梁: BRIDGE
景点: LANDMARK

N

13

19

15

16

17

18

19

PASSPORT

United States
of America

20

Union européenne
République française

PASSEPORT

uropéenne
ue française

PORT

21

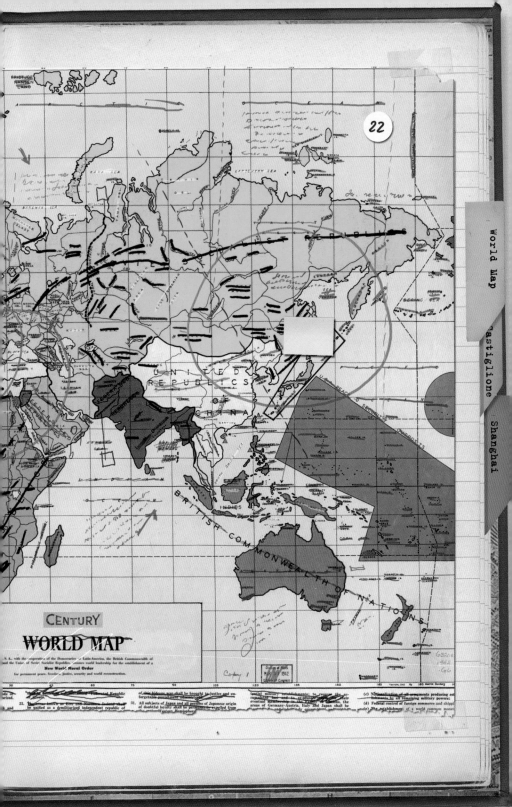

CENTURY

WORLD MAP

New World Moral Order

for permanent peace, freedom, justice, security and world reconstruction.

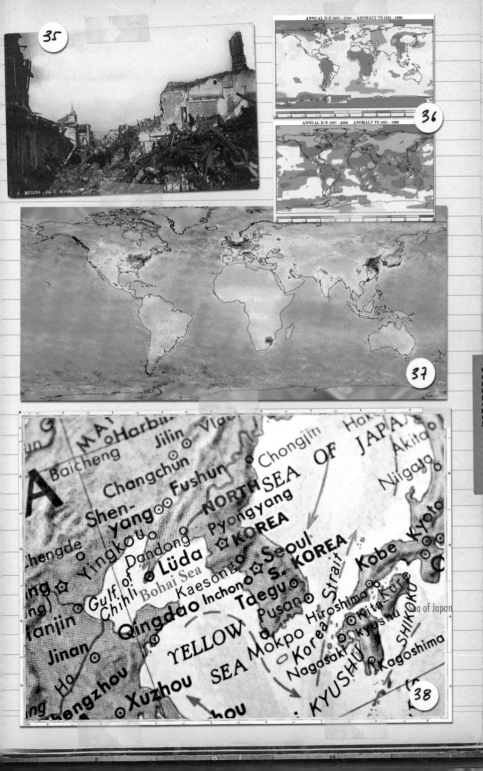

35

ANNUAL D-N 1891 - 1900 . ANOMALY VS 1951 - 1980

36

ANNUAL D-N 1997 - 2006 . ANOMALY VS 1951 - 1980

37

MA Harbin Jilin Vla Chongjin Ho OF JAPAN Akita
Baicheng Changchun Fushun NORTH SEA Niigata
Shen- yang Pyongyang KOREA Seoul
hengde Yingkou Dandong Lüda Kaesong S. KOREA Kobe Kyoto
ing Tanjin Gulf of Chihli Bohai Sea Inchon Taegu Pusan Strait Hiroshima Kita-Kyu
Jinan Qingdao YELLOW Mokpo Korea Kyushu SHIKOKU
Ho SEA Nagasaki KYUSHU Kagoshima
hengzhou Xuzhou hou Sea of Japan

38

INDEX

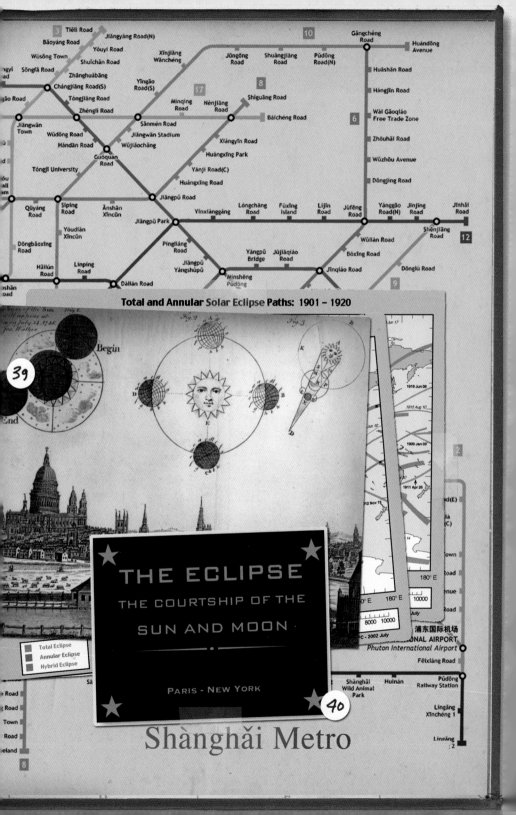

Total and Annular Solar Eclipse Paths: 1901 – 1920

| Total Eclipse |
| Annular Eclipse |
| Hybrid Eclipse |

THE ECLIPSE
THE COURTSHIP OF THE
SUN AND MOON

PARIS – NEW YORK

Shànghǎi Metro